WINDHAM WEREWOLVES

THE COMPLETE COLLECTION

NEW YORK TIMES BESTSELLING AUTHOR

SHAWNTELLE MADISON

VALKYRIE
RISING
PRESS

This story is a work of fiction. Names, characters, places, and incidents are the product of the author's imagination or are used fictitiously. Any resemblance to actual events, locales, or persons living or dead is purely coincidental.

The Hunter's Moon

Copyright © 2014 Shawntelle Madison

The Hunter's Alpha

Copyright © 2015 Shawntelle Madison

The Hunter's Pack

Copyright © 2015 Shawntelle Madison

The Hunter's Clan

Copyright © 2015 Shawntelle Madison

The Hunter's Mate

Copyright © 2015 Shawntelle Madison

Version 3.5

All rights reserved. Except as permitted under the U.S. Copyright Act of 1976, no part of this publication may be reproduced, distributed, or transmitted in any form or by any means, or stored in a database or retrieval system, without prior written permission of the author.

THE HUNTER'S MOON

PART I

[1]

On most mornings after her chemo treatment, Cynthia woke up at home with a mouth scratchy like cotton and a hammer-struck headache.

This morning, however, her eyes shot open, and she sat up alert. Something was wrong. Darkness filled the bedroom's corners. Only the light coming in from under the single doorway to her left cast a glow along the floor. Post-chemo, her room was usually pitch-black. Light-sensitive migraines were fairly common for her.

The blankets, which should've been smooth cotton, were stiff. Instead of refreshing, cool air from a humidifier, the air was dry and warm, with the subtle scent of white pines and fir trees, almost as if she were in a cabin.

Why wasn't she in her room? She would beat the hell out of her brother for letting her recover in some off-the-wall bed-and-breakfast where they served sunshine happy face breakfast platters.

"Zach..." Her brother's name died on her lips as a familiar jolt to be alert for danger folded over her. She moved her hand first then a leg. Every limb was stiff as if she'd slept for longer than usual. A search along the sheets only revealed someone had left a warm spot next to her side. She hadn't slept alone.

She fought the fearful swallow that danced along the back of her throat. If she weren't at home, she wouldn't have any weapons. A hunter always carried something useful, but she had no idea where her bag was.

"I know you're awake," a deep male voice said from the darkened corner to her right.

As quickly as she could manage, she shuffled out of the bed toward the door. By the time she had taken a few steps, her body rebelled. Her stomach clenched tight as a wave of nausea coursed through her.

Not now. Not now. Not now.

After each therapy session with a lovely cocktail of drugs, she was one of the lucky ones to have severe nausea. And every single time, she puked her guts out like a binge-drinking college dorm boy bending over a porcelain altar to worship. Intensification therapy for cancer sucked ass.

The sound of her retching must've spurred the stranger into action. In seconds, he was at her side, a bucket in his hands. After so many hospital visits, the shame from such a personal act was gone. Nurse after nurse had seen her spew. Another stranger didn't matter much.

He supported her with a strong arm around her waist and helped her hold the bucket. Even as her knees buckled, he held her. Far too easily.

"I gotcha," he said softly. "It'll be over soon."

When she finished, her head rolled back. Episodes like this always took what little strength she had left.

"You shouldn't have gotten up." He picked her up and laid her on the bed. Once she was settled, he left the room with the bucket and returned shortly thereafter. All the while, her heart raced. It wasn't the smooth lilt to his voice that alarmed her, but the heat radiating from his skin. She had lost a bit of weight, but he lifted her as if she were nothing. Had the werewolves captured her while she was so vulnerable and weak?

"Where am I?" She stuck with a safer question instead of asking, *Who are you?*

He chuckled. "Safe, Cynthia."

So, he knew her name. "'Safe' isn't a good enough answer."

"You've been sleeping for nearly twenty-four hours after your chemotherapy treatment in Vancouver. If you were in danger, you'd be dead already, *hunter*."

"Where is Zach?" She tried to keep the quiver out of her voice.

The man didn't reply.

Her eyes had finally adjusted to the darkness. A single heavily draped window and the door were the only exit points. Each required at least five footsteps. She wore a thin T-shirt and a pair of shorts. Depending on the wintry conditions outside, she wouldn't last long unless she took him out and found adequate clothing.

Her fingers twitched. A year ago, before her cancer diagnosis, she would've used a gun strapped to her thigh to turn him and every thug werewolf into Swiss cheese. At least two silver bullets to his chest would do the job.

"Did you kill him?" she asked slowly.

"No."

Cyn could faintly make out the man who leaned against the wall. He stood tall, with broad shoulders and a lean waist. She couldn't make out the color of his hair—matter of fact, the only features she could discern were his eyes. In the dark, they reflected like a canine's eyes, like those of a predator. She tried to hold his gaze, but the intensity in his eyes forced her to blink. *Stay sharp, Cyn.*

"You're after a ransom, aren't you?" she managed. "Bring down the weakened hunter and use her to cushion your bank account?"

He folded his arms. "Not even close."

"Then what do you want?"

"I want you to calm down first. Your heartbeat is too elevated."

As if he cared. She made a rude noise. His kind lived to conquer and dominate. Ever since the world had discovered that werewolves roamed the cities, the hunters had had to step up their game to clean up the carnage from the rogues who trailed after trouble.

"I don't have any drugs for arrhythmia if your heart goes out, so you need to chill," he added.

Cyn turned his way. Was he a doctor? As much as she wanted to leap out of the bed, he was right. After practically living in the hospital a few times, she wasn't eager to go back.

Silence crept between them. The nagging need to ask questions didn't stop. How did she get here? Where the hell was *here*? What had happened from the point when she got her treatment to now?

"Where is my brother?" she said with clenched teeth.

"He's not here." The man left the wall. With a sweep of his hand, he opened the curtains to reveal the night sky. Instead of the Vancouver skyline, there was nothing but mountains and endless trees dotting an expansive valley with not a single sign of civilization.

"Your brother returned to Vancouver," the man said. "We brought you to my cabin in the mountains."

KADEN WINDHAM TRIED TO READ THE DARK-HAIRED woman who lay in his bed, staring wide-eyed out the window of his cabin. A rainbow of emotions crossed her ruddy features: indifference, anger, fear, doubt.

Her mouth formed a straight line, yet her brow furrowed as if her sickness were beating at her. To the wolf in him, her body was weak. Before Kaden had healed her, her scent had been bitter and strong, almost like black licorice. Every time she exhaled, her body recited a list of problems. The list led to one obvious conclusion: she was dying.

And yet, the fierce resolve in her voice said otherwise.

"My brother would never abandon me with you *people*." She spat out the word *people* as if it were an expletive. "Why were you lying next to me?" She didn't look at him when she asked.

"I had to heal you."

"You're not that good. I still feel like shit." Her chin tilted upward, and he caught the hint of amusement in her light gray eyes.

"You don't believe me."

"Alpha werewolf healing is bullshit. It's just a rumor you spread so you can get sympathy or justify your existence." She dared him to deny it with her hardened gaze.

He took a step toward her, a growl forming in his chest. She froze. Her hands clenched the blanket and the muscles in her legs tensed as if she *really* planned to attack him. This determined streak of hers was entertaining only for so long.

Minutes passed. Her body trembled, but she wouldn't stand down and look away.

He advanced on her faster than she could blink. In one moment, he was across the room, and, in the next, he had her pinned to the bed with his body over hers. Not to hurt her, but to make a point.

"Don't make me regret my decision to help you, hunter," he growled.

This time, he had her attention. She tried to move him

but failed. Her feeble push was nothing, even compared to a man's thrust. She turned her head to the side, baring her neck like a pup as if she'd been taught such. When he had lain next to her during the night, at first, he'd gotten close enough to touch, but not much more. But as the night grew deeper and the cold seeped through the cracks, he sensed the chill along her skin and couldn't help but draw her to him. He surmised she'd lost weight, but she still had womanly curves. His arm had rested along the gentle slope between her waist and hip. A perfect fit.

"And what do you get for helping me?" she finally asked him.

Was that all she cared about? Answering her wouldn't make any difference; she'd already judged him the moment she figured out that he was a werewolf.

When he didn't answer her, she remained silent. He took that as defiance.

Her stomach growled, but she refused to ask for food. Even though anger floated off her in waves, she wouldn't be much of a threat. For now. He rose off her and left his bedroom for the kitchen in the adjoining room. Time to fetch what she needed. He returned to the bedroom to find she hadn't moved. She remained still as he got close.

"Drink." He tilted up the cup until she was forced to quench her thirst. Then he presented a few pills.

She paused and looked at them suspiciously.

He snorted. "It's Zofran, just in case you want to stop puking. Your choice."

She glanced at the white anti-nausea pills in his hand then peered at his face.

Her hand hovered over his open palm. The faint white scars along her knuckles resembled claw marks. When she caught him looking at her hand, she quickly downed one of the pills.

Noises from outside the cabin piqued his attention, maybe a deer passing by. If it were one of his friends, now wasn't the time for them to be nosy. "I'll be back."

He checked out the living room window that faced the peak. Beyond the trees, he couldn't detect anyone, not by sight anyway. If someone were close, whoever it was didn't want to be spotted. He grinned. If he did have a visitor, he'd contend with them after she rested. He returned to the room to find her lying in bed with her arms crossed and belligerence all over her face.

"Your brother warned me," Kaden said. "But I didn't expect you'd be as stubborn as a cross-eyed rabbit getting dragged into a carrot patch."

"What reason do I have to believe you're not lying?" Her heartbeat stuttered and her breath caught in response. "That you haven't kidnapped me from the hospital?"

He needed to heal her again, but he had an inkling she wouldn't be a willing participant.

"You need to rest now. I'll answer any questions you have later."

She rolled her eyes. "If I had a weapon right now—"

"You'd be using it to prop your eyes open," he supplied.

The woman inhaled sharply, her eyes blinking. The scowl she tried to hold in place drooped. "What did you give me?"

"Something to help you relax. Because any minute now you're gonna *try* to take me down."

"That's right," she mumbled. "Just gimme a knife." Her quickened heartbeat reached a steadier rhythm.

He counted down to ten, but she faded to slumber long before he reached seven. A few strands of her black hair had fallen into her face. He reminded himself, as he moved her hair out of the way, that he was being nice to her and that their first night together side-by-side in his bed had been nothing.

Every time he helped her, his attachment to her would grow stronger, but bonding with her wasn't going to happen. After his ex-girlfriend Hayley had left over a year ago, he'd told himself he didn't need another distraction, especially if that distraction could potentially bring his pack's downfall.

Also, adding a former hunter to his pack wouldn't go down well with the others and would create dissent, even though her brother had promised to help his pack in exchange for her life. He'd heal her to the best of his abilities, and, when the time came, he'd send her on her way. Anything else was unacceptable.

[2]

WHEN CYN WOKE UP AGAIN, THE PAIN WAS GONE. THE familiar aches in the muscles along her arms and legs that greeted her every time she moved weren't there anymore. The pains would've been a distant memory if she hadn't experienced them not too long ago.

Someone lay in the bed with her. The werewolf.

The back of her head rested against his chest and his thick arms enveloped her. He had splayed his right hand across her stomach. Silky warmth spread from her stomach and extended blissfully into her limbs. Her muscles turned to liquid and her bones to smoke. As much as she wanted to break his arm and run away, she hadn't felt this relaxed in so long. She had endured month after month of waking up feeling like utter shit, day after day when it got harder to think about the doctor's prognosis:

"You have less than a year to live, Miss McGinnis. Maybe only months."

A familiar ache hit her chest, piercing and deep, every time she remembered that morning: the doctor's cold room, his messy desk, the way the world slowed down to a frame-by-frame movie.

After she'd learned her fate, she isolated herself as she adjusted to her new circumstances. How long had it been since she'd gotten this close to a man? The last one had been a year ago, before her diagnosis. Michael. She pushed thoughts of him away. He was too precious for this place. Yet, she missed being held. During chemo, her brother often held her hand to comfort her, but that wasn't the same as having someone wrap their arms around her as she shivered and ached.

The werewolf next to her made her feel protected, but that was an unwelcome feeling from the likes of him.

With the patience of a mongoose waiting for a viper to strike, she slid his hand from around her waist. Stealth was a hunter's lesson from day one. The werewolves had far superior hearing, but with a planned approach, an experienced hunter could outwit them.

She rolled off the bed, each movement done bit by bit. Time stretched along until she was standing. She waited. He lay in the bed on his side, his chest rising and falling in rhythm. Any second now, he'd probably open his eyes and grab her. But he never did.

She backed toward the door, hoping and praying the cold wood under her feet didn't groan. By the time her fingers brushed against the doorknob, enough time had passed for him to stir, but he continued to slumber. The knob yawned a bit when she turned it. His hand twitched, but that was about it.

As fast as she dared, she opened the door and raced out. The room beyond the bedroom was far larger than she'd expected. A quick scan revealed five exit points: three windows in the living room, a doorway to what had to be the kitchen, and the front door. Time to run.

As tempting as it might be to go into the kitchen and hunt down a blade, she still wasn't in any condition to take down a healthy werewolf on his own turf. She had a better chance of tackling the sad guy who wore wolf costumes at Playland in Vancouver.

So, supplies first. With a part of her attention on the bedroom door behind her, she checked around the simple cotton couches until she spotted a familiar bag. *Bingo!* She snatched up her hospital bag and opened it.

Not a single weapon inside. Even the Swiss army knife in a side pocket had been taken. *Clever little wolf.*

At least the clothes she'd changed out of at the hospital were there: a pair of jeans and a T-shirt, her long underwear for when she had the chills, but no jacket, though. The tall rack next to the front door only had one thick coat. She checked it out. The coat was far too big for her and smelled like him. Her hand paused, touching the downy material used to line the inside. His cologne wafted from the folds, smooth and rich like bay rum.

Damn it all to hell, she didn't want reminders of this guy during her escape, but she'd do what was necessary. As quickly as she could, she threw on the long underwear and then her clothes. She shrugged on the coat and it nearly swallowed her whole. The tips of her hands poked out of the sleeves and the bottom reached her knees. Ehh, she'd need protection from the elements anyway. She grabbed her bag and headed for the door. The werewolf had left her post-hospital snacks inside the bag—they'd last her a while until she reached Prince George. With a soft click, she unlocked the door and made her way outside.

She was greeted by something bright and blinking in the way. Red and green lights flashed on the Christmas tree that blocked the path to the porch steps. Her mouth dropped open. There were four days until Christmas and now she was seeing this?

What was this doing here? Was this some kind of sick joke?

Every ornament was all too familiar from her childhood. The popsicle stick wreath she'd made in first grade. The tiny plastic bells her dad had brought home from a long hunting trip to Florida. Even the crimson ribbons tied at the end of the branches. She glanced from the plastic star at the top, down to the only object underneath. Someone had left a folded piece of paper tied to a rock.

Her name had been written on the outside in Zach's neat handwriting. She'd recognize it anywhere. The ribbon holding the note to the rock gave way easily. She quickly read the note:

This is the only gift I can give you this Christmas. No matter how much you hate me, you have to live on and protect Ty when you get better.

Zachary

[3]

If Zach had been in front of her right now, she would've beaten his ass and then shot him dead. Fury pulsed through her, forcing her to clench her fists. How *dare* he make such a decision for her? Her life was her own and how it ended was her choice.

Just looking at the tree twisted her stomach further into knots. It was the same plastic tree her parents had used. Not too tall and not too short. As hunters, her parents didn't possess much. Living on the road was often necessary to keep her siblings safe from the inner-city werewolf gangs.

When they moved, Mom and Dad never left the tree behind. It was a tradition that was always kept to give them some sense of continuity and normalcy. Thanksgiving Day was optional. Why not have a turkey sandwich? Labour Day was just an excuse to sleep in. But Christmas was different and Zach had left this tree here to make his point crystal clear: leaving her with that werewolf had been his decision. Damn him to a burning hell with pools full of hemorrhoid-inducing fire.

She sucked in a few breaths and clutched her bag and the

note until her fingers went numb. Her vision blurred with tears.

How could you, Z?

The chill in the air turned her exhalations into mist. Eventually, she released the note and let it drift away with the breeze. As much as she wanted to leave, many of these ornaments belonged to her, and her idiot brother had given them to the enemy. She stuffed what she could into the bag.

Then she walked south and didn't look back.

CYN'S LUNGS BURNED, BUT SHE HADN'T RUN A SINGLE mile yet. *Keep going. Don't stop.* The mantra was all too familiar, especially when running was more advisable than fighting.

She kept going downhill along a snowy path. Patches of dead grass among the slushy snow made it easier for her to traverse. The light from the rising sun guided her to the southwest. She'd find Prince George if she didn't give up.

As a child, she'd visited the city with her family during an endless road trip to Alaska from Seattle. The journey had been long and boring, but she remembered the mountains fondly. To the south was Longworth Peak and Fraser River. The clearest skies could be seen now along with the haze from the Aurora Borealis. This early in the morning, the dancing lights could be seen from miles away. But now wasn't the time for sightseeing. As much as she didn't want to admit it, that werewolf had done something to her. Each steady footstep in the snow told her as much. A few days ago, she had to be wheeled into the hospital as the lucky soul who got to have chemotherapy right before Christmas, a lottery ticket she'd wanted to refuse.

"We could always do your treatment after New Year's," her doc had suggested.

"I think that's the best option, Cyn," Zach had said.

She snorted as she focused on the tree line ahead. Her brother had been planning her capture the whole time. He'd known damn well she'd take the treatment. For a fighting chance at remission, she had to have it, even if she would've returned to her family very sick, forced to spend the holidays resting. Anger pulsed through her again, but she slowed down when a feather-light sensation brushed against the back of her neck, that tingling feeling when someone was trailing after you. Years of running away from her prey forced Cyn to listen to her body. That human instinct that alerted her to danger wasn't something to be ignored.

Cyn kept her stride casual and her eyes forward. She couldn't tell how many people were following her or how far they were behind her, but the one thing that was obvious was how difficult walking had become. The snow along the cliffs began to blow to the east. The skies to the west were still dark from the night, but instead of wasting away at the light from the rising sun, the darkened skies to the west grew more ominous.

She drew in a deep breath, cursing with each step. Guessing distances was a knack she was good at. You had to be when you tracked enemies who travelled quickly on foot. From where she stood to the nearest highway, which led to Prince George, had to be at least twenty miles. The path was nothing but forest. On a good day—when she was at her prime—twenty miles could be done at a steady run.

A chemo patient with an oncoming storm, and an unknown enemy on her tail, was another matter entirely. A breeze, cold and bitter, ruffled her coat and she shivered. Was the werewolf following her? Could she run if need be? How far would she make it? Only a fool would keep going under these odds. And her mother hadn't raised one.

She turned around and saw that no one was behind her. Peering through the trees, she surmised that either she was alone or whoever trailed after her was damn good at hiding. Carefully, she made her way back toward the cabin. As much as she wanted to find Zach and keep him from doing something foolish, Cyn wasn't in any condition to go all the way to Prince George and elude whoever was behind her.

Damn it. Damn it.

She shook her head and tried not to smile. At least Zach had been thorough with his plan—which showed he still owned a pair of balls. He'd left her isolated and with someone who had medical training of sorts. But what did that werewolf get for healing her? She wasn't exactly wife material. Nobody did something like this for free. She'd yet to meet a humanitarian among their ranks.

She was getting closer to the cabin now. The house should've been dark, but the lights from the kitchen were on, as well as the living room. Snow was beginning to fall and the wind had picked up even more, whistling through the branches. She zipped up the coat even farther until a small hole for breathing was all she had.

Carefully, she approached the porch and peered through the window. No one was stirring in the living room. The Christmas tree was gone now. In the time since she'd left, he had taken it into the house and now the tree sat in one of the corners. All the ornaments she hadn't taken had been arranged again. Not in the right spots, but they'd been hung with care.

So he'd been awake the entire time and he'd let her leave.

Why?

The chill in the air swept into the gap and coursed down her throat. She couldn't stay out here like this. Heading inside to attack him was an option. She had a few ornaments in her bag. She could tackle him and throttle him to death with holiday cheer and broken glass. As much as she wanted to go in, she decided to go around the house to see if she could find a weapon like an axe. There wasn't much. A tiny shed with a massive lock was right behind the house. The cold padlock was as big as her hand. Beyond that, the trees were hard to look past.

What she found fascinating was the lack of a generator and power lines. Where did the house draw power?

Her legs buckled, a warning that she'd been exposed for too long. Time to face him again. She walked through the front door; why bother trying to sneak in when her previous ninja-like attempt in leaving had failed?

The moment she opened the door, a cloud of warmth bathed her face. The fireplace at the other end of the room had been lit and the heat was welcomed. And the smells! Fresh hot soup and bread.

She could use some real food after walking. Sounds from the kitchen revealed the werewolf's location. With caution, she left the coat on the sofa and she took a seat near the fire to warm her hands. The bag was in her lap, close by in case she had to make a quick decision.

"Did you have fun on your little hike?" the werewolf's voice called out from the kitchen.

"It was...educational."

"Do you want something to eat?"

Her first thought was no, but her stomach thought otherwise and growled.

"I'll take that as a resounding yes." He came out with two bowls of food and followed with drinks. She spotted wet footprints on the floor. So, he'd been her little tag-a-long. Quite a fast one.

"I don't want your food."

"Suit yourself." He took a spot at the tiny table on the opposite side of the room. His stance was casual. He even placed warm bread and a knife on the table. The blade was large and he turned his back on her to go to the kitchen.

Did he really believe she was that harmless?

"How long have you been awake?" was what she asked instead.

"Long before you moved, I caught your intentions."

Now that's not good.

"You're the noisiest hunter I've ever met," he said.

"Oh, really?"

"You hit every floorboard between here and the door. Not to mention how you danced around the porch grabbing those ornaments."

She rolled her eyes. *Stupid werewolf hearing.*

He sat down, and not long after his first slurp of soup, her body rebelled. Hunger sliced through her insides. In the past, she would have been so nauseated, she'd refused food, but now was different. The werewolf had done something to her, and whatever gift of energy he had given, she wasted it in her futile escape attempt, and now she was a husk.

While avoiding his gaze, she got up and took the only spot opposite him at the table. He continued to eat, not even looking at her. Even the bread and the knife had been left on her side of the table.

This had to be some kind of test. A hilarious one at that. No more than two feet separated them. All she'd have to do was grab the knife and aim for his chest. Maybe even dump the hot soup over his head for good measure.

"Your blood sugar is getting low," he grumbled.

The hand that was supposed to stab him shook slightly. That was a bad sign. He pushed the glass of juice toward her. "Drink." The command was firm.

She hesitated, tapping the tabletop with her fingertips.

Giving an alpha control was never a good idea, but her body won out. The cool liquid slammed down her throat. The effect didn't take long and, soon enough, a heady rush hit.

Next, he slid a pill across the table.

Oh, hell no. She laughed. "I'm not falling for that shit again."

"You drank the juice, didn't you?" His eyebrow rose.

Clever little soon-to-be dead wolf. Was there anything in the juice this time? Her fingers inched toward the knife. He left the pill next to the bread and continued to eat.

"Was there anything in the drink?" she asked.

"Cut me off a slice of bread, would you?"

He had massive balls. Even her other brother Ty never pulled that kind of shit.

She flipped the knife in one hand and slammed it down into the loaf. The table shook from the blow.

"Is that how hunters cut their food?" He hadn't flinched, not so much as a twitch.

"You wish." She took a bite of her food in a huff. "Hey, werewolf, how about a little Q&A?"

"There was nothing in the juice. Just pulp, orange juice, and water. You drank the last of what I had." He reached for the bread and tore off a slice. "What more do you want to know that you haven't learned already? You saw the Christmas tree. You can't tell me you didn't feel a little different post-chemo. What is there to know?"

Everything. "The reason. Zach sent me here to be healed, but c'mon, there's no way a werewolf would agree to such a thing. Not from a hunter. I've heard the rumors. That an alpha without a mate would consider human women, especially the ones with incurable diseases. They turn them into werewolves to heal them."

He shrugged. "Sounds about right."

"Zach is like me. He has wanted for years to take down

the gang who killed my parents, and now that I'm out of the way, no one can stop him from exacting his revenge."

"So you think I fed him intel on how to find the gang?"

"You bet your hairy ass I believe that's what happened."

He sighed. "Would you ever believe that maybe he did it because he loves you? That he wanted you to live instead of finding your parents' killer?"

A part of her believed that. During all the appointments —the ones she'd let him attend—he'd been her driver and supporter. But underneath it all, anger had begun to build in his blood. Before she'd gotten sick, a lead had surfaced to the gang's location, only to disappear along with her health.

"Your face tells me you have doubts," the werewolf said quietly. He tore off another piece of bread and placed it next to her bowl. Reluctantly, she took a sip of her soup and held back a sigh. So delicious! Just the right thickness for a beef stew.

He'd asked her if she had doubts. She was swimming in doubts galore. If what was happening was true, her brother had left her here to mate with a werewolf. The very idea made no sense. Did Zach think she'd agree to this? That she was *that* hard up she'd need to jump into the sack with this dude and mate with him? The guy did live out in the middle of nowhere, but it wasn't because he was so ugly he'd have to wear a paper bag. If he'd been a human, the huntresses would be all over him, sizing him up as a future husband. But he wasn't human. He was the enemy. And, unfortunately, a good-looking one at that.

Now that they weren't in the dim bedroom, she tried to avoid taking him in. He had the kind of chin most men would envy, strong and assured. The T-shirt he wore did little to hide the firm muscles along his chest and arms. The light from the overhead lamp hit the top of his thick hair. *Thick enough for a woman to grip while he kissed her.* The delicious thought coursed through her and she slapped it away before her eyes went to his mouth.

Kissing, my ass.

She scraped the bottom of the bowl. How had she eaten the soup so fast? The bread was just as good. She tried to yank off a piece and failed. Even the bread had it in for her. She used the knife instead. When she handled the blade, he didn't even look up.

"Whatever you're hiding, I'm going to cut it out of you." She played with the hilt. Still no reaction.

Then she stood, and he got up.

Now we're talking. Instead of coming at her, he rushed to the windows.

Now that was unexpected.

"Oh, shit," he breathed.

She followed him, seeing at just the right moment—not right in a good sense—as a wall of white rushed at the cabin and the cabin shook. In one moment, sunlight poured through the windows, and, in the next, snow and ice covered them.

[4]

"WAS THAT WHAT I THOUGHT IT WAS?" SHE ASKED IN A quiet voice beside Kaden.

"Unfortunately."

His hands formed fists and he took a deep breath. At his side, the hunter still held the knife, her gaze centered on the window and the blanket of white covering it.

Instead of standing there like a fool, he got to work. When he'd first moved here, this had happened a couple of times. A great deal of snowfall high up in the mountains and a trigger often sent snowdrifts plunging toward the lower-lying areas. What he hadn't anticipated was this happening again after he'd cleared most of the drifts over a week ago.

And what was he doing a week ago? Planning a kidnapping in exchange for the safety of his pack.

He stormed to the front door, only to find, when he pulled it open, another wall of white. He went from window to window. Through each room and the result was the same. Most of the time there was at least one free crack, a place where the house wasn't covered.

"Hey, werewolf, you got a loft hatch?" she asked from behind him.

"I had plans for one someday, but it never happened. A cellar seemed more practical for food storage." Right above them was the roof, nothing more. With the right tools, they could break through it if they had to. Too bad those tools were in the shed.

Her face had grown pale since she'd eaten.

"How claustrophobic are you?" he asked. He reached out to touch her, but stopped himself in time.

"Not at all. You wouldn't believe the places I've had to hide to ambush my targets. I once hid in a garbage dumpster—"

"We'll have to dig ourselves out. Or should I say, I'll have to dig us out."

"What about air?"

"We should be fine for a day or two, but we can't have a fire." He immediately put out the fire to conserve their oxygen.

She appeared calm now, taking the news far better than he'd expected. But he wasn't worried about Cynthia as much as he was the people outside of his home who most likely had been hit by the same avalanche. He had to get out to check on them.

First things first. He gathered as many pans as he could from the kitchen cabinets. If she attacked him, he'd tie her to the bed if necessary. Instead, she hovered close, watching his progress. He returned to the doorway, scooping up as much snow as he could into the containers. A few of them he left near the fireplace to melt while he dumped the rest into the sink.

During his second trip, the lights went out, leaving the house pitch black. He had no trouble making out a few shapes here and there in the darkness, but Cyn would need light.

She bumped into the table as if to prove his point. A cup of water fell off and rolled under a chair. "Shit!" she mumbled.

He fetched a flashlight from under the kitchen sink and handed it to her.

"What's the power source to this place?" she asked as she cleaned up her mess.

"A cable from a generator in a shed north of here." He returned to the door to get to work.

"Which means something happened to that shed."

He nodded, digging even faster. This wasn't a good sign. Something bad had happened and he'd been too distracted with the hunter for upkeep.

She plodded over to the door. "Do you want help?"

Why couldn't she go to bed already? Was it that easy for her to forget she was a terminal leukemia patient? "Grab a blanket and keep warm. The temperature will drop soon and you're not well."

She took one of the bowls and the flashlight's beam danced about as she moved. "Didn't you heal me, though?"

He held back a grumble. "Unfortunately, it doesn't work that way. It takes time...among other things. All I did was give you strength you didn't have before."

"My arms are starting to hurt again. Not too bad, though."

He paused in the middle of working. The need to touch her and heal her nipped at him. "Take the aspirin on the table."

"So that's what that was."

"No sedative this time."

"Did Zach honestly believe I'd stay with you?"

"I guess he did."

"This will backfire if I kill you."

He chuckled. He had yet to meet a hunter like her. "You and what army?"

"I'm not at my peak anymore. Even I know that." She ran her fingers through her short-cropped hair. Most of the cancer patients he'd encountered during his internal medicine residency had made a pre-emptive effort to cut off their hair, but she'd left herself with a simple style. She leaned over, resting her head on her hands and her hair flopped over her face. Would it have been thicker before her chemo? Her cheeks fuller? Her hips wider?

After she had taken the pill, she fetched the bowls he'd filled.

"Do you have a shovel?" she asked.

"It's outside with everything else of value. I left one knife in the house for practical purposes. It doesn't cut worth shit, though."

She grinned. "So you don't trust me with a knife."

He rolled his eyes. "Just sit down and stop trying to help me."

But she persisted until he smelled her exhaustion as well as something else ominous. The effects of the chemo crept in. She stumbled with a pot on the way to the sink.

In a few footsteps, he caught up with her and snatched the bowl away. "No more. Go sit."

She glared up at him. "Are you serious? I'm not a dog."

With ease, he picked her up and headed for the seat farthest from the drafty fireplace. She was just as light as he remembered from when he'd carried her up the mountain to the cabin. Zach had trailed after him with the Christmas tree box. At the time, he thought the human had gone daft. Why not just leave his sister a note and be done with it? Now that he'd spent time with her, he found the man's idea was necessary. He had yet to meet a woman so stubborn. She wouldn't let up on her questions, either.

He almost put her down, but, on second thought, he grabbed a blanket from the closet. After sitting her down, he covered her with the blanket. There, now he could get some real work done.

Her hand locked on his arm. He stilled.

She twisted her face away as if she didn't want him to see, but he smelled her suffering, quite strong to his nose, like bitter chives.

"What's wrong?" Asking questions instead of assessing patients through their scent and body language was what humans did and her kind expected it. Most of his patients never knew he was a werewolf and it was for the best. He would've been denied the opportunity to attend medical school.

"The pain has started again." Her voice seemed strange, as if a knife's edge cut through her. "Please don't leave me."

"Have you been in pain all this time?" He sat next to her on the sofa. Close enough for their shoulders and knees to touch.

"Zach said I'm an expert at hiding it at this point."

"I can get you stronger pain medication if you want." He tried to get up again, but the grip on his arm persisted, even tightening for a moment.

"I can ride through it. I've done it before."

The pain had to be worse. He could practically feel the nerve endings firing against his skin where their bodies made contact. "Where does it hurt?"

"Does it matter anymore? I've lost track of all the report results. The blood cultures. The *stool* samples." She grimaced.

"I can only imagine." He glanced at her face and she stared into a dark corner. The flashlight on the coffee table was aimed away from them, but he could make out every feature on her beautiful face. He itched to check her, to gather her in his lap and place his palm on her body. Would she accept his healing?

"Please let me examine you." He rarely asked when it came to his pack. Most of the time orders sufficed when someone was in need.

"Zach always held my hand," she finally said. So he took her hand. The palm was cold, so he gathered her small hand in his larger one.

"You got a name?" She had been calling him *hey, werewolf* for a while now. He couldn't help smiling.

"Kaden."

She mouthed his name. Her breathing was far more audible now. And the snow continued to cover all the openings in the house. If he worked all day he could clear a hole, but even the needs of the others beyond that door didn't compare to those of the woman beside him. So he sat.

Silence filled the room, except for the occasional sound as someone shifted on the couch.

She hissed at his side, clutching his hand tighter. *Fuck it.* He gathered her into his arms. He didn't give a damn if she didn't want to be healed or be close to him. Let her fight.

But her head fell against him instead. She rested her cheek near the pulse point at his neck, her breaths steady on his bare skin. Every inch of her was cold and he fought the building desire to carry her to his bed and warm her properly.

"Have you ever been sick before?" she asked, ending the silence.

"Never."

"You're lucky."

"I was born this way." As were all his younger siblings. Living in northwestern Canada had been harder, but his pack had been safe, compared to those who lived in the south in the cities.

"My brother Ty had always been the sick one," she said. "He has diabetes. One would think that would make him sympathetic to others who cared for him, but he's always been an asshole."

He couldn't resist smiling, trying as covertly as he could to move the arm under her legs to cover them. "I have a sister like that, too. She has enough baggage to start a luggage store."

"As the oldest one, I used to be the strong one everyone depended on. I've never broken a single bone in my body. All those missions, and the most I've dealt with was a chest cold." She snorted. "Karma's an evil, vile bitch with a crooked toe."

"Now, that I agree with. As the eldest, I was expected to take care of the others and clean up their messes." He sighed. "My kind has made too many mistakes. The packs were supposed to reveal our existence under peace, but a few mongrels have rampaged and now we're hunted like animals." His right hand was closer to her stomach now. Bare skin would be perfect, but she'd never let him get that close. Mere inches separated his hand from where he needed to be. Wanted to be.

"You're so warm," she breathed.

The rise and fall of her chest drew his gaze. The T-shirt she put on covered her body but still revealed the curve of her breasts. Her nipples jutted out and his imagination went wild, feeding him images of his mouth licking at her sweet skin. She'd cry out each time his tongue circled the peak. He inhaled deeply, trying to resist the wolf that stirred within him, the feral part that wanted to take this strong female and bond with her. She had endless drive—only an alpha female would possess such a thing. But she was also a hunter.

Keep your pecker in your pants, pal. "Rest now."

Her breathing slowed a bit. His fingers inched over her hip, traveled underneath her T-shirt to her stomach. He stifled a growl when her bottom brushed against his groin. Almost there. The heavy cloth of long johns blocked his access, but he was close enough. *Hold your breath. Don't move.* His fingers spread out wide and he closed his eyes, focusing on the growing tension in his head, the tightened bow that, when released, would feed healing magic into her body. A part of him would become a part of her. Healing others took concentration, but he couldn't help but relax as she softened in his arms. With the right person, the pleasure bounced right back at him. A moan escaped her mouth and a shiver pulsed through him.

Suddenly Cynthia's hand that held his left hand let go and clutched the one on her stomach.

"I'm *grateful* and all, but I'm not interested in what you're selling me, Kaden." She was breathless, but now a harder edge lined the words. She'd just wanted him to comfort her and nothing more.

"I'm not selling anything." He could shove her hand away with ease but didn't.

"I don't want what you're offering."

His jaw twitched. "You don't want to live?"

"Oh, I want to live." She grew more animated by the minute. "And once I finish my chemotherapy, I'll be fine."

His eyebrows rose. She needed to work on her lies. "You're not doing well." What should have come out was, *You're dying*, but she didn't need to hear that. She needed to hear him say he was willing to do anything to make sure she survived. "And whether you like me or not, I'm compelled to heal those who are hurt. Have you ever thought about how your brother feels and what he might be willing to sacrifice to save you? I've seen the families suffering firsthand back in the cities where I used to work. Have you seen the desperation a father has to heal his child or that of a husband for his wife?"

She visibly swallowed. Then, moving faster than he'd expected, she tried to remove his hand from her stomach. "I don't care," she bit out. "I don't trust any of your kind and I don't need you to fix me."

He didn't fight her, even when she tried to head-butt him. The swipe to his head missed and she hit the couch instead. When she did get close enough to strike him with her fist, he snatched her forearm in mid-swing.

"Enough!" he thundered. His whole body tensed; the wolf writhing under his skin was hungry for a fight. There was no way she could stay here with him. "If that's what you want, I won't touch you ever again."

She didn't move in his lap, merely staring back at him with as much ferocity as he threw at her. The moment he let go of her arm, she scrambled off his lap and sat in the darkness of a far corner.

[5]

THE MOMENT HIS ASS FELL ASLEEP, CYN WAS GOING TO reduce the werewolf population in the area by one. That is, if she didn't fall asleep first. But he didn't go to sleep; matter of fact, he scooped bowl after bowl of ice, clearing a path until a spear of light penetrated the room through the front door. So much time had passed and now the setting sun was the last of the light they had, which most likely meant they'd spend the night in the dark.

He never looked her way the whole time. Scoop after scoop, trip after trip, he got rid of enough snow to reveal the outside. The cold air swept in and even the blanket around her shoulders didn't keep her warm.

As to how long she'd stay mad at him, forever didn't seem like a great option. Forever in a dark corner didn't fill her belly or make the ache go away. With each passing minute, she felt closer to nausea, closer to the moment she first woke up in Kaden's bed.

But wasn't that what you wanted? she thought. Hadn't she told him she didn't want his help? In essence, wouldn't she rather die than let a werewolf heal her? All her training, all the words her mother had taught her about werewolves fought against what she'd experienced for the last twenty-four hours.

"They have a driving need to dominate and deceive, Cyn. Don't fall for their smooth words and tricks," her mother used to say.

She hadn't been harmed, though. Her gaze flicked to the couch. Not more than a few hours ago, they'd been sitting there with her on his lap. And damn it all to hell, but he'd made her feel good.

While Kaden was in the kitchen, a shadow passed over the opening. She tried to back toward the wall, immediately realizing there was no place to go. Was someone out there? Not just someone; two shadows passed by.

"You're scaring her. Back up," Kaden called out.

Her head whipped to the kitchen. *Scared? Pffi!* She wasn't on her deathbed yet.

"Are you all right, Kaden?" a woman's voice asked.

"Still alive and kicking." He sounded bored.

"For half a second, I was concerned that bitch would hurt you."

Bitch? Cyn sucked in a deep breath.

"Watch your mouth, Naomi!" Kaden marched into the living room and walked right past Cyn.

"What?" the woman said. "You told me she's a hunter. You can't throw one of those crazies without getting cut in the process."

Kaden's frantic digging cleared a wider opening until he was able to crawl outside. She peered with curiosity as he spoke to whomever was outside. She strained to hear, but couldn't catch what was said.

She slowly stood, making her way toward the opening, only to have to back away as a woman made her way in.

"Who are you?" Cyn whispered. "Are you Naomi?"

This woman had to be another werewolf. There was something about the dark-haired woman's stance, the smooth way she angled herself through the hole and slid inside. Her features were familiar. Cyn had seen that perfect nose and cleft chin before, the same black hair and green eyes. Was the woman related to Kaden?

The werewolf didn't answer her question. Instead, she silently studied Cyn.

Not far behind the person, who *had* to be Naomi, someone else appeared, a tall, bald black man. "I told you not to rush in here," he barked.

Who are all these people? The man took in Cyn. Not with curiosity—his eyebrows were lowered and his cold black eyes stared her down as though he'd determined every possible way to dissect her. His skin was light brown, while the stubble on his face had hints of red and brown. His stance was stiff, yet self-assured. Men like him had 'hired killer' written all over their faces.

Kaden came inside last. The chill from the outside followed him.

Since the others weren't feeling too chatty, she kept her mouth shut.

"How bad is it out there, Sinister?" Kaden asked as he shrugged on his coat.

"Shitty," the man mumbled. His eyes never left hers.

"Any estimate on how much time it will take to bring back the power?"

"Nope." Evidently, he was a man of few words.

"Let's go check the generator shed." Everyone clamored outside. With only the blanket, Cyn shivered against the wind. The avalanche had cleared so many trees, leaving a streak of bare land from above. Without all the trees in the way, she was surprised to see more cabins uphill, at least seven of them. All this time, the trees had hidden them.

Kaden stared up the hill and cursed. "This isn't good. We're exposed now."

"To who?" Cyn asked.

"To anyone who has the means of finding hidden packs," Naomi snapped. "People like you."

Cyn knew very well what kind of people Naomi was talking about. Freelancers. Not all werewolf hunters had clans. The freelancers picked away at the werewolves who fled the cities and exterminated them for rewards from the larger clans. If the landslide had occurred less than a day ago, there was no telling when a freelancer might find this hidden set of buildings.

From the ground, Sinister picked up a Mossberg sniper rifle, a beauty. The tall man eyed her as if he practically dared her to dive for it.

Kaden placed his coat over her shoulders, but she declined the offer. "Go back inside," he said. "I have work to do, and you're in no condition to stand out here."

He did have a point there. Reluctantly, she returned to the cabin through the opening in the snow. She was surprised to see Naomi following her. Did Kaden think she needed company? A nurse wasn't necessary at this point.

The inside was colder now. Darkness was spread like a cowl over everything. She made her way to the couch and sat.

Naomi continued to stand there.

"My brother will be busy for a while, hunter." Her malevolent smile spread wide. "He never should've left you alone with me."

[6]

"This doesn't look too good, Windham," Sinister mumbled to Kaden.

Kaden waited at the entrance to the generator shed. The only part the avalanche hadn't caved in. Tension filled him to the point where he gripped the door tight enough to bend the metal. The snow had brought down trees, which in turn had decimated the generator shed's roof and the far wall.

No power meant no refrigeration. Any food could be moved outside or to the cellar, but the medical supplies that required a constant temperature of 40° were another story, especially if Cynthia needed them. And, at the rate she was going, any minute now that hunter would hit him over the head with a medical emergency.

He tried to push thoughts of the hunter aside. "How bad is 'doesn't look too good'?"

"We need to clean the carburetor and the spark plugs. Clear out the snow and patch the walls. If I ditch guard duty for a few days, it'll take me at least seventy-two hours."

"Shit." At least wood was plentiful for the fireplaces.

"Yep."

There wasn't enough time in the day for what had to be done. He'd come to depend on Naomi for a few things. If his sister hadn't been so bitter after she returned to him a few months ago, the situation wouldn't be so complicated. Hayley was a part of that problem. Memories of that woman dampened his day even further.

Sinister glanced up. "Is the hunter better?"

"Not really." He wished he could say yes. Cynthia made things harder than they had to be. "How's your shoulder?"

"A mosquito bite. Your sister didn't hurt me."

Kaden chortled. He wouldn't call a stab wound to the shoulder a mere mosquito bite, but Sinister wasn't like most human men. A few months ago, when Naomi had shown up on his doorstep, she'd found Sinister at his cabin instead of him. When he returned from his two-day fishing trip, he'd found Sinister chopping wood—and bleeding—while his sister cooked dinner.

As hard as he tried to pry what had happened out of the two, his sister had refused to divulge the details.

A beeper attached to Sinister's hip went off. Only twice since he'd moved here had he heard the perimeter alarm go off. *Shit.*

"Looks like a freelancer has come to play," Kaden said. Uncertainty flickered through him. Fear was something he rarely entertained unless he feared for the life of those close to him.

Sinister cocked a grin and pulled the rifle off his shoulder. "What about Naomi and the hunter?"

"They'll be fine. Naomi will take good care of her."

"WHAT THE HELL IS THAT SUPPOSED TO MEAN?" CYN bit out.

"Something happened to him after Hayley left," Naomi said, her voice calm and cold. The werewolf strolled away from the only light source in the room, the way out through the partially covered door. The darkness in the corner swallowed her. "He's gotten all soft, thinking he could protect the pack if he sent us away until he found a safer place."

Who the hell is Hayley, and what does that have to do with me?

Cyn shrugged to keep a straight face, but warning bells rang loud through her skull. She had a werewolf in the middle of a power play, poor lighting conditions, and only one way out of the house. "That sounds like a personal problem between you and your brother. What do I have to do with any of this?"

"You're not strong enough to be his mate," Naomi said from the corner. Cyn couldn't see her anymore. "Our pack is weakened right now, and if you just…died…there would be one less weak link among our ranks."

Was this the sister Kaden had been talking about who had issues? She didn't know the details going on between Zach and Kaden. Time to set things straight. "I don't know what you might be thinking, but I have no *interest* in staying here. The way I see it, we should join forces and beat up Kaden. After that, we hunt down my knuckle-headed brother who helped him."

"I don't care how much he likes you. My idea is better," Naomi growled. Her head emerged from the shadows, revealing her bright yellow eyes.

At a time like this, Cyn couldn't afford to do any stupid shit. Walking in here without knowing her environment was a deadly game, but what she did know was the layout of the room before the lights went out.

Naomi pounced and Cyn sidestepped out of the way. Using Naomi's momentum, Cyn tossed her across the room onto the kitchen table. The sounds of broken glass and splintered wood bounced off the walls. Naomi was far faster, maybe even a bit stronger, but she didn't see the bag full of Christmas joy before it hit hard across her face.

Cyn cringed at the sound of ornaments breaking. She stepped back, ready to swing again, but Naomi threw a hard jab and connected with her face. The punch to Cyn's cheek rocked her hard and sent her sprawling into the nearest wall. The hardwood wasn't forgiving. Damn, she was rusty. That's what sitting around did to you.

She got to her feet as fast as she could and threw up her hands to protect her face. Naomi's blows grazed her forearms, but they still hurt like hell. There was no finesse in the way the young woman fought; maybe it was the lack of formal combat training. Punches were thrown in abandon without technique or precision.

When an opportunity came and the werewolf exposed her side, Cyn came at her with an uppercut followed by two right hooks. Unlike Cyn, Naomi didn't block when Cyn clocked her across the side of her head. After a few more hard hits, Naomi added some distance between them.

Cyn took a second to catch her breath. Not bad for a chick who'd staggered to bed every day last week.

"Don't get cocky," her dad used to say. *"Keep reassessing your battleground and your target. They're most likely pissed and ready to rip out your throat after you kick them down."*

"You're not good enough for him," Naomi spat.

"And you're one to judge?"

"You're weak. I can smell death all over you."

Cyn chuckled. "You must be referring to all the werewolves I've killed. You wanna be next?" She had no plans to kill Naomi, but if push came to shove, she'd have no qualms about knocking her out.

Instead of letting Naomi recover, Cyn charged at her,

running across the room. They crashed into the Christmas tree and ended up on the floor. The one place Cyn didn't want to be: in the dark rolling around on the hardwood with a werewolf. One deep scratch to her back and a bite to her shoulder sent Cyn into a rage. She rolled on top of Naomi's back and secured her hands around the woman's neck. With a last-ditch tug upwards, she forced Naomi to arch her back as a grunt was torn from the woman's throat.

"You bitch!" she groaned.

Naomi twisted and jerked to get out of the camel clutch, but Cyn had executed this move far too many times to make mistakes. Naomi twitched and then passed out. Cyn immediately released her and staggered to stand. A quick check of Naomi's pulse revealed a steady heartbeat.

"I think I was good enough…for now." She walked away from Naomi, her legs wobbling a bit. The adrenaline in her body would fade away soon, leaving her vulnerable. She rubbed the throbbing sore spot on her cheek. How had she gotten into this shit?

Her damn brother.

If her chemo treatment recovery had gone as planned, she'd be sitting at home, chain-watching shows on Netflix with an industrial-size bag of movie theater popcorn. The thought of blowing through the whole season of *Firefly* seemed much more appealing. She welcomed the rest now.

Everything should've been quiet in the room, but her head darted up when she heard gunfire.

By the time Kaden reached the ridge above the cabins, a growing rage had built in his stomach, clenching tighter and tighter. This place was meant to be a safe haven. A territory he'd established for his pack.

Shots were fired to his right southward, at least a mile away. He spotted someone hiding among the trees with a long-range rifle in hand. So that was his target. The wolf in him pushed him forward. *Seek out your prey.* The full moon was coming and it had been a while since his need to hunt had been sated.

The guy in military fatigues darted even closer, searching for an ideal position from which to fire. No one else was coming, but the man was heavily armed.

Crouching low, Kaden shrugged off his coat. He glanced at Sinister and they exchanged nods. Next came the rest of his clothes. Pinpricks danced along his skin as the need to transform folded over him. Claws bit his fingertips and sprang forth first. That was but a momentary pain compared to the broken bones and shifting flesh. He endured the discomfort each time, the price he had to pay for the wolf's power.

The forest blossomed into vivid colors and his target's scent became all too clear. Kaden didn't have to see him as he raced southward in a wide arc. He'd find him by scent alone. Gunpowder was sharp and metallic on his tongue and the scent grew stronger the closer he got. By the time he was behind the freelancer, a clear trail of footprints led Kaden toward his target. He slowed down, eagerness making his heartbeat race.

Almost there. Up ahead, he could clearly see Sinister taking aim with his Mossberg sniper rifle, waiting for an opportune moment to fire. The freelancer was behind a rocky outcropping and hard to see.

Movement from the cabins made Kaden freeze. Cyn emerged from his cabin with no blanket and a stagger to her step. She scanned the horizon as if searching for the gunfire's source.

The freelancer cocked his head and looked up. "Cynthia?

What the hell?" The guy reached for something on his hip: a gun or a radio; Kaden didn't care. He surged forward, ramming the freelancer into the outcropping. The hunter's long-range rifle clattered to the ground. What he should've done was subdue the older man, but freelancers were all the same. If this guy knew their position, he'd report back, and more men would come. More death.

Kaden clamped down on the hunter's throat and watched the hunter's eyes roll back in his head as Kaden cut off his air supply.

One life in exchange for many was something Kaden would have to live with.

The freelancer stilled and Kaden left him behind to hurry up the hillside to Cyn. She was still outside and had seen the whole exchange, which was most likely why she was staring at him. A hint of her fear reached him, sour like sweat, and gathered along her temple. He caught the bruising along her cheek and held himself in check.

The cabin was silent except for a steady heartbeat from someone inside. Flashes of what could have happened stumbled before his eyes and it took everything he had to keep himself from storming into that cabin to reprimand his sister. *Focus on Cynthia*, he reminded himself.

Cynthia kept backing up until she reached one of the trees near the cabin. All the while, her gaze never left his. The anger simmering under her skin cooled and was replaced with something else: exhaustion. Her knees sagged first and she grasped the tree for support. He took a step toward her and she stiffened.

He froze. Every part of him sensed what was coming. Her heartbeat slowed. She gasped for every breath and blinked as if she clung to consciousness with her fingertips. The moment she closed her eyes, he transformed back into a man.

When Kaden picked her up, she didn't stir. Her fight was gone. *For now*, he thought with a frown. He'd told her he wouldn't touch her anymore. He'd have to break that promise soon and there'd be consequences.

Whether you heal her or not, you know you want her, he thought.

A shadow crossed him. Sinister didn't speak. It was for the best.

"Go into the cabin and check on Naomi," Kaden said. "She did something very foolish, and if I speak to her, it will be in anger." He trembled, fighting to keep his grip around Cyn not too tight.

[7]

This time, when Cyn woke up, she rose to a noisy house and a pounding headache, the normal kind folks have when they'd slept for too long. She didn't feel like shit, though. There should've been a huge-ass bite mark on her shoulder, but there wasn't. The lump under her eye was missing, too.

What became her immediate concern were the blankets. They weren't Kaden's. The jovial pink pattern with flowers didn't seem his taste. The furnishings were minimal, just a dresser and chest.

Beyond the closed door, she heard voices.

"Just because she's awake doesn't mean we have to go," a woman's voice barked, Naomi's. "This is my home!"

"Do as you're told." This time, it was Kaden's sharp voice.

Naomi laughed. "I'm still against the idea of bringing a hunter here to endanger us."

"A bargain has been made and I'm prepared to live with the consequences."

"And will those consequences affect the entire pack? Will

that affect all the work we have put into this place, your Shangri-La in the mountains?"

Cyn rose from the double bed. Naturally, it creaked. What were they talking about? What bargain had been made? She knew her brother had made a bargain of some kind with them for her life, but she didn't know the details.

She strained to listen further, but when she got to the living room, she found only Kaden sitting on the couch. He sat back, his feet propped up on the coffee table.

"Where are they?" she asked him.

"I heard you wake up, so I told them to leave." This protective streak of his bothered her, but there was nothing she could do about it.

"How long did you let me sleep this time?" she asked him.

"As long as was necessary for you to recover. A few days."

She harrumphed. "There's not enough time to scratch the surface of that problem."

She took a seat on the opposite side of the couch. Some distance would be good until she sorted out what was up between them. She sat for a bit, almost waiting for him to say something. Wasn't he an alpha? Didn't he want to take control of the situation?

"Look, as much as I want to hunt down your sister and beat the crap out of her for punching me, I can be the grown-up and let it go. What I can't let go is that you and what's going on at this place are bigger than I can even imagine. I suspect you're making a safe haven for your pack."

"An attempt of many," he replied drily.

"Do you think more freelancers will come?"

"Probably not. If someone sounded the alarms, more than one hunter would have come for us."

She nodded, recalling the man she'd seen before Kaden had

killed him. Gregory was a bat-shit loner who only showed up during large hunter gatherings every couple of years. The chance of single-handedly taking out an alpha was too delicious a kill to share with others. But then again, Gregory had seen her. What if Kaden hadn't killed him before he reported her whereabouts back to her clan? She was a hunter living in a werewolf's den. *A traitor.* Her stomach soured at the thought, but it was the truth.

"I shouldn't stay here," she finally said. "I'd endanger everyone."

"Bullshit." He scooted closer to her. She tried to shift the other way, but there was no place to go.

Her head whipped to look at him. "I'm a hunter, Kaden. My people hunt yours."

"Not here."

"In your—as Naomi would call it—Shangri-La, a utopia for werewolves? The way I see it, there are too many bad eggs in the box to push the bad feelings away. There's money to be made hunting your kind."

His mouth formed a hard line. "Did you ever collect a paycheck?"

She didn't look away. She refused to be ashamed for doing what she'd thought was right.

"Personally, I don't care if you got paid. What matters is right now. Your brother asked me to save your life. He said his big sister was more precious to him than even his clan. At first, I didn't believe him, but now I do."

She rolled her eyes. "You've known me for what, two or three days? How do you know what kind of person I am?"

The mischievous smile on his face widened as his eyebrows lowered. He leaned toward her, close enough for her to smell the whisky he'd been drinking. "For most werewolves, they can sniff out the useless ones after a midnight run. It's different with alphas. It's my job to assess. One night with you was more than enough for me. You're amazing in more ways than one."

"I still can't stay." She tried to be vehement, but having him so close was doing something to her insides. "I'm not gonna lie. I'm attracted to you, but you and I can't have a relationship." She sighed. "I even had to let someone else go."

"Why did you let him go?" he asked softly.

"He was perfect."

He chuckled.

"Not in the way you'd think." She paused. "Michael had the kind of life I could've had if I hadn't become a hunter. I'd wear heels to cocktail parties. Yacht rides on the bay. An apartment in the city. But I turned it all away. I had to."

"Why?"

"Because I made a choice, Kaden." Her voice became strained. "I chose to protect him from my lifestyle. Even if I'd married him, what would he do if the werewolves came for him to blackmail my clan? What if we had children and they ended up dead like my—"

He caught her arm. "That would never happen if you were with me. I'd protect you, us. Every single night you've been here, you've lain in my bed in my arms. It felt right." His fingertip brushed against her knee. "Give me one good reason why you *shouldn't* stay."

She had a million and one but couldn't speak. Finally, she said. "You told me you wouldn't touch me anymore."

"After your fight with my sister, I had to do what was necessary to keep you alive. Even if I'm fighting the need to make you mine."

Her stomach dropped and she sensed his heated gaze. He placed his hand on her knee. The warmth from his palm should have angered her, but she felt pleasure instead. Somehow, she had to drive a wedge between them before she gave in to what she was feeling, too. Here she was, sitting next to an alpha, and she wasn't fulfilling the duty her parents had drilled into her every day: *exterminate the vermin*. Falling for one of them was unforgivable.

"You don't get it, do you?" She took a deep breath. "If I let you heal me completely, I give up my humanity. I have to give up the cause I've fought for years to defend."

His grip on her knee tightened. There was no place for her to go. "I want you to stay—I told myself it was my drive to heal you. The need to help another person, but every moment we're together I want more." His gaze raked over her from her face down to her legs. "You smell so good. You're driving me crazy."

"What are you saying?" she breathed. *What if* came to mind and she couldn't shake it. What if he could be the normal she needed?

His lips were almost close enough to brush hers, but he didn't fill the gap.

"I care for you." He sighed. "And I want to touch you again, but I'm willing to wait until you're ready to come to me."

[8]

Cyn couldn't believe he'd said that. He cared for her? Had he lost his mind? But as her hand rose to rest on his chest, the same question could be asked about her. His heartbeat thundered under her palm. She was the one who was doing that to him.

The man whose lips hovered above hers wasn't the same man she'd met when she awoke in bed. The hidden layers she hadn't known about were now bare for her to see.

Even after she'd seen him attack that hunter, she could still see his real side. He wasn't a brute or a conman like the men she hunted—so what was he? And what place could she have in this new life?

He was waiting for her. She had to be the one to bridge the gap.

She stood, as if turning away from him would make him disappear. But she still caught his scent, and the warmth from where he touched her lingered. He was standing behind her now, his breath fluttering against the top of her head.

Maybe if she faced him and told him she planned to leave, he'd let her go. *Good luck trying.* When she met his gaze, the raw intensity of his green eyes dissolved any words she had gathering on her tongue.

Say it. Tell him you're leaving.

Instead, she pressed her lips against his. *Bliss.* A second later, her back was slammed into the wall. The Christmas tree shook, making the red and green lights dance against the walls. He smothered her body with his. Every hard inch of him, from his chiseled stomach muscles to his legs, held her in place. His breaths were hard and heavy, the primal part of him evident in his lidded eyes. With one hand, he stretched her arms above her head, granting him access to her neck. His mouth drifted from hers to nibble over her jaw down to the sensitive skin along her neck and back to her mouth. She struggled to touch him, to feel his face or explore the width of his back.

He growled against her mouth. "No moving. I want to taste every part of you."

Her head naturally tilted as the kiss deepened. His tongue brushed against hers, commanding and bold. With each stroke of his tongue, his hand, which had rested on her hip, snaked under her T-shirt to yank it upwards. The moment his hand touched her skin, honey-like warmth radiated from his palm. Strength surged into her limbs and her body trembled from sheer pleasure. But it wouldn't be any fun if she just hung out like this all night while the good doctor healed her.

She grinned. *Oh, no, you're not gonna be captain of this ship for very long.*

She managed to twist one of her wrists from his iron grip. With one hand free, Cyn grasped his arm and curved it with a jerk behind his back. He grunted, not in discomfort, but surprise, especially when she shoved him away. Now a few feet separated them. He waited, their breaths heavy in the silent room.

Now this game could be played on her terms.

"Cyn..." he gasped. The thick muscles along his forearms twitched and his mouth parted to reveal clenched teeth. Was he hanging on a thin thread like she was, straining to make this moment last instead of screwing without a care?

Their gazes locked. She took a step toward him. Placed her index finger on his chest and pushed him backward until the backs of his legs hit the couch. He sat down and she straddled his lap. Off came her T-shirt. She grasped at his shirt and when the buttons gave her trouble, she ripped the shirt open. Screw the buttons.

He was sheer perfection with hard abs and a delicious V-shape to his hips.

She sampled his skin, kissing, sucking, and nibbling at his lips. With every lick, she tasted him: the saltiness around his neck, the dry bite of whisky along his lips. He was just as eager. His hands were everywhere, grasping at her hips, unhooking her bra, kneading her ass. Every touch added fuel to the frenzy growing under her skin.

All the while, she rocked her hips, rubbing her core along the bulge under his zipper. She eased herself slowly back and forth. Jerking against him until his hands locked on her hips and he thrust upward.

"Cyn," he hissed, "you're making it hard for me to control myself."

There were too many pieces of clothing between them. She wanted everything from him. No boundaries set by hunters or werewolves.

He pushed her up, and she shrugged off her jeans and panties. Now she was bare before him. She expected him to carry her to bed, maybe even bend her over the couch and plow into her. But he sat there. Still clad in his pants—a matter she'd remedy soon—and all he did was stare. He took in the curve of her bare breasts. His eyebrows rose with amusement and his tongue darted out to lick his lower lip, then his attention turned to the gold ring jutting out of her belly button.

Next his hand rose and he brushed his fingertip against the elaborate tattoo on her hip, the red paw print that was the symbol for her hunting clan. "Nice tat." He swiveled his fingertip over her nipple and she gasped. Then he dipped his fingertip into the moist seam between her thighs.

Just that one caress from her nub to her channel's entrance made her moan.

He tried to draw her down to him, but her gaze flicked to his jeans. "Too many clothes."

His half-grin did something to her insides. Without a word, he unbuttoned his pants and pulled them off. The ladylike thing to do would be to meet his hungry gaze eye-to-eye, but she wanted to see what she'd been grinding against for the past few minutes.

Off came his briefs, and now he was naked before her in all his glory. Hot damn on a stick, he was a tasty holiday treat waiting to be devoured.

"I think we're about even now," she whispered.

She pushed him back on the couch and he drew her toward him. She eased down on his length, her core stretching to accommodate his girth. Over the years, she'd had a lover once in a while, never a one-night stand, but all of them had been humans. She'd never felt so tightly wound, so ravenously hungry to make love.

His hands tightened on her thighs as she slowly rose again. Heat seared her skin from where he was continuing to heal her.

"Oh, Cyn…you're beautiful."

She lowered herself again, savoring how much he filled her. As agonizing as the slower pace was, there was something so intimate about facing him. Lips against lips. Her cries of pleasure sucked into his mouth.

She climaxed; her stomach muscles locked as her body shook.

"Up." When she didn't move, he lifted her off him with ease. Her legs barely held her, so he picked her up and marched to the bedroom.

He was between her legs before she had a chance to scoot all the way onto the bed. In one hard thrust, he was inside. He growled and all she could do was cling to him.

Every thrust stole her breath, her body rising to the heights of bliss. So high, she might not ever come down.

She reached the peak first, but he kept going, feeding the overflowing fire in her.

"All mine," he said, his whole body shuddering. Then he lay quietly with her; the only sound in the room was their quickened breaths.

"Are you all right?" he asked.

"I don't think 'all right' really is the best word for what I'm feeling right now."

"So what then?"

She thought for a moment—which was rather hard. Cyn wouldn't be the last gal to turn down rough sex once in a while, but what had just happened was beyond mind-blowing. Every bone in her legs had no substance; her throat was raw from screaming out his name. And even with all that, her core clenched again in anticipation. Instead of answering, she kissed him. In response, his shaft hardened and he thrust again. Ever so slowly.

Damn insatiable little wolf.

[9]

THERE IS NOTHING IN THE WORLD QUITE LIKE WAKING up and feeling ready to kick the ass of everyone who'd ever pissed you off in the past. Strength pulsed through Cyn. Even her hair had the sheen and volume from her high school days. But one thing was for certain, she wasn't a werewolf yet. He hadn't offered to change her and she hadn't asked. Getting up and dressing was just like any other day.

Kaden rolled over onto his back and placed his hands behind his head. He was awake. One glance at him was one too many for her. The muscles in his arms flexed and she had to look away. He was sheer perfection from his chest down to the place where the covers hid the best part. She stood beside the bed waiting for him to say something, but he didn't. When she took a step to leave, the bed groaned as Kaden got up. She didn't look back.

Would he try to stop her? With each footstep, she reminded herself she wasn't the same woman who'd had to be carried into the cabin. She was well enough to take care of her brother and come back.

She would come back, wouldn't she?

The living room was dim. Kaden maintained a respectable distance behind her. All the curtains had been left shut and only streaks of light peeked through the cracks. Something new over the fireplace drew her attention. A set of stockings. Four of them with names stitched into the top. Make that three. She had one, as well as Kaden and Naomi, while Sinister's stocking was oversized and bright white with his name written in pen at the top. She snorted, not surprised. Someone, most likely Sinister, had come in while they were busy in the bedroom and had left candy—real candy—in the stockings.

Someone had left her bag by the door. She fetched it and put on her boots.

It was Christmas Day. Every single Christmas, the McGinnis kids would gather wherever the family deemed was safe and they'd open presents and eat some kind of burnt bird. Zach made the most horrible cook, but he tried and they made an effort to choke down a bite or two, except Ty. He just complained.

This Christmas was different, though. The broken-down tree was in the wrong place. There were no presents. The lights were dimmed. She opened the window for good measure. There was a fresh layer of snow outside. Perfect Christmas weather.

She shrugged on Kaden's coat, refusing to look at him. She sensed his unwavering gaze. If she looked at him, she suspected her resolve would melt away, and all these new feelings she had for him would cloud her judgment.

If she left now, once she reached the highway and then Prince George, she could reach Vancouver in about ten hours. It wasn't like she hadn't hitchhiked before.

She grabbed her bag and left the house. The sounds of the door opening and closing behind her could be heard. Any moment now, she expected him to grab her arm to say something to stop her. To her surprise, it was the dark wolf that ended up walking beside her. He was massive. Something to be feared, but now, she only felt safe.

Her hand brushed against the soft fur along his flank.

She couldn't help thinking about what had happened the other day. Kaden had killed someone to defend his pack. He'd protected his loved ones as he'd told her he'd do. *He'd protect you too*, a voice whispered in her head.

The wolf remained at her side as she trudged through the snow. The landscape was beautiful. The morning light reflected against the snow and a gust of fresh air blew across her face.

Contentment filled her and that overwhelming feeling made her stop walking. This was her first Christmas without arguments, without an upcoming assignment nagging at her. The cabins were small, about the size of her apartment, but when you lived so simply, why would you need more? She could stay here. No more hunting. No more hearing about dead family members. But could she stay here with Kaden? Michael couldn't give her a normal life and neither could Kaden, but the werewolf was someone just as wonderful. She could not deny or ignore the way he made her feel safe, the way he'd given a part of his soul so that she could live longer.

The wolf circled in front of her and blocked the path. She could go around him if she wanted to do it, as she had planned when she first left the house. But at that moment, she knew she was done running. She was done searching for the normal. Instead of dying, she could live on with someone who cared for her and understood her circumstances. And whatever dangers they faced, they could face them together.

Instead of going around Kaden, she picked up some snow. She didn't have any gloves, but she didn't plan to hold the snow for very long. With a mischievous grin, she lobbed the snowball at him. Before she caught the wolf's reaction, she turned around and made a run for it. What kind of fool would just stand there?

Laughing felt good. When was the last Christmas she'd had a snowball fight with her brothers? It had been so many years ago, she'd lost count. When she reached the cabin, she turned to see she was alone. She scanned the valley and couldn't spot him.

The snowball that hit her on the side of the head came out of nowhere. Ehh, she'd deserved it. Kaden emerged from the trees, quite naked, and marched over to her holding more snowballs. "Are you done?" he asked with a grin.

"Since you're naked—very much so." She held up her hands in surrender. Damn, he didn't even shiver. He dropped the snowballs and walked up to her. Silence passed between them, but all the while, she took in his gaze. The hint of a smile on his beautiful face. Was this what it felt like to fall for someone, this feeling when you could stand out in the cold and not give a damn, as long as that special someone was right there with you?

"Aren't you cold?" she finally asked him. She opened the coat and invited him into her arms.

"Not that much." He wrapped his arms around her waist. His heat radiated against her skin as she rested her cheek against his chest. She inhaled. He smelled delicious. All male.

"You don't worry about shrinkage, do you?" she blurted. She had to say it.

"So you noticed." His eyebrows danced.

Smart ass.

He used his hand to tilt up her chin and he kissed her long and slow. For a moment, she forgot about the cold, the fact that she was a hunter, and any other misgivings. Only this perfect sliver of time, this moment with Kaden, existed, and that was more than enough for her.

[10]

CYN HAD ALL THE ENERGY IN THE WORLD, YET SHE slept better than she had in years. Maybe the man who held her close made that possible. There weren't any antiseptic smells, no cold, white hospital room, no heart monitor beeps.

If she stayed here, she'd be free of that, and she'd have him, too.

"You keep squirming," he said against her forehead. His breath was warm. "If you keep it up, I might have to make love to you until you fall asleep again."

Now that was an offer she wanted to consider. "I've slept for long enough, but I'm not ready to get up."

He chuckled, running his hand up and down her arm. The firm touch formed goose bumps along her skin.

After they had made love again, they lay naked, limbs intertwined. It was Kaden who broke the silence again. "My pack is coming here. Your brother has…done his part in terms of our agreement."

She visibly swallowed. "Will they accept me?"

He kissed her forehead, slowly. "You'll be my mate soon,

and once that happens, I'm never letting you go. No matter what happens, you'll be by my side."

"And what if I try to leave again?" She sensed his smile in the darkness.

"I followed you twice before to let you decide on your own, but you won't be so lucky if you try again." He kissed her neck, drawing her leg over his hip. "You're mine now."

She laughed. "A real fight. Very nice. I wouldn't have it any other way."

THE HUNTER'S ALPHA

PART 2

[1]

"A PACK DINNER?" CYNTHIA SOMEHOW MANAGED TO keep a straight face. She had a feeling though that Kaden would read through any clever ruse she might create. "Are you sure this is a good idea? I think your pack needs time to get used to me."

Kaden had spent most of the day helping his pack settle in, now that they'd arrived. An introduction tonight seemed fitting—other than the fact that she was a hunter going to a pack event.

Honestly, Cyn wished she were back home in Vancouver so she could at least make a better impression. The only clothes she had were a couple of T-shirts, a pair of shorts, some women's thermal underwear, and jeans from her hospital bag. She had to wear them over and over again.

She tried to remember the last time she fussed over her appearance in the bathroom mirror. At least a year ago? To hunt werewolves, she needed guns and not glamour. Brushing her black, chin-length hair was useless. The ends pretty much went in every direction except down. With a sigh, she gave up.

"Stop tripping over how you look." He snuck up behind her and kissed her cheek. "You're beautiful."

He tugged her hand to make her leave the bathroom. "C'mon. I'll protect you."

She laughed. "From over ten werewolves?"

His right eyebrow rose. "As if you can't handle them yourself. You were twirling the steak knives the other day like they were batons."

"A girl's gotta stay fresh."

Cyn didn't have a proper coat yet, so Kaden helped her put on his spare coat. He paused when he touched her concealed weapon.

"Do you seriously have a metal meat hammer attached to your back?" He sighed and extended his hand. "Where did you get it—don't answer. You got anything else?"

She might as well be honest. Begrudgingly, she flashed the switchblade strapped to her ankle. "I sort of borrowed that from you."

"Is that it?" he asked.

"Of course."

He tilted his head. "You don't lie very well."

Clever little wolf. She pulled him toward the door. "Let's go."

He gestured with his fingers for more. When she didn't move, he did it again. "I can't protect you properly if you go ape-shit on the family during our first dinner together."

"Oh, c'mon! I don't even have a gun and silver bullets."

"As if that makes a difference." There was amusement in his voice.

"Don't you trust me?"

He ran his fingertips down her arms, but she backed away.

"I don't trust human nature," he said.

"Human...nature?"

"Werewolves still have a human side," he explained. "That's the human nature I'm talking about. People say and do things they believe are right, but, in the end, things can still go wrong."

"Throw me a bone, Kaden. And yes, pun intended. Let me have something."

His hands went up in surrender. "I'll concede if you do the same. If you're willing to leave a few toys here, I'm willing to back down."

"No strip searches?"

"Would you like one?" His voice became silky, and she laughed.

"As nice as that sounds, that would make us late. Ugh, just give me a second." She went into the bedroom. From her ankle, she plucked the switchblade. Just the knife. At least she conceded *something.*

There was no way in hell she wasn't going into the werewolves' den without some insurance against injury.

THE NOISE OUTSIDE THE CABIN WAS A PREVIEW OF WHAT was to come. The largest cabin was filled with werewolves. The moment Kaden walked through the door with her trailing behind him, Cyn expected silence, maybe even furtive glances in her direction, but the unexpected happened. No one looked her way.

"Kaden!" one of the men called.

Kaden leaned over to speak into her ear. "That's my brother Rhys. This is his cabin. My other brother Bastian is sitting with Naomi."

"Finally made it!" a blonde woman said as she darted between the tables set up for dinner.

"And that's Rhys's mate, Eva," Kaden added. "The two boys who are here are hers. She has an older son somewhere."

Even though no one greeted her, she had to admit that so far, the gathering seemed like one from a hunting clan: loud and rambunctious. Eva's two youngest boys chased each other around the tables. Naomi, Kaden's sister, argued with a dark-haired man on the other side of the room. The dark-haired guy must be Bastian.

Almost like home. She smiled. Her brother, Zach, was always the loud one, talking to everyone and making others feel at home. Back home, the newer hunters sat on the outer tables and took turns working as servers. That was the way of the clan. You worked your way up in rank and proved yourself in the field.

Compared to Kaden's simple home that didn't have any personal photos or knick-knacks, Rhys's home had family photos, hand-drawn pictures made by the kids, pretty much all the things that made a home comfortable. She took a deep breath, sucking in the decadent smell of fresh bread and all the fixings of what could be an excellent meal.

One figure in the corner though caught her eye. Compared to the others, this man had pale skin and snowy, white hair that fell to his shoulders. He was an albino werewolf. She was sure of it. The young man talking to the albino kept up their conversation, but the moment she got closer, the albino's red-eyed gaze seemed to focus on her. A cold feeling brushed over her, but she ignored the sensation. Deadly predators roamed this room, but showing any fear wasn't wise.

So she focused on learning what she could. Like the hunting clan, the werewolves appeared to have a pecking order below the pack alpha. The table where Bastian and Naomi sat had to be where the dominant werewolves ate.

There was only one free seat left for Kaden by the time they got there.

Kaden glanced at his sister. "This is rather preschool of you, Naomi."

"I didn't set up the table. It was Eva." Naomi didn't even look at him.

"So that makes it better?" he said tersely. "As much as you'd like to have things be difficult between us, this is the way things are. Help me out here."

He waited. This scene felt familiar, too. How many times had Cyn fought with her stubborn brother Ty? Well, when he decided to show up, she got to fight him.

Naomi stood and adjusted the placement of the plates. And gee, there happened to be plenty of room for another place setting.

"There," she said with a voice drenched in sarcasm, "I made a place for the *hunter* to sit."

That was when the place went dead silent. Even the two dudes eager to feast stopped in mid-stride.

Shit.

"Are you crazy, Kaden?" Eva nearly dropped the bowl of food she held and bared her teeth. With one glance at her children, they ran to her. The other pack members all looked at Cyn as if she'd pulled a gun.

Kaden closed his eyes for a moment, and then flashed Naomi a dark look. Even Cyn sensed the searing heat radiating from him. His sister looked at her plate and didn't move.

"They deserve to know from the beginning what she is, Kaden," his sister whispered. "I have nephews to protect."

"So violence instead of meaningful conversation is the best approach?" Kaden's gaze flicked to Eva. "Cynthia McGinnis is under my protection." His voice grew sharper. "Anyone who touches her will have to face me."

The tension in Rhys's body didn't ease, but Kaden's brother nodded. "I've always trusted you, Kaden. My mate and I will do as you command. But, I expect you and I will be having a long conversation on this matter."

Eva briefly looked at her mate Rhys with a question in her eyes, but she let go of her boys.

Tension knotted Cyn's stomach to the point where she lost her appetite. Slowly, everyone began to move again, but the vibe was different. Almost as if she'd sat in the room with a ticking bomb in the corner.

Kaden directed her to her seat next to Bastian and leaned over to kiss her neck. "You're gonna be fine. *Relax.*" He even massaged her shoulders a bit. They had to be bricks by now. "I'm going to get you something to drink and make sure it's not poisoned."

She laughed then stopped. Was he serious?

So...here she was, sitting at a table as the odd woman out. Making conversation with Bastian and Naomi wasn't gonna happen. For a moment, they stared her down, but she didn't look away. This was the first time she'd seen Kaden's brothers up close and she could see the resemblance in their faces. They had the same dark hair, handsome angular lines on their faces, and strong chins. But that was where the similarities ended. Kaden didn't smell like a high-class stripper joint or wear clothes better suited to picking up chicks.

Naomi's Cheshire-cat grin widened. "Cynthia," she whispered, "it's all downhill from here."

"Oh, really." After the fight she had with Naomi a few weeks ago, she expected as much.

"There's a bunch of snow cabs outside now. It might be in your best interest to consider using one of them someday." As Naomi spoke, Bastian began twirling his spoon on the wooden table. The noise was rather annoying. Was he trying to prevent Kaden from hearing their little conversation?

"The one in the back has plenty of fuel," Bastian added.

"How helpful of you." As much as she disliked Naomi, she did have a point. One of those snow cabs could take her home. They'd help her reach Prince George and, from there, find her way to Vancouver. Once there, maybe she could help her brother Zach. Since she'd been gone, she couldn't stop worrying about him. As a fellow hunter, Zach got into trouble more times than she could count.

When Cyn continued to stare right back at them, they gave up and began to annoy each other again as if she weren't there. They really needed to find a better way to pass the time.

"I'm surprised you didn't bring a little friend with you to dinner," Naomi said to Bastian.

"As much as I'd like to find a mate, there are too many vixens who need my attention," he replied smoothly.

"What about that girl you left behind in Toronto?" Naomi smirked. "She wasn't enough to tame the bad wolf in you? Or was it easier to just mess everything up with her father and have Kaden come clean up your mess?"

Bastian paused. "That's a low blow for even you, sister. What about you and your past lovers? Isn't it sunnier back in Los Angeles? Or maybe the reception there is too cold for your taste?"

Her body tensed. "You're an asshole."

Apparently, both of them had enough baggage to fill an airport terminal.

Not too long ago, Kaden had told her about the problems he had taking care of his siblings. Bastian seemed as troublesome as Ty was for her.

"The past always clouds our judgment. Especially when a lost love and a betrayed brother are involved," an unfamiliar voice said from close to Cyn.

Cyn turned to see the albino right next to her. *Holy shit, she hadn't even heard him walk over.*

He leaned in closer to her, and she caught his scent: sweet pine resin. How strange. Unlike most werewolves with flawless skin, this particular werewolf had a long scar from the corner of his eye down to his chin.

"Uncle Damien," Bastian said with his gaze fixed on the table.

He shifted to Bastian's seat right beside Cyn, and Kaden's younger brother swiftly vacated it. "I've yet to have the pleasure of dining with a hunter. In the past, I've dined *on them*, but we won't let that get in the way of pleasantries, will we?"

Awkward pause.

"Of course not," Cyn managed to murmur. What in the hell could she say? The dude sounded dead serious.

Damien looked around the table with a broad grin. "I've tried to teach these two tact, but they're rather incorrigible." He leaned his head toward her as if to share a secret. "In all honesty, they're pretty harmless. Naomi used to only eat ketchup as a child, and Bastian likes to eat his peanut butter and jelly sandwiches inside out."

"Oh...How do you eat them inside out? What about Kaden?" Cynthia tried to hide her amusement. She even ignored the exasperated expressions on Bastian's and Naomi's faces.

"I have countless stories to embarrass him! He used to sleepwalk as boy and we'd find him curled up in the dryer." Damien laughed. "I love conversations like this. Our hunter here makes for the most satisfying meal. This is more fun than the time your aunt Becca streaked naked across the front lines in World War II!"

When everyone looked at her as if it were her turn to say something, Cyn glanced away to see Kaden returning. *Thank goodness.* He was the tallest guy in the room, and he was so beautiful. Even among werewolves, he had something she couldn't place, a charisma that made her want to listen to him, to follow him wherever he went.

For the first time, she wondered what she would've done if she'd met him on the street. Would she have asked him out? Maybe spoken to him? Relationships for hunters were rare, though. She lived a life in which she wasn't home often and her last boyfriend wouldn't have understood her lifestyle.

Once Kaden put some punch into her hands, Cyn pushed thoughts of her past boyfriends and her strange company away.

"So we have punch now?" she asked. The liquid was red and smelled sweet.

"They snuck up some additional provisions," Kaden replied, "including liquor and a bunch of other things I wouldn't have recommended."

She took a sip and enjoyed the fruity taste. Not bad.

Dinner was served and everyone ate, including Uncle Damien, who ate far slower than anyone else. Between the smacking and clatter of utensils, bowls were passed around, but no one touched her. Matter of fact, they went out of their way not to touch her, except for one of Eva's kids.

"Hey, you want a rock-hard biscuit?" he asked. The blond-haired boy appeared to be no more than ten or so.

"Sure, why not. Thanks."

"I've never met a hunter before. You sure don't look like one," he remarked.

Now, that made her laugh. "Yeah, I've heard that before." From her targets, anyway.

"I'm Peter," he said, extending his hand. He was bold. She liked that.

"Nice to meet you, Peter. I'm Cynthia." She shook his hand.

"Yeah, I caught that already." He leaned in to put the

biscuit on her plate. "Be careful with Mom's cooking. She kind of experiments in the kitchen."

"Peter!" The sharp word came from the other side of the room. "Get away from her and get back to work. You should mind the company you keep."

Cyn's grip on her punch glass tightened.

Kaden glanced at Eva. "Don't start tonight, Eva," he said between clenched teeth.

Eva looked at Cyn then Kaden. "I'm Peter's mother, and I'll protect him as I see fit."

The conversation wasn't loud enough for Cyn to hear, but, then again, reading Eva's lips wasn't too hard. Cyn was surprised she hadn't outright called her that *hunter bitch.*

"I won't tolerate her," Eva added.

"I want peace, Eva," Kaden said. "This place is a haven."

"And it can be."

"As long as you get what you want." Kaden gripped the edge of the table until his knuckles turned white.

Eva stared him down and a standoff ensued. Many others in the room looked away as if to ignore them. Only Damien smiled as he continued to eat. The two glared at each other until Eva finally glanced away. A moment later, she stood and stormed out.

Cyn took a bite of the casserole and forced herself to chew. The food had a strange texture. Almost as if the chicken used for the dish had pieces that were overcooked and other pieces that were slightly undercooked. Chewy yet crunchy. Peter wasn't kidding. But for damn sure, she'd smile like crazy Uncle Damien and show these werewolves she wouldn't back down for anyone.

[2]

THE DINNER HAD ENDED—WITH EVERYONE STILL ALIVE—but the night wasn't over for Kaden.

He still had work to do.

Eight months and three days ago was the last time he'd seen his pack on a rain-soaked road in Seattle. When the werewolf hunters got too close and began killing his people, he sent them away to safety. Their return should've been a special day—until he had a suspicion that something was up. While he was greeting his pack and getting them settled, he never had a chance to inspect everything.

As the others retired to their cabins, Kaden walked over to the snow cabs. Not more than ten feet from the one in the rear, he caught a strange stench, oh so faint, yet quite familiar: death. It didn't have the musk of an animal, but that of a human.

The bitter Canadian cold couldn't mask the scent of dead human flesh.

He marched along the snow cabs, checking between each to see where the smell came from. So far, so good. But as he approached the one in front, the putrid odor grew stronger.

Once he reached the snow cab in front, he spotted something strapped to the cargo hold in the back: a dead body.

Who in their right mind brought a dead body to a safe haven? Didn't he always tell them missing humans left trails that only led to ruin? With werewolf hunters on the prowl for rogue werewolves, the world wasn't a safe place anymore.

Kaden's nostrils flared and the wolf within him churned, ready to strike. *How dare they do this?* The layers of plastic weren't enough to keep the smell hidden.

He approached the wrapped up plastic. Whoever lay within the layers was now stiff as a board, yet the corpse stank like rotting meat. No lingering perfumes or colognes. To a werewolf, even the dead told tales. His pack would have to know that. He reached for the body, but a figure approached him from behind.

The wind brought the werewolf's scent to Kaden's nose and the tension that filled him rose. Only one man would wear such expensive cologne in the far Canadian north where he'd be miles away from civilization and any women he'd want to attract: Bastian.

"What are you doing, Kaden?" Bastian's loosely cropped black hair ruffled in the wind. Bastian grinned at him and his green eyes shined as if such a gesture could make what was strapped to the snow cab disappear.

"Would you prefer 'Good evening, Bastian'? Or maybe 'What the hell is a dead body doing here?'" Kaden asked. He was proud he didn't sound too pissed.

"We ran into trouble on the way here," Bastian said.

Kaden reached for the plastic to unwrap the body but froze as suspicion hit him. His brother didn't stop him this time.

Bastian grew quieter. "Micah wanted to rip him to shreds, but I stopped him and did what was necessary to protect everyone."

Micah was Eva's eldest son. Protecting the boy was important, but a terrible mistake had been made.

"This man is a hunter, isn't he?" Kaden asked slowly.

Bastian hesitated before he inhaled. "How did you know?"

So Bastian had killed a hunter. Kaden remained still. If he moved, it would be to throttle his brother. "This is the wilderness, Bastian. Most trouble for our people involves hunters."

He was tempted to search the body for a clan tattoo, but he needed time to process the whole thing. A shit storm was coming soon. There was no way he could tell Cyn about this.

"What happened?" Kaden asked. "Tell me everything. And I mean everything."

"A biker was following us on our way to Prince George. At a rest stop, he followed Micah and me into the woods. We confronted him and killed him."

"Is he a freelancer?"

Bastian glanced toward the woods and took a deep breath. "I don't know, but he—"

"So it's possible a hunting clan might be looking for him?" Kaden asked.

Bastian didn't blink. "I did what was necessary to protect the pack. I'm the *one* who's been with them for the past few months."

Kaden snorted. His brother's attempt to cut him down wasn't gonna work. "You forget your place. I put Rhys in charge. Not you."

"Well then, maybe, as alpha, you made a *poor* choice."

Kaden advanced on his brother, ready to snap.

Bastian hesitated, then took a step back.

The need to strike down Bastian was overwhelming, but fighting without understanding the whole story wasn't wise.

"We'll discuss this later," Kaden said. "I need to investigate the matter further."

All Bastian did was nod.

"If you touch this man before I've had a chance to look at him, you'll have to answer to me." As the eldest, Kaden had a good five inches on Bastian and he was taller than Rhys, the middle child in the Windham family. "This mess better not blow up in our faces."

Bastian swallowed but otherwise didn't move. "This isn't Toronto. Everything will be fine."

As Kaden backed away from Bastian, he had a feeling more sacrifices would have to be made in the future, and he'd have to be the one to make them.

[3]

Morning came and Cyn woke up alone. As much as she wanted to hang around and wait for Kaden to return, she grew restless. Back when she lived in Vancouver, boredom could be easily fixed by going out the doors of her apartment. Along Granville Street, with all its fine restaurants and trendy bars, a younger crowd roamed the scene. Want to eat? Head down to The Refinery. Need to vent out some frustrations? Head to the dartboards over at Brazenhead Irish pub on 5th Ave.

That was her life. Before cancer, anyway.

Cyn got up from the couch and donned her coat. It was far too easy to fall into old memories.

A few weeks ago, she could barely get up, much less chew people out. Zach often came to her apartment to keep her company. Once in a while, he forced her to get out.

As much as she didn't want to do it, she touched her face. She used to be much thinner. All this time, she'd avoided the mirror in the cabin's bathroom. After she began losing her long hair, she taped wrapping paper over the mirror in her apartment in Vancouver. It was easier, in the beginning, to assume everything was fine and she could continue to hunt.

She stopped by the kitchen and tucked the metal meat hammer and a simple kitchen knife into her coat pocket. Kaden hated that she carried the thing around. A meat hammer was better suited for beating steaks into submission, but it was better than walking into a fight barehanded.

By the time she strode to the door, she'd shaken off what tried to drag her down. For now, she was stronger, and she was here with Kaden.

Cyn left her cabin and headed to the others. Cold air bit the exposed skin on her face. The air was crisp and fresh, nothing like the city. She had come to love that about the mountains. Maybe she'd see Kaden and they'd go for a walk like they did a few days ago. She didn't expect much more than that. What she did find, as she walked up the plowed path toward the hidden cabins, were the two boys she'd seen during dinner. Another older boy stood beside them with his hands in his pockets. They stopped tossing a ball back and forth to peer at her with curiosity.

She offered a casual wave, and only one of them waved back.

Eva probably told them to leave her alone and stay away from the deadly werewolf hunter. Yep, she was sure feeling dangerous and ready to prepare a barbecue feast for herself.

A ball soared over her head and fell into the snow behind her. With a few hops into the deep snow, she managed to fetch the ball. The boys had good taste. It had been a while since she'd seen a high-quality Diamond baseball. Back when she was a tomboy, she used to play catch with Zach. He sucked at catching, but he threw quite well. She turned around to see someone waiting close by.

It was Peter, the one who had spoken to her last night.

She threw the ball and he caught it with ease. "Thanks," he said quietly.

"Not a problem," she replied.

He seemed to consider something for a moment. Other than his blond hair, the boy took after his father, Rhys. "Would you like to play catch with us? My younger brother Phil isn't too good and Micah is still being a jerk."

Cyn laughed but paused when she caught the dark look Micah threw her way. "Thanks for the offer, but I have things to do. Just give your brother some time and he'll figure it out. My little brother was the same way."

"Okay."

"Why don't you ask Micah to teach Phil how to play?"

"Mom forced him to go outside and play with us. He's about to go through his first transformation into a werewolf, so he's very *moody* right now."

"I see." So many new things for her to learn.

So the older boy was Eva's eldest son. The way he stood there, stiff with his eyebrows lowered, made her stomach tighten. Only his eyes moved as he watched her.

"Try to have fun if you can then. See you later, Peter."

"Bye, Cynthia!" He waved and ran back to his brothers.

As soon as she passed, she smiled as she watched them start up again. As expected, Micah just stood there while Peter tried to teach Phil a thing or two.

They had little to fear from her, and she was glad that at least the kids weren't afraid. To her hunting clan, hunting werewolf pups were strictly off limits.

Sadly, other hunting clans didn't have such rules.

"Not everyone believes as we do," her dad used to say. *"Also, it's important to decide for yourself before you make a decision based on what your clan says you should do."*

As she walked along the edge of the cluster of cabins, she caught the glimmer of a conversation. The sounds of a television or radio bled through a cracked open window. The tranquility of this space had been shattered, but after living in the city, she welcomed the noise.

Cyn spotted the door to the power generator shed and headed that way. After a snow avalanche had knocked out the shed a few weeks ago, Kaden had worked diligently to get the power restored.

When she wasn't far from the doorway, a figure emerged, closed the door, and made her way to the other cabins: Naomi. What was she doing in the generator room? Was she there to cause trouble?

"Helping out a bit in the generator room?" Cyn asked with a small smile.

"Mind your own business," Naomi said. For once, Kaden's sister retreated after snapping at Cyn. Matter of fact, her cheeks reddened as if Cyn had caught her doing something secret. Now what could that be?

Naomi kept going, not even looking over her shoulder to see if Cyn would follow.

Instead of finding Kaden, she ran into another familiar face. Sinister, the only other human in the camp, could often be found either performing guard duties or tinkering away to get the community's power supply back up. Apparently, he'd been entertaining Naomi as well.

The plot thickens…

The moment she'd met Naomi and Sinister for the first time, he'd been very protective of Kaden's sister. As to why the tall black man liked her, she had no idea.

"Windham isn't here," he grumbled.

No shit.

In the space of the shed, the bald man stood with his back toward her. The generator rumbled and hummed, all cleaned and fixed. Sinister's thick coat was hung on the metallic wall on a hook. Wasn't he cold?

"How was your visit with Naomi?" She didn't expect him to answer so she kept going. "It's not often that I see her blush about something. She's usually cold to everyone."

"No, she's not," he quickly bit back. "Don't go spreading rumors about someone you don't understand."

"So he speaks…Look, I don't kiss and tell—"

"There's nothing to tell…yet," he said quietly.

Cyn couldn't resist smiling. If she were back with her hunting clan and he was one of her friends, she'd tease the hell out of him, though. A girl never blushes unless she has a reason to do it.

Her fellow human didn't say anything else as he fumbled with some part in his hand and continued to work. As the only other human around here, she expected him to have an air of caution now that the other werewolves had arrived, but he appeared the same. That perception was an illusion, though. A brief sweep over him revealed concealed weapons she hadn't seen before, such as a knife on each ankle. His wide back wasn't as flat anymore. A bump on the middle of his back betrayed where he held a gun.

"I'm surprised you're still here after what happened at the dinner," Cyn said.

He grunted and shrugged. "They're just gnats."

Cyn scoffed. *Rather large hairy gnats with massive teeth.*

During her time here, Sinister had said little and revealed less. When she'd prodded, even Kaden hadn't said much. Yet now she knew.

"Do the others know what you are?" she asked him.

She leaned against the wall and caught his profile. He had the hint of a smile. A rarity for him. "Maybe. I don't give a damn."

"All this time, I thought you were a drifter with combat skills, maybe even a classmate from Kaden's college days. But you're a hunter, too. How the hell does Kaden get caught up with people like us?"

He didn't nod or show any sign of acknowledgment. She'd met men like Sinister before. Combat veterans made ideal hunters and her clan actively recruited them. So why would a hunter come here willingly? And, more importantly, did he have any hunter clan associations? Perhaps the deadly Carmine clan from the southern U.S. or even the Cerulean clan from Calgary. There were so many in the world now. There was no way he'd flash his hunter tattoo even if she asked.

So the question remained. Why was he here? Naomi? He was quite protective of her. Cyn couldn't hold back the laugh. *To each his own.* "Once they find out you're a hunter, you're going to be the hunted one, too. We need to be careful."

"I'm not worried one bit about them," he murmured. "Outsiders are the problem."

Cyn stood straighter. What the hell was up with this guy? Had he been sniffing the fresh air for too long or were his balls that huge?

"You look like you'd come from the Carmine hunting clan," she remarked. "Maybe the Cerulean clan."

"Do I look like Cerulean scum?" he ground out. "They always come to collect what they're owed and their debtors pay in blood. I don't associate with bottom feeders."

Well, at least she knew he didn't have an allegiance to her Red clan or the Cerulean clan.

His head slowly turned to her. "This 'us' thing don't exist. You need to watch your own back, *hunter*."

"I see." Like Sinister said, Kaden wasn't here, so she was just wasting her time. She turned to leave, but he grunted again.

"Wait."

He went to his coat and retrieved a leather bundle from

the inside. Casually, he unrolled the pack along the top of the generator. "Take one before I change my mind."

Cyn's eyes widened, and she couldn't hold back her admiration. "Look at those deadly dames…Military-class Fox hunting knives." One blade with a serrated edge glinted from the single light bulb overhead. "A five-inch titanium blade…" She ran her fingertips over the molded rubber on the fiberglass handle.

"Why are you letting me have one?" she asked. Was this some kind of test, and could she take *more* than one?

"The little butcher knife in your pocket won't cut shit. I have a feeling you'll stay out of trouble unless trouble comes looking for you."

Did he have x-ray vision or something? "How did you know I'm carrying a weapon?"

Another small smile. "A good hunch. It's what I'd do if I didn't have anything."

She laughed again. *There might've been no more 'us,' but a hunter is still a hunter.*

[4]

A FEW DAYS PASSED WITH SNOWSTORMS THAT blanketed the mountains with snow and kept everyone inside. By the fourth day, Cyn woke up to find clear skies and Kaden long gone. She told herself he had pack business to settle, but other ideas came to mind and none of them were good. *Had another freelancer come for them? Would another avalanche occur after so much snow had fallen?*

Controlling the situation seemed far easier in the city than in the mountains.

Instead of pacing and waiting for him, she settled on the couch and continued her current project: creating a spear. Might as well be prepared for anything.

One moment she was sitting on the couch, sharpening the end of a spear from a sapling she'd cut from an ash tree, and the next, she awoke after dozing for several hours. By the time she opened her eyes, only darkness lingered outside the windows.

She'd faced the doors the whole time, but no one had come to pay her a visit.

Including Kaden.

She got up but sat back down. Her senses danced for a bit, but her disorientation quieted once she rose at a steady pace.

Countless times, Kaden had used his healing abilities as pack alpha to fight back the cancer that had almost killed her, but if he skipped a few days, her recovery regressed. There was only one solution to become cancer-free: she had to become Kaden's mate and turn into a werewolf. The decision should've been simple—but once she became a werewolf, she'd have to cut off ties with her old life. Right now, her brother was bent on finding the people who killed their parents, and Zach wasn't good enough to take on his enemies alone. It was her duty, as his big sister, to protect him.

As of late, she wasn't doing a good job.

She was almost finished with the crude spear. With the addition of Sinister's serrated blade and a switchblade, she had a few toys to protect herself. She balanced the spear in her hands. The weight was ideal for a rapid-fire offense, but against a pack, a steel spear with a silver tip was ideal.

The wood planks on the porch groaned. Cyn strolled to the window and pulled the curtain to the side. Someone was walking to the door. She paused, holding her breath.

It was Eva. Now this was unexpected. Rhys's mate even knocked on the door.

Cyn opened the door. Instead of a greeting, Eva gestured toward the seats on the porch. "I'd like to speak to you for a moment."

It was bitterly cold outside. "Could we talk inside?"

Eva's fingers trembled. Her normally light-blue eyes seemed darker, sharper. She'd been far more relaxed during the dinner. "I wouldn't advise that."

What did she mean by that?

Eva took a seat on one of the lawn chairs on the porch.

Rhys's mate didn't move as Cyn approached her and took a spot on the free chair close by.

"It's the full moon tonight," Eva said.

"I didn't know that." Tracking the moon now that she didn't live back home was harder. But now that she knew the date, she understood why Eva's behavior seemed different. Werewolves were far deadlier once per month.

"Changes are coming for my family, and I'll have to make decisions as a mother. As much as I'd like to ignore the fact that you're here, I can't do that."

"I don't understand."

"During the full moon, not all of us will assume our true form; only the mature adults will."

She didn't elaborate, but Cyn was a fast study. Eva's boys wouldn't be running with the pack tonight. If Eva left them behind, they would be vulnerable.

"As much as you all seem to hate me, I have no ill-will toward of any of you," Cyn began.

"I don't hate you," Eva finally said. "I hate what you represent and the people you associate with."

"So I represent all hunters?"

Eva smiled. "You might think you're one of the good guys, but I fought countless hunters before I met Rhys and had my children. They hunted us like animals, even though we lived our lives like humans do."

Cyn wanted to speak, but something told her now was the time to listen and let Eva get what she felt off her chest. This was the first time she'd ever had such a conversation. Usually, if she were like this, she'd be interrogating a werewolf gang member or questioning someone for information on a fugitive. But this was...unexpected.

"Rhys and I did all the right things. We gave into the white picket fence dream and lived in a subdivision with a pool and all." She paused for a moment. "Every now and then we messed up. Rhys got caught butt-naked by the elderly lady down the street and I got arrested for indecent exposure during the full moon."

"You wouldn't believe how many guys I've captured without a stitch of clothing on."

Eva snorted and Cyn did the same.

"And what do you do with the men you captured?" The serious vibe came back real fast.

"You know what happened to them."

"That's my point. You've been trained to murder. From the day you were born, you were prepared to be a hunter and to *kill* werewolves."

Cyn's mouth opened to speak, but she immediately shut it.

"Before we rejoined the pack, we got into a bit of trouble. My mate and I had been out hunting in the woods and we tangled with a few deer hunters. One of them died when he tried to shoot me; Rhys killed him to protect me. That man's death was an incident I regret, but, after that, the hunters came and we had to leave behind everything we'd built. The house, our belongings, the kids' toys..." She bit her lower lip.

"I have three boys. They can be trouble, but I'd do anything to protect them. Kaden told me they'd be safe here. That we wouldn't have to run anymore. But with you here, anything can happen."

"I'd never harm a child, Eva. There are clans that have strict rules on interacting with pups. In my Red clan, the penalty is death for harming children." Only one member of her clan would disregard that law, but right now wasn't the time for her to think about her brother Ty.

"That sounds honorable and all, but are you a mother?"

Eva knew the answer to that question so she didn't bother to wait. She continued. "You talk a good game, but if the moment came, and you had to strike, you'd do it because that's what you're trained to do."

Cyn wanted to ask about defending herself, but arguing was futile. A mother protecting her pups was another thing entirely. "So what do you expect me to do? Do you want me to leave?"

Eva sighed. "That would be an easy solution, but not necessarily the right one. Kaden hasn't been happy for a long time, and you're the reason why we're together again."

"So what can I do to earn *your* trust?"

"I don't think that's possible. The only way I'd rest easy is if you were dead." A wall seemed to fall between them again.

"If I were dead? Sorry, I'm too attached to this body."

"Look around you, and tell me you don't feel strange living in the same space as your enemies. You don't belong here, Cynthia. The moment you realize that, both of us will sleep better."

Eva got up and continued. "If you touch my children, I will tear you apart. This will be your only warning." As she walked down the steps, she said, "If you do decide to stay, the day may come when I'll have to challenge you to protect what's mine. And there's nothing Kaden can do about it."

THERE WAS SO MUCH TO DO TODAY NOW THAT THE FULL moon had arrived. As Kaden's pack grew restless, he felt the same. The time had come for Micah's first transformation.

There also hadn't been any time to check on the dead hunter attached to the snow cab. If he were a hunter from Cyn's clan, he'd have even more problems.

From the morning to the early evening, he'd patrolled the perimeter of his territory to check for danger. If they hunted tonight, he didn't want any unforeseen problems coming up.

As he checked every corner and cliff, anticipation built along his skin. The wolf within him stirred, almost pacing like an animal in a cage. He needed to hunt. He needed to mate. The last time he was like this, he'd kept his distance from Cyn. The last thing he wanted to do was frighten or hurt her.

A brief stop at their cabin, before he helped with the preparations, was the best he could do. By the time Kaden approached the door, he practically vibrated with need. Cyn was in the living room on the couch. Her scent had changed, too. His keen nose tonight would make staying away from her much more difficult. She smelled delectable and most likely had no idea. His groin tightened.

She crossed her arms the moment he came inside. She was probably still concerned about going to see her brother.

He joined her on the couch, his long body covering hers.

"Now that was unexpected," she remarked after a long kiss. "You're warm."

"Like always." Wasn't this supposed to be a brief visit?

She wrapped her arms around his waist and any thoughts he had about leaving faded for a moment.

"I'd like to make love to you and heal you right now, but I have to help prepare the bonfire," he managed. "It's time for Micah's transition into adulthood."

"So that's why I keep seeing pack members carrying wood toward the camp."

"Yes, they're building a bonfire for the celebration." He couldn't stop looking at her lips. They looked like they needed to be kissed again.

When she parted her lips and her tongue slipped out to wet her lower lip, he growled in frustration. She fumbled with his pants, but he managed to twist his hips out of the way. He chuckled. "Damn it, Cyn... You're making it hard for me to leave. I just wanted to check on you."

"And I appreciate that." She nipped at his neck and he

held tight with a firm grip to his resolve. Wasn't he supposed to be telling her to stay inside tonight? Right now, she was making that far harder. She pulled off his shirt and ran her fingertips over his nipples. Her hands trailed over his stomach and his body quivered from her touch.

She pulled him closer so she could run her tongue from one nipple to another. His body quaked from the warmth of her mouth on him.

"I see all of this as a part of my recovery program." She leaned upward to kiss his mouth. "The more time we spend together, the more often you can heal me."

"As much as I'd like you in my bed, I want to know you better. As in talking—"

She unbuttoned his pants and reached inside. With a devilish grin, she grasped his length.

He hissed.

"I can talk now if you like." She stroked him, working him gently at first until his teeth clenched from the intense pleasure. He was close to taking her right then and there on the couch. She stroked faster, going from the tip down the bottom. *Oh, mercy.* The wolf writhing under his skin didn't make his agony any easier, sending him images of Cyn shoved over the side of couch, her ass in the air, his hands on her hips as he thrust into her. Her cries for release would fill the room.

When he spotted hair growing on the back of his hand, he pulled off her and rose. She wouldn't understand if she saw him lose control.

"Okay. Break's over." Of course, his pants fell to the ankles.

"I don't think every part of you thinks that." Her gaze was fixed on his lower half. Damn traitor. "Five minutes won't hurt."

"It's gonna take me *much* longer than that, sweetheart."

At least an hour to do all the things he wanted to do to her tonight.

"I'm a gal who likes to hedge bets. You won't last five minutes with me."

He loved when she got cocky like this. "You'd be scared to see what I wanna do to you." On the couch. On the bed. In the shower… He reached for his jeans.

"One minute," she boasted.

Someone knocked on the door. This would probably be the only time in Kaden's life when he'd be grateful for an interruption.

"Oh, you gotta be kidding me," Cyn groaned. "Can we ignore them?"

Naomi whispered a curse on the other side of the door. "Damn bitch."

"No," Kaden said as he adjusted his clothes, "we can't ignore people who can hear everything we say."

Cyn scooted to the corner of the couch and refused to look at him. "You have a job to do, and I understand that. Just go take care of it."

Even though her tone didn't project anger, her body language said otherwise. He'd have to make up for his absence later. He kneeled before her and dared to put his hand on her knee. She didn't shrink away. "I'll be back tomorrow morning. Can you stay inside for the rest of the night? Lock the doors?"

"Why?" She finally looked at him with suspicion, then glanced away. "What will you be doing outside?"

"All the adults will change tonight, including me."

"I know." She stiffened a bit.

"I want you to be safe." He paused for a moment as a thought came to mind. "Someday I'd like for us to run together," he admitted.

A part of him wished that the next words she'd say would be, "Of course," or "In time."

She sighed instead. "It's not that simple, Kaden. You know that."

"So you still plan to help Zach? If you leave, even for a few weeks, you'll begin to die again." He sucked in a breath. He didn't want to think about the symptoms returning—the organ failure, the weakness, the shortness of breath. That was what leukemia did to people. As a physician, he often had to separate himself from what was happening with his patients, but Cynthia was different. She had a terminal disease he could cure. He wanted her by his side, but the choice to become a werewolf had to be hers.

"Your brother made me promise to save you," he added.

"And you did."

"I'm merely keeping you alive. That's different."

Naomi knocked again. Now she was bothersome, and she damn well knew it.

It was time for him to handle pack duties, even though handling the problem he had with Cyn was far more important to him. But as the pack leader, it was his duty to attend the ceremony and run with Micah during his first night, which meant he couldn't watch over her and make sure she didn't bolt. *Damn it.*

"C'mon, Kaden, the others are waiting," Naomi shouted. "Not everyone has time to screw around here." He was really getting tired of reprimanding Naomi. He was grateful to his sire for teaching him patience above all things when it came to guiding pack members. Any other man would've lost what little patience he had left.

Once he composed himself, he said goodbye. "I expect to see you when I return."

"I'll be here." She still wouldn't look him in the eye. He didn't know if she were lying or telling the truth.

[5]

Kaden joined the others gathered around the bonfire. Smiling faces greeted him. Rhys and Bastian kept the fire going while Eva roasted marshmallows for s'mores with her younger boys.

Seeing everyone here took away a bit of the ache in his heart after talking to Cyn. He missed feeling the pulse of his pack, the power of their very presence.

Not far from everyone, Sinister sat on the steps of a nearby cabin. The small cabin seemed to suit him just fine and he looked on with a beer bottle in one hand and a rifle in the other. Even though they celebrated, someone had to be on guard duty. Sinister never seemed to get off it.

Micah stood near the fire, his coat discarded. All the young man wore was a pair of jeans and worn tennis shoes. Just seeing Micah reminded him of his first night experiencing the change. *Boy, what a night!* It was as if he'd seen the world through a glass door since birth and now that the door opened, every secret had been revealed. Sadly, after his parents died he never had a ceremony like this one.

Rhys's eldest son trembled and his scent flared like bitter sweat. The time had come.

Kaden raised his hands and the conversation around him ended. "The time has come for our brother Micah to join us in the forest."

The adults around him nodded. "This is a solemn occasion that happens only once in a lifetime. He will experience pain and then joy." He approached Micah and laid a hand on his shoulder. The young man jerked away and stared hard at him. The dark flash in Micah's eyes made Kaden pause. It seemed almost as if Micah would snap at any moment.

"Micah?" he asked with authority this time.

The boy didn't answer.

What the hell is going on here?

Micah vibrated and the heat from his skin seared Kaden's hand. The time was coming. The change would happen whether something was wrong with Micah or not.

He nodded to Rhys who quickly stepped forward and pressed his hand to Micah's chest. Bastian came next.

Suddenly, Micah bent over, his face turning into a grimace. He didn't cry out though.

Naomi, the highest-ranking female, approached.

From the corner of his eye, Kaden spotted a figure in the shadows near his cabin. So Cyn decided to witness this event, after all. Did that mean she wanted to watch or that she had something else in mind?

A trail of pack members walked up to Micah and touched him. By the time the last member walked by, the boy was on his knees, his back bent toward the cloudless, dark sky.

Kaden continued to rest his hand on the young man's shoulders. When Micah's shoulder blade popped and the young man screamed, Kaden remained to offer support.

"Ride through it," he advised. "What comes next is the most beautiful thing in the world."

Micah spasmed and jerked, his nose elongating into a snout. A sheen of sweat covered his brow as jet-black hair sprouted along his back. Everyone remained close, but Kaden could smell their anticipation, feel their need to join Micah.

By the time a wolf stood where a young man once had been, over ten minutes had passed.

The newest shifting pack member was ready to run with them.

"Took you long enough," Bastian said with a snort.

Micah huffed.

"It took *you* half an hour," Rhys said to Bastian.

"Who the hell is in a hurry to get broken down and rebuilt again? If I had my way, I would've been drunk off my ass." He downed the last of the beer can in his hand as if to make a point.

Kaden shook his head. A drunken werewolf? Now that wasn't something he wanted to witness. In the past, he'd seen others do all sorts of things to dull the pain, but for him, the pain was a necessity. Life had painful moments, and he had to be ready for them. For him to deny the process was to turn a blind eye and assume nothing bad would ever happen. Those in denial wouldn't survive too long in his world.

Micah circled the camp, first sniffing the ground along the campfire. Peter tossed him a s'more, and he gulped it in one bite.

Kaden checked and Cyn was still rooted to the same spot. Their gazes locked. Did she have unease? He couldn't tell from so far away. Maybe she was curious. Was this her first time seeing a transition?

He took a step toward her but stopped when he spotted Rhys taking off his shirt. Bastian followed. The wolf churning in his stomach nipped at him to change. The moon had her sway over him, but his control exceeded the others who discarded their clothing.

Cyn emerged from the shadows and half her profile was revealed. As the others transformed around him, he wished she were coming with him. He wished he could expose the world to her as he saw it. He wished she could see and believe how truly beautiful she was to him both inside and out.

Eva's children continued to play as their mother transformed. After she was done, her youngest even wrapped his arms around her massive neck and hugged her. She pushed him over and proceeded to lick his face. He giggled madly.

Kaden took a step toward Cyn. She took a step back. His control was as thin as a thread now. The change was coming. The nerve-endings in the muscles along his legs were firing again and again, registering as pain. Claws bit his fingertips and sprang forth first. His pulse raced. His incisors lengthened in his mouth. Many wolves circled him now. Bastian ran after Micah past Cyn into the woods. The others trailed after them.

Sinister had disappeared from his perch.

Only Eva was left now. She herded her children toward their cabin. The children would remain inside for the night.

Now it was just him and Cyn.

Would she watch what came next? She'd never seen him do it before. Would she watch his face and hear him grunt from the pain that always came? By the time the wolf stood where the man had once been, he looked up to see she was gone.

[6]

After a long night of hunting, Kaden wanted nothing more than to crawl into bed with Cyn and wrap his arms around her. Maybe for a moment, he could forget about her desire to return to Vancouver and the dead hunter in his camp.

Not long after he walked in the door, he heard a knock. No rest for the weary. He was surprised to see Rhys and Eva.

"I found you." His brother appeared alarmed and a bit breathless. Eva resembled stone, but she smelled like fear.

"What's wrong?" Was there something else now for him to deal with?

"Micah hasn't returned yet," Rhys said.

"Have you checked your cabin?" Kaden asked.

"We went there first," Eva said, "but he's not there."

"So what happened last night?" He beckoned them to come inside and sit down at the kitchen table, but his brother refused and waited near the door. His mate did the same.

"After you had separated from the pack to hunt, I followed Micah and Bastian," Rhys said. "Not long after midnight, I lost track of them. When I got back to camp, only Bastian was here."

"What was Bastian doing?" Cyn asked. Kaden turned around to see her standing in the bedroom doorway. Her hair was a mess and she wore nothing more than a T-shirt and shorts.

"Nothing special," Rhys said with a bit of exasperation. "He talked about getting some sleep."

Kaden stood. There'd be no sleep for him today. Finding Micah was more important. "Let's go find him."

He put on boots. By the time he stood, Cyn was dressed and putting on a coat.

"What are you doing?" he asked her.

"I can help."

Eva made a rude noise. As expected.

"Are you sure that's wise?" It was Rhys who spoke. He stared Cynthia down.

Cyn rolled her eyes. "Enough with the drama. Looking for people is what I do. It's what I'm good at. Let me earn your trust and help you find Micah."

"There's no way I'd let you—" Eva began.

"She will be with me the whole time, Eva. I will find your boy," Kaden added.

"Fine." Rhys left the house, but Kaden didn't miss the stiff way his brother replied to Cyn. Rhys didn't trust her at all.

Eva continued to stand in the doorway. "Remember what I said, Cynthia. I meant it."

She quietly closed the door, leaving him alone with Cyn.

"Do I have to ask what that was about?" he asked. "Should I talk to her?"

"No," Cyn said firmly as she put on gloves. "She's just protecting her family, and she has a right to do it."

As hard as he was trying to bring everyone together, he'd

just have to be persistent and force everyone to lay their grievances on the table and talk it out. The time was coming soon for that to happen.

By the time Kaden and Cyn walked outside, they'd formed a simple plan. They'd take one of the snow cabs to the last place Kaden had seen Micah, and, from there, they'd try to track him on foot.

Their plan took a sudden detour when Kaden walked up to the first snow cab and noticed something was missing. He froze and stared hard at the back of the cab.

Damn it all to hell.

"What's wrong?" Cyn asked.

"It's nothing," he murmured.

When he tried to walk away, she pushed against his chest. "Wait a second here," she said. "You're surprised and angry about something. I can tell."

She searched his face, and he tried to hide any feelings that surfaced.

"The pack brought a dead man with them," he finally said.

Her mouth dropped. "What?"

"They encountered a drifter on the road, ran into trouble, and the human ended up dead." Now wasn't a good time for the whole truth. If he told her, she'd be angry and most likely leave. Especially, if the hunter were from her clan.

If she left him, she'd die.

He managed to continue. "I told Bastian to leave the corpse alone until I had a chance to investigate the matter."

"Apparently, he didn't listen."

"No, he didn't. He has a history of causing problems." Time to settle the matter. Immediately.

He left the snow cabs and marched straight to the cabin where his brother stayed. Cynthia walked beside him without speaking.

He didn't bother knocking and walked right in. No one was home. The whole situation was going downhill fast.

Cyn touched his back. "I'm sorry, Kaden."

At least he could tell her about his past history with Bastian. "None of this should surprise me." He had to keep his voice down but found the volume of his voice rising again. Just thinking about what he might have to do to fix this mess further angered him. "After my parents died, Bastian kept making messes for me to clean up. Namely, falling for women who were nothing but trouble."

He'd have to make a choice now whether to search for Micah or find his trouble-making brother. He'd decide after he spoke to Sinister. Maybe during the night, Sinister had seen something he'd missed.

On the way, Kaden continued, "Back in Toronto, Bastian fell hard for a wealthy businessman's daughter. Turns out, that man was a gangster and he had no interest in letting his little girl associate with vermin like my kind. Long story short, he put out a kill contract on Bastian, and my brother lied for months that everything was fine!" He snorted. "I had to negotiate for his life in blood. I had to *kill* another piece of shit criminal to save his life." He briefly glanced at her, hoping she wouldn't think of him differently. He'd taken the Hippocratic Oath to "never do harm to anyone" as a doctor, yet he killed to protect his sibling.

After he had spoken, they walked in silence for a bit until Cynthia intertwined their fingers together like she did not long ago. Just the warmth of her hand eased him.

They ran into Rhys again before they reached Sinister's cabin. At least Kaden could question him on the latest developments.

"The body's gone, Rhys. Is there something you need to tell me?" Kaden stepped up to his brother.

"No!" Rhys immediately tilted his chin toward the

ground and averted his gaze. "Bastian took care of everything! I don't know what's going on. I wasn't even there when the pack was attacked. The only people who saw what happened were Bastian, Micah, and one of the younger females. That's it." Rhys spoke what he thought was the truth, and, unfortunately, he revealed what Kaden suspected: Bastian was trying to take over the pack as alpha.

"So what do we do?" Cyn asked.

Now that was the million-dollar question. "First, I'll have to track Bastian." He turned to his brother. "Rhys, you should continue to look for your son. I'll join you once I see where Bastian's trail leads."

With a nod, Rhys headed north as Cyn spoke up. "See where Bastian's trail leads? He could be halfway to Prince George by midday."

"It doesn't matter. He has to get rid of the body first, and he can't burn it, or we'll see where he is."

Naomi emerged from the woods and walked up to them. Seeing his sister filled him with unease. Did she know anything about Bastian's treachery? He had yet to question his sister. He cursed inwardly.

"Where's Rhys going?" she asked.

"Micah is missing and he's gone out after him."

Naomi shrugged. "It's Micah's first run. He'll be gone for a long time." She didn't appear concerned at all.

"A wolf never hunts alone during their first time," Kaden said.

"You did it." Naomi had a hint of an amused smile.

"My situation was different. I didn't have anyone, and I made mistakes I regret."

Naomi still crossed her arms and stood there as if there were nothing to be worried about. "If you're concerned, then we should send out a few search parties to check on him, although I believe you have nothing to worry about. For all we know, his nose is stuck inside a hibernating beaver's hiding spot and he's spent the night trying to dig them out. We might be worrying about nothing."

"I'm serious, Naomi. Worry first. Laugh later. Search to the west for me."

She slowly nodded. "Understood. I'll do what I can." Her playful tone was gone, and, for once, he saw the mature woman he'd respected before she left for Los Angeles.

They didn't encounter anyone else on the way to Sinister's cabin. After Kaden knocked once, Sinister opened the door.

"Have you seen Bastian?" Kaden asked.

The hunter shook his head. "The last time I saw him was early this morning. He was heading southeast out of the camp." Sinister's gaze flicked from Kaden to Cyn. "Is there a problem I need to know about?"

"We got problems." Kaden tried to hide his building anger but failed. "Big ones. Cyn and I are heading out to track him."

"Wait a sec." Sinister disappeared into the cabin and returned with a rifle. Instead of tossing the weapon at Kaden, he handed it to Cyn. She didn't hesitate to use the strap to place the rifle over her shoulder.

"Fully loaded and ready," he said evenly.

She placed the cartridge he gave her in her pocket.

"You know what to do if I don't come back, right?" Kaden asked Sinister. Every time he left during a dire situation like this, he asked the same question.

"You'll be back." Sinister gave him a hard look and shut the door.

So his friend still believed in him. Even after everything that went down between them before Sinister arrived on his doorstep.

[7]

CLAD IN A WARM COAT AND ARMED WITH A SINGLE RIFLE from Sinister, Cynthia joined Kaden to find Bastian. After a short ride in a snow cab, she followed him into the forest, heading southeast.

Light snow began to fall, and, no more than ten minutes later, the cloud cover from snow reduced visibility. In wolf form, Kaden's pace was relentless, even in such weather.

The trees and snow obscured most things, but hunting in these conditions wasn't so bad. Countless times, she'd chased her prey into buildings with dark nooks and crannies. The open forest was the easiest place to track and seek your target. She glanced up to see the dark gray wolf was farther ahead. She needed to stop getting lost in her own thoughts and focus on what needed to be done. Find Bastian.

With the snow falling, tracking any wolves by their tracks wasn't an ideal choice. Based on the path Kaden took, he was leading them by scent. If she were hunting prey, she'd guess that any werewolf trying to run away would head south toward Prince George.

Eventually, once they cleared the forest at the edge of the

mountain, the path to the south was clear. As far as she could see, there was nothing but snow-covered hills, rocky outcroppings, and more forest.

The endless fields were tranquil in a way. Before she knew it, she began to speak. Maybe for her own benefit. "I could never imagine living out here. It's way too easy to get lost in your own thoughts and lose yourself."

Kaden paused for a moment. Even though he couldn't use words, she found him to be quite expressive. One of his ears twitched. He had the same green eyes, although the shade was darker.

"I bet you've gone hunting out here and asked yourself, why do I go back to being a human when I can just keep going?" She touched one of the trees. "I'll be honest; I've thought of that, too. I've wondered what it's like to be a wolf. To see the world out here through your eyes."

They kept going.

"Since my dad died, I regret not asking him if we killed werewolves because we envy them. Do we hunt them because they possess the immortality we'll never have?"

Kaden huffed, but he didn't stop moving.

"Ty and Zach never asked those kinds of things. They just did their job, cleaned up the rogues, and collected their money…"

Soon, they reached the next forest, far denser than the first one they crossed.

"Now that I have a terminal disease, I think about my mortality every day. Even more so now that I'm surrounded by beings who won't age like humans do—"

A twig snapped in the distance and the sound echoed. They both froze.

Kaden veered to the left, but Cyn suspected the sound came from directly ahead. They walked a bit, still within sight of each other, until Cyn saw a dark spot in front of them. The form was close to the ground and couldn't be mistaken for an elk or moose.

Cyn slowed down, her boots going into deep snow as she took a path near trees for cover. Each step was taken with caution.

The closer she got, the more she could make out her target: a single midnight-black wolf with his nose along the ground. Was that Bastian? The wolf's coat was quite similar to the unruly mop of hair Kaden's brother had.

To not spook him, she slowly approached until a strange feeling clenched her stomach. The chill from outside slithered down her bones and a hunter's intuition slammed into her.

She stopped again, her finger resting on the rifle's safety. From behind her, she caught a faint sound, so faint anyone else would've called it the wind or the sound of snowfall. Another crunch in the snow was closer, a tentative step from her right.

She squeezed her eyes shut and bit her tongue. She was a fool to separate herself from Kaden. A trap had been set and she'd strolled right into it.

[8]

The black wolf Kaden and Cyn had been tracking edged his way farther to the south. Kaden crept toward his target, trying not to frighten Micah. Instead of finding Bastian first, they'd run into Rhys's son.

Micah's ears stood up so Kaden waited. The key would be to trail after him, reestablish himself as the alpha, and then force Micah to return with him.

All-out chasing him wasn't wise.

He remembered his first night well. The experience had been intoxicating. During the full moon, the need to give into the wolf was undeniable, but it was also the deep end of the ocean where the weak-minded could get lost.

He should've been the one to keep an eye on Micah and not Rhys. He'd caved in so that as Micah's sire, Rhys could be a guide to keep Micah in check, but apparently Micah had eluded his father during the long night.

Kaden had left his siblings on his first night. He'd had no choice. At the time, Uncle Damien was traveling through Europe and they had no close relatives. Kaden's error had dire consequences. He didn't return home for a month, and it was Bastian who finally found him wandering in the wild.

Cyn better be keeping up with his pace. He refused to let Micah have the same fate.

~

CYN SUCKED IN A DEEP BREATH. *RELAX, YOU'VE PLAYED this game before. Now is not any different than before.* She'd lost count of how many times she'd been ambushed. The key wasn't speed. It was to anticipate and to feel. Experience was her advantage.

The first attack didn't come from the front or the back but from the side. *Amateur.*

She twisted hard to the right, rifle turned to the side. She was ready. The sheer force of her attacker sent her sprawling onto her back, but Sinister's rifle didn't break. The gun shook hard in the wolf's mouth. The beast tried to force her to let go, but she'd wrapped the leather strap around her torso, which meant whoever was attacking her was up close and personal.

"C'mon, you bastard!" she screamed. The wolf snarled and hissed, fighting hard to bite through the rifle. Pain from scratches blossomed along her sides, but she ignored the pain.

Time to get out of this mess. She tucked her legs toward her chest and kicked hard in the wolf's gut. She had to move fast. Wolves never hunted alone. When another kick didn't work, she rammed the hard edge of the rifle into the side of the wolf's head. While it was stunned, she pulled a switch-blade from her leg, swiped hard against the side of the wolf's snout, and then drove the blade deep into its shoulder.

For her, it was all about muscle memory at this point, striking while she had the advantage.

She yanked out the blade and aimed to come down again, but something rammed her hard in the back, sucking the air out of her lungs. *Well, hello wolf number 2.*

She hit the ground face first, but staying down would be fatal, so she immediately rose, nose bleeding and all, to aim the gun.

Suddenly, Kaden jumped on the second wolf and the tawny beast ran away. The one she stabbed lay still on the ground.

She prepared to fire at the retreating one, but with one glance from Kaden, she stopped.

In moments, all her pain came in a flash: the burning sensation along her sides, the ache in her arms from the jolts while holding the gun.

All the while, Kaden continued to approach her first attacker, who lay unmoving on the ground.

Had she killed him? She couldn't have. She didn't make a single killing blow. Yet, the wolf's chest moved at a snail's crawl.

Had she done the one thing Eva said she'd do?

"You talk a good game," Eva had said, *"but if the moment came and you had to strike, you'd do it because that's what you're trained to do."*

Instead of examining the fallen wolf, Kaden ran after the wolf that was escaping.

Cyn began to follow after Kaden, but her legs wobbled and she collapsed as she gasped for breath. *I didn't kill him. I didn't kill him.*

But what if it's one of the females. Eva or even Naomi?

She looked back at the injured wolf. Her vision jostled for a moment and she took in a few cleansing breaths. When everything cleared, it wasn't a wolf that lay on the ground anymore.

It was a naked man who stared her down with a malevolent smile that doused her with cold water.

"Bastian," she gasped.

"The little hunter is all alone again." He made a tsk tsk sound. "For once in my life, I gave someone else an out, but they didn't take it."

"How lucky for them..." Cyn said.

Seeing a naked, bleeding man walking through the snow was rather disturbing, even more so was the way he spoke with a mouth filled with sharp teeth. The wolf was still in control. He took a wide berth as he approached her, but every step was just as menacing. All the while, she was amazed to see how quickly his wounds began to close. How the hell was he doing that?

"Just like my brother, I've changed into a healer." He glanced at the wound she took in. "While he was searching for a new home for the pack, I was taking my proper role as the alpha. Not in name naturally; the hierarchy was there. The control was there. As a true alpha, I grew stronger and my healing abilities began to show. I'm no doctor, but I have to admit, my handiwork is rather good, isn't it?" He was closing in now. Her fingers had gone numb from the cold, but she had enough feeling to reach for the gun's trigger. All she had to do was aim and fire. A few bullets should shut him up.

"You should've left when I gave you the chance, Cynthia."

She was still breathless, but she managed a half-smile. "I'm stubborn like that."

He chuckled. "You would've made a fine alpha female. It's unfortunate you were born as a hunter, and you'll have to die like one."

He was right in front of her now. She'd almost killed Kaden's brother. Could she do it for real to defend herself?

She had killed many times before without hesitation, but, this time, she paused.

In a flash, Bastian's right hand was around her throat, his other hand locked on her wrist that held the gun. He lifted her with ease off the ground until her legs dangled like a rag doll. Her body shook. Her free hand grasped and clawed at him desperately. Her chest burned as dark spots began to pepper her peripheral vision. She'd been a fool to hesitate.

"Put her down! Now!" a voice thundered from behind them.

The moment her body hit the ground, everything went black.

[9]

If Bastian weren't his brother, Kaden would've struck him dead where he stood. His brother didn't say a word during their march back to the cabins. Bastian merely stayed a few feet ahead of him as he carried Cyn back in human form.

She was alive. He'd been foolish to chase after the other werewolf who'd attacked Cyn, but he was furious that anyone would dare to ignore his orders.

While he was away, Bastian had tricked him again. Thankfully, he returned just in time to save her. But that also meant he had to stop chasing Micah.

Whatever relationship he had with Bastian was torn and scattered across the mountainside.

His brother stood there while he did mouth-to-mouth to help her start breathing again. He was too angry, too unfocused to heal her the proper way.

Cyn made a strangled sound, and he released his tightening hold on her.

He'd settle things soon enough with his brother.

Once they reached the cabin, he placed Cyn in their bed

and returned to find his fuming brother where he'd left him. Bastian had put on the clothes he'd given him.

"How do we move forward from this point?" Kaden asked. He knew the answer, but he might as well ask.

"We don't. The moment you left the pack behind to find a new place, you surrendered control." Bastian slowly turned his face to him, smug as usual. His parents hated Bastian's attitude, and so did Kaden.

"An alpha is the leader of his pack no matter where he lives. All I did was allow Rhys to make decisions in my absence!" He took a step across the room, but stopped himself.

Bastian grimaced. "Rhys is weak. He has always been weak. I made the hard decisions! Not him." Bastian decreased the space between them. "He's a family man now, not a killer. When the pack got into trouble, it was me who stepped up to the plate."

"So you're saying you're the alpha now?"

"Pretty much." His brother smiled and Kaden's heart sunk. "You're weak now. That *bitch* has made you weak." Bastian tried to advance again, but Kaden's words stopped him cold.

"Call her a bitch again, and I'll end you, B."

Bastian motioned him forward. "Let's go at it then. I'm tired of you making me feel guilty. For once, I was the one to take control, and I believe I should be pack alpha."

"So be it." Kaden moved first. Maybe if he smacked some sense into his brother, Bastian might come to his senses.

He threw a hard right hook, followed by a left that knocked his brother into the wall. His younger brother shook off the blow with ease. "About time we settled this between us like men."

Bastian was quick to respond, bringing up his leg in a kick. Kaden blocked it.

Every time they had fought as kids, Kaden had been the victor. Only once had Bastian won by playing dirty and throwing sand into Kaden's eyes.

With a snarl, Bastian came at him again with a combination: a right hook, a brutal uppercut, and then a right jab that dazed him for a moment. When his momentum propelled him left, Kaden twisted downward, sweeping his brother's left leg and bringing him down.

"Argh!" Bastian crashed hard onto the shelf next to the front door.

"Are you done fighting me?"

"Why don't you come find out…" Bastian staggered forward, wiping off blood from a cut on his forehead.

He slammed into Bastian, shoulder to chin, as hard as he could, and his brother tumbled onto the kitchen table, whacking his head on the hard surface.

Bastian scrambled to stand, his red face contorted into a snarl. Among the debris on the floor, he reached for a kitchen knife

"So it's come to this?" Kaden whispered. At this point, he was willing to fight Bastian until he acquiesced, but his brother was willing to take things beyond the point of no return.

Bastian nodded. "Damn right it is. Only one of us is leaving this cabin alive."

Kaden didn't budge. Suddenly, he spotted a weapon in the corner, Cyn's spear. He grabbed it.

Slowly, his brother closed in on him. "The end's coming for you soon, Kaden." Bastian laughed as if he found the situation funny. "I'll tell everyone you snapped and tried to kill me."

He's lost his mind… Kaden's legs tensed and he tightened his grip on the spear. Could he really kill his brother?

Bastian's jaw twitched as he clasped the blade with his

trembling hand. With a roar, Kaden surged forward and sprang into the air. He aimed at Bastian's mid-section, but Bastian glanced off the blow with a swipe of the steel blade. Unfettered, Kaden twisted hard to the right to swing the spear back around in one smooth motion. With a hard thrust forward, he stabbed Bastian in the belly.

"Ahhh!" Bastian reached for him, grasping and clawing. Unable to get past the spear's length, his brother slammed his fist down the middle to sever the staff. Kaden grabbed the jagged edge, ramming his brother into the closest wall. The scent of Bastian's spilled blood filled the air.

"Give up, Bastian!" Kaden kept one hand on the broken spear and the other was used to twist Bastian's right arm behind his back.

When he pushed the spear a bit to the left, his brother cried out in pain. "Kill me then, you coward!"

With every jerk, Kaden felt like he was stabbing himself. Just seeing his brother's face filled him with remorse, but he had to do this.

"Go ahead and do it, Kaden," he goaded. "Or are you too weak to lead and do what must be done?"

"The easy route would be to watch you take your last breaths. To end this back and forth between you and me." Bastian squirmed and tried to push them backward, his face reddening, but Kaden's grip on him was too tight. "But after Dad died, I promised Mom I'd protect you. I'm willing to do what must be done to uphold that promise." *Damn it, Brother, stop fighting me!*

Instead of pushing the spear right or left, Kaden pushed upwards until his brother howled.

Just when he thought he could do no more to bend his brother to his will, Bastian finally relaxed and his head tilted to the side. Bastian bared his vulnerable neck, the ultimate gesture of submission.

Kaden immediately released his brother and staggered backward as if he was the one who'd been stabbed. Bastian fell to the floor in a heap.

"Damn you for doing this, Bastian…" He pulled the spear out of his brother and threw the broken stick aside. The back of his throat burned. Pain coursed through him, but it wasn't the pain from his injuries. It was the pain of betrayal. "Leave the body on my porch. I don't want to see your face again for a *very* long time."

Kaden didn't move after that, even after Bastian stumbled to stand and limped out the door.

The sound of the front door shutting had a dead finality to it.

[10]

CYN STUMBLED OUT OF THE BEDROOM INTO WHAT WAS left of the living room. The kitchen table couldn't be called such, one of the walls had holes in it, and there was blood all over the floor.

If she hadn't seen Kaden slumped over on the sofa, she would've assumed the worse.

"What happened here?" she asked, joining him on the couch. She examined his body, checking every limb for injuries. Not a single bruise marred his perfect face.

Yet, only a wounded man would stare at the door with the blank expression Kaden had. "We fought and I won. He's gone. It's over."

He didn't protest when she eased herself into his lap. Each movement was painful, especially her throat when she swallowed. She'd worry about her wounds later. Kaden needed her more than she needed him.

"Close your eyes," she whispered. "Rest now." When he didn't obey, she used her fingertips to lower his eyelids.

"There now, my stubborn little wolf." She snuggled against his chest, resting her head on his shoulder.

Soon enough, his quickened heartbeat slowed down and he appeared to doze off. No matter the pain, it was easy to relax against him. She closed her eyes, too.

Time passed from day to night. Cynthia was on the edge of slumber when a honeyed feeling enveloped her. Pleasure coursed from her stomach and spread into her limbs. When the sweet bliss snaked down to her core, she opened her mouth to moan.

"Mmmm," she murmured.

The discomfort in her throat faded away. The scratches that burned her sides became a faint memory.

"Cyn…"

She opened her eyes to see Kaden looking at her. The heat in his gaze further inflamed her desire for him.

"I need you, Cyn," he whispered. "Only you."

She didn't speak as he carried her toward the bedroom. None of the lights were on, so she trusted his eyes. With every footstep, anticipation filled her body. Usually, they had a game of dominance to see who would give in first. Would she be the one on top? Would he be the one to make the calls in the bedroom?

But tonight was different. He was the wounded one.

Once inside the bedroom, he immediately shut the door, leaving them in complete darkness. Instead of heading to the bed, he set her down in the middle of the room and directed her to the far wall. He enclosed her in his arms and bent his head until his forehead pressed against hers. His arousal brushed against her leg and she couldn't wait for their clothes to come off.

This was the moment she enjoyed the most, the anticipation, not knowing what he'd do next. But she had to admit one thing to him.

"Thanks for leaving the light off," she whispered.

"Why is that?" His lips were on her neck now, slowly

trailing to the most sensitive part near her pulse point. Each nibble ignited the need for release.

"I probably look horrible right now with all these bruises. And, well, my body has changed since my first night here." Now that she was on the path to recovery, she didn't have a toned body anymore.

Kaden ran his hands over her shoulders. From there, he lightly brushed his fingertips against her waist and hips. "You were unhealthy before, but your body is much better suited to your height. I love the way you are now: delicious and curvy."

Before she could protest, he lifted her shirt and his mouth was on her bare breasts. He rained soft kisses along every curve. "I want to stay right here. I can make every doubt and pain you have go away." His mouth traced a circle around her bright pink areola. "So soft."

"I'm not stopping you…" she managed.

In the darkness, she felt him suck and nip at her most sensitive places. He paused for a moment to kneel before her to better position himself. While he drove her crazy with his mouth on her body, all she could do was reach for him. She ran her fingers through his hair, unable to hold back the moan stirring at the back of her throat.

He sucked hard at her nipple, forcing her to release the breath she held. Suddenly, his hands were at her hips, tugging her pants down. She complied and stepped out of them for him.

"Kaden…"

"I've dreamt of the day when you became well, and I could see what you truly looked like." He chuckled. "Minus the bruises." His warm breath was on the soft curve of her stomach. Slowly, his tongue dipped into her belly button, eliciting a squeal from her. "Ticklish, are we?"

She tried to push him back, but he continued to lick her until she laughed out loud. *Naughty little wolf*, she thought.

Next came her panties and now she was naked.

She expected him to stand so she could reciprocate and give him pleasure, but he remained where he was and tugged one of her legs over his shoulders.

"Kaden, what are you—" The moment his mouth brushed against her core, her legs trembled.

"I can't tell you how much it turns me on to hear you scream," he murmured. With one long lick, he fired every nerve ending between her legs.

"Oh, God!" she gasped.

Kaden was relentless with his tongue and sampled every part of her. She screamed his name again and again as a climax swept over her. By the time she slumped against the wall, he had backed up. The sounds of his discarded clothes meant one thing.

"Should we go to the bed—" He pressed his fingertips against her lips. The time for words was apparently over. With one swift movement, he had her up against the wall, her legs wrapped around his hips, and then his hard length was inside her. *Finally!* She cried out from the first thrust and her core tightening around him.

Then she had no place to go but to hang onto him as he thrust into her again and again.

THE MOMENT KADEN WAS INSIDE HER, HE COULDN'T stop himself. He'd wanted to take things slow and show her how much he wanted her. How much he needed her to be with him.

His hips pushed upward until she took all of him. She was so tight. So perfect. He savored the closeness they had now. There was hardly any space between. His mouth was on hers. Her arms were wrapped around his neck, locking him in place. Everything was perfect.

"Yes…yes…yes!" Her cries drove him crazy, urging him to move faster, to go harder. As much as he wanted to go all out, he didn't want to hurt her.

She was so responsive, and he tensed as her next climax approached.

"That's it," he urged. "Come for me, baby."

She obliged, crying out his name again. He wished Cyn could see how beautiful she was to him. In the dark, he could make out every feature on her face. When she climaxed, her lips would part and her light gray eyes formed slits. Every defense she put up collapsed as she exposed her true self to him.

That was the woman he wanted by his side.

As she relaxed, his own release came swiftly and his body stiffened against hers. Every worry that plagued him vanished for an exquisite moment and only the two of them existed. "Mine," he whispered.

Gently, he carried her to their bed and placed the covers over them. Time passed and he enjoyed having this moment of peace. As her body relaxed against his, he expected her to fall asleep, but she spoke instead.

"There's something I've been wondering for a while," she began.

"Hmmm?"

"What did Zach do for you as a part of your agreement to save me?"

He brushed her dark hair out of her face. "You've been thinking about the arrangement a lot, haven't you?"

"It's been hard not to."

Kaden drew in a deep breath. He'd been avoiding this subject, but Cyn was relentless in her search for answers.

"Zach promised to oversee this territory in exchange for your life. In order to save you, I must take you as my mate."

"So that means my clan would control all freelancer and hunter activity in the area."

"Precisely."

"That's too much for him to handle. You're both crazy."

"Crazy about *you*, Cyn." He kissed her cold nose. One of the short strands of her hair curled around his finger.

She paused and chuckled. "You weren't *crazy* about me in the beginning."

"No, I wasn't," he admitted.

She sighed. "You can't keep healing me forever until I make my decision."

He let go of the strand he'd held. "What you're truly saying is you don't want to be my mate and become what I am." Which meant she didn't truly accept what he was. He had no idea how to convince her under their current circumstances. Cyn's life among the pack would become more difficult before it became easier.

"Don't do this to me." She stiffened against him. "If I could be with you *and* protect my family, I'd do both in a heartbeat."

"He's a grown man, Cyn," he growled. "You have to let him go and make his own decisions…and mistakes."

Her eyebrow rose. "Like the mistakes Bastian has made?"

He winced. Bastian gave him far too many burdens to carry. Just thinking about their fight gave him physical pain.

"Are you all right?" she asked softly.

No, he wasn't. "I'll be fine." He covered her body with his and sampled her lips. He would kiss her until she understood that she belonged here with him and nowhere else.

After the kiss had ended, she tried to hide a smile and failed. "You're so bad…I still can't believe it's only been a few weeks and our relationship has progressed this far."

"When a werewolf attaches to someone, letting go is next to impossible."

She sighed. "I never believed in that mated for life stuff. So, you're telling me that's all true?"

He took her hand and kissed the back. The intensity of her gaze made him want to take her as his mate right then and there. "Yes, it is."

"But you said *next to impossible*."

His past relationship with Hayley briefly came to mind, but he pushed the thought away with ease. Hadn't he attached to her, too? And yet, she'd left him behind as if their bond had meant nothing. Which meant his assertion could be a lie.

His grip around Cyn tightened as a wave of possessiveness blanketed him. *No, she belongs with me.* Even with all these obstacles in the way, he'd see things through to the very end.

Finally, he managed to speak. "Keeping you safe from the others will be hard, but not impossible. Get some sleep. We need to find Micah soon, but we need to recover first." He closed his eyes and listened. Just hearing her steady heartbeat took some of his worries away. He could keep healing her and protecting her, no matter what danger may come for them. While he had strength in his body, he'd never fail her.

[11]

Cyn woke the next morning to find a note from Kaden on the dresser next to their bed.

I'm heading out to find Micah. Get some rest. I still need you.

She read the note again and again. By the third time, she was laughing and smiling. He hadn't outright told her he loved her yet, but the fact that he needed her almost felt the same.

That tricky little wolf is making me fall in love with him.

After everything that had gone down with Bastian, at least Kaden was safe. She sat quietly on the edge of bed, lost in her own thoughts until she heard a knock on the front door.

She spotted a tense Sinister on the porch. He was leaning over an open bag containing the body.

Why was the body on the porch of all places?

Tentatively, she approached him.

"Kaden told me to bury the body like I did the other one," Sinister said. "I was about to do it when I got curious and examined it. I noticed something weird."

Cyn approached the corpse from the other side. The blond man, who wore a thick, black coat and tattered jeans, had been sliced open along his belly. The sight was gruesome, but she'd seen victims like this before.

"This man was slaughtered," she whispered.

"He has bits of skin under his fingernails, though. Whoever killed him took a few hits," Sinister observed.

"If he attacked the pack, he was a drifter who tangled with the wrong people."

"Oh, no, Cynthia. Look closer," Sinister advised.

Along the opening on the side of his body, close to his chest, Cyn caught a glimmer of dull color, a light blue. Using the switchblade strapped to her leg, she tilted the dead man's shirt open to reveal a tattoo. A light-blue tattoo.

No way. No freaking way. She pulled the shirt open wider to reveal light-blue werewolf paw prints. She knew that tattoo well.

The Windhams had killed a hunter.

Did Kaden know this entire time?

Not only was this man a hunter but he was also a member of the second most dangerous clan of hunters: the Cerulean clan. They had money, influence, and power.

The intensity of Sinister's gaze burned the side of her face. His eyes slowly closed to slits. His jaw twitched with building anger and his words the other day bounced around her head: *The Cerulean clan always comes to collect what they're owed. The debtors pay in blood.*

There was no way in hell the Windham pack wouldn't pay for this.

THE HUNTER'S PACK

PART 3

[1]

THE BLACK WEREWOLF IN FRONT OF KADEN GROWLED and bared his teeth. His back arched and his wild eyes flared from dark yellow to sun yellow. Kaden sensed the lunge coming.

His nephew, Micah, was too far gone. After following him for three days in wolf-form, Kaden suspected that, each day, the wolf within the boy took his nephew farther away from him.

Shifting should've been a gift, but the process had been too much for Micah.

The muscles in Micah's front legs tensed. Kaden froze, but alarm cut through his insides. If Micah struck him, he'd have to strike back to bring the boy under control.

So far, patience had been the key here, but every single hour that passed plagued him to no end. They were far to the north now. At least over the next mountain.

You've left your woman alone for too long, he told himself.

Micah snapped at him, but didn't budge from his perch on a lower outcropping. There wasn't any place for him to go.

Either he went over the cliff to a sure death or he fought Kaden.

Every single day, Kaden had to make the same choice, either continue to follow Micah and drive him back or return to protect Cynthia. Tracking Micah had been arduous, but now that he was at this point, he knew, for a fact, that Rhys wouldn't have had the strength to bring his son back. Only an alpha was capable.

Kaden slowly crept forward, his tail high. If this was the place where he needed to make his final stand, so be it. *Prepare yourself.*

Countless times in the past, he'd protected his pack. He tried to remind himself that everyone was valuable. Returning without his younger brother's son wasn't acceptable.

The moment he surged forward, Micah reared back, his mouth open wide. The younger wolf tried to bite his flank, but Kaden came down hard on his back. With a twist of his neck, Kaden managed to bite down on the back of Micah's neck.

The boy yelped and jerked to free himself, but Kaden wouldn't let go. Micah managed to squirm free to back up, but, with nowhere to go, he veered closer to the edge.

Kaden nipped at him to get him away from the cliff.

Submit, damn it.

When Micah snapped at him again, he growled and pinned him again.

The process continued until, by the third time, the boy finally stilled.

The end of the day had snuck up on them with the sunset looming to the west. He peered at the boy and finally saw recognition in Micah's eyes. The wolf within him had retreated. For now.

Hopefully, it wasn't too late for him to return home to Cyn.

[2]

EVEN COLD-HEARTED HUNTERS ENJOYED A WARM BOWL of oatmeal before they searched for their prey.

Cynthia McGinnis never thought of Sinister as an oatmeal person, but, as she sat down to eat breakfast with the only other human who lived in the werewolf camp, she had to admit the dish looked and smelled damn good.

"You even have walnuts, strawberries, and cinnamon sprinkled on top," she murmured. She took one quick glance at the black man across from her, who, just fifteen minutes ago, declared that they needed to eat breakfast before they went on patrol around the camp.

"If you're gonna help me, you'll need strength," he'd said. His expression was dead serious. Like always.

As Sinister shoveled his first bite into his mouth, Cyn slid her fingers across the worn table to grab the scratched-up spoon. The utensil and table weren't the only worn things in the room. When she first approached the fellow hunter's cabin, she expected a simple room and nothing else. Most hunters, such as the man across from her, had foul-smelling clothes and weapons strewn all over the place, but Sinister had a tidy bed, an end table, a table, a small kitchenette with a mini-fridge, and not much else. No nudie posters or pictures, not even a book. She didn't ask where the two doors in the back went.

The whole place smelled like aftershave. A bachelor pad.

Something bumped her calf under the table. She leaned back to glance at her feet.

"That's Captain Crunch," he said.

Captain Crunch? She spotted a hazel-eyed cat peering up at her with his one good eye. The light from the window behind her shone on the cat's glossy coat.

Yep, Sinister even had a tabby cat.

"I'm not giving you any of my bacon," Sinister grumbled to the cat. His pet meowed in response. "So wasteful." He glanced at the full bowl of cat giblets in the corner.

"How did you get him up here?" she asked. They were deep in the Canadian mountains far north of Vancouver.

"During the last supply run to Prince George, I found him roaming the streets."

"Ahh." She blew on her steamy spoonful of oatmeal and took a small bite. The food had just the right thickness and flavor. The good stuff. However, the undercooked bacon, which she usually loved charred to a crisp, didn't look as appealing. She picked up a piece. With a deft twist of her wrist, the flabby meat slipped to the side, and she strategically let the portion fall to the floor. The scamper of claws told her Captain Crunch had pounced on his target. *Atta boy.*

"You done?"

She glanced up to see Sinister had finished his food. Every last morsel.

"Not yet." She was far too distracted today. She scooped up another bite and froze when the curtain behind her slid shut. The only light left came from a tiny lamp on the end table next to the bed.

"You never told me we had a guest, Sly." The voice was a mere whisper behind her back, but Cyn recognized the smooth timbre from her first dinner with the werewolves. An itch along the back of her neck urged her to turn around and face the werewolf, but she didn't move. "Sorry about the curtains, but my albinism gives me a bit of a skin condition. I avoid direct sunlight."

A pale hand with long fingers reached around Cyn to grab one of the slices of toast from a plate. Next, the man took two pieces of barely cooked bacon and placed them on the bread.

"Damien," was all Cyn said. *Was he a werewolf or a vampire?*

There were only two seats at the tiny table, so the albino werewolf stood at the side without a seat.

"You can call me Uncle Damien, if you like." Damien wasn't as tall as Sinister. Matter of fact, unlike most of the werewolves Cyn had hunted in the past, Damien had a thinner, more compact body. Compared to Sinister's simple flannel shirt and jeans, Damien was dressed in business casual with dark slacks and a sweater. Almost as if he planned to entertain company with cocktails.

"You'll be family soon, after all," Damien added.

"Of course." *Right after she patrols their territory due to a slain hunter.*

His head tilted a bit. "You don't sound sure."

Lying to werewolves was next to impossible. "Not all the Windhams want me here."

"I've learned over the many years I've walked the earth that what might seem insurmountable is a mere whisper of a challenge to face."

A mere whisper? Fighting Kaden's younger sister Naomi

had been one thing, but facing someone like Eva, a high-ranking werewolf who wanted to protect her family, that was something entirely different.

"So you're giving up without trying?" Damien asked.

Bitter words swirled around her tongue, but she didn't say them. She didn't want to try as much anymore. Kaden had lied to her about the dead body. Betrayal settled like a weight in her stomach and made her feel queasy.

Maybe Kaden had a reason to lie to her? She sighed. He'd withheld information before and the reason was always clear: if she had found out, she would have left. Which meant he didn't trust her judgment.

The one person who *should've* trusted her didn't. So why was she staying here?

It most certainly wasn't the breakfast options.

"You don't seem like the type to give up without a fight, Cynthia McGinnis." At the sound of her name, Cyn glanced up at Damien. The prominent scar along his cheek drew her eye. You couldn't miss it. It was if someone had taken a blade and tried to slice his face open inch-by-inch.

Cyn slowly rose. "I'm not a quitter, but I do know when I'm in too deep. Especially when it comes to people like Kaden Windham."

Sinister wiped his mouth off with a simple purple napkin. "We got work to do. Whatever shit you got going on with Windham can wait." He leveled her with his gaze. "We clear?"

Did he have an idea what went down? "Crystal."

Sinister jerked his head toward the far wall with the two doors. One of them was open a crack. Was that the door Damien had come out of?

Her host gathered the plates while she made her way toward the open door. By the time she touched the cold doorknob and peered inside, she was surprised to see the tiny cabin hid even more secrets. Beyond the tiny room, lay a far bigger one.

Not a single light illuminated the room except the dim light from the other room. Were there any windows? Sinister's room was darker now that Damien had removed the sunlight.

She took a single step inside. Then another. To keep herself from running into something, she reached her hands out. A few steps inside and her hand hit a pull chain, only to have another warm hand slide across hers.

"Whoa!" She jumped left.

"Need help?" Uncle Damien's smooth voice asked.

With a strong jerk, light filled the room and Cyn gasped.

A hunter's fantasyland unfolded before her very eyes.

Shelving along the walls held ammunition and weapons. *Oh, the guns!* She stifled a giggle. One shelf had a full row of professional grade Glock 17s and Korth pistols. High durability weapons. A box of Barrett 50 caliber mounted sniper rifles lay in one corner next to a lovely stack of Bouncing Betties.

It was like friggin' Christmas at the McGinnis household.

"Oh, look; it's an M-16. I got a rifle like this for my fifteenth birthday," Cyn said with pride. The year before that her parents got her make-up. That nonsense gathered dust on her dresser and they ended up gifting her a 9mm Beretta. A much more suitable present to blow your enemies away with.

Just thinking about the money necessary to buy all this was mind-boggling for such a small camp. Her werewolf-hunting group, the Red clan, with hundreds of members, had this kind of arsenal. A camp of less than twenty people had some crazy firepower.

In the middle of all of this was a single twin-sized bed. Perfectly made with a navy blue wool bedspread. Was this where Damien slept? Why wasn't he surrounded by family in one of the other cabins? Older hunters weren't treated like this.

"Why are all the weapons in here?" Cyn asked. Over the last couple of days, Sinister had given her everything she needed. She hadn't seen this room before.

"I didn't want the kids getting into trouble," Sinister replied.

She nodded. Good point.

"I sleep here to keep the curious away," Damien said. While she looked around, the elder werewolf sat down on his bed, crossed his right leg over his left and began to read a hardback book: *How to Tell if Your Cat Is Plotting to Kill You.*

Umm-kay. Captain Crunch is totally plotting their demise.

She shifted her attention elsewhere. On one shelf, she spotted an older weapon.

"A Thompson machine gun? It's barely usable." She eyed the machine gun. "This is pretty old. Who do you plan to kill with this thing?"

"It's from World War II, but she still fires." Seeing Sinister smile for once was a bit disarming, Cyn had to admit. He frowned far too often. Up close, she caught the faint reddish-brown stubble on his light brown skin and she hid a grin. Was this what Kaden's sister Naomi saw that no one else glimpsed? Sinister the human?

"Want to hold it?" Sinister asked with a bit of reluctance in his voice.

She wiped her hands on her jeans as if she were preparing to hold a newborn babe. "Come to mama."

After she had checked out the weapon for a while, Sinister gave her a full tour until she was comfortable with what was available and could fetch what she needed if the time came. Captain Crunch leaped onto one of the boxes and watched their progress. His tail flicked back and forth.

"Our time is running out. You gonna be ready for what's coming?" Sinister asked.

Now she definitely was.

Doubts still plagued her, but if hell was coming for them, hell better bring some backup. "I'm more than ready. I was born with a silver blade in my hand."

[3]

THE SKY TO THE WEST DARKENED FROM GATHERING murky gray clouds. The thickening cloud line stretched as far as Cyn could see. By the time Cynthia and Sinister returned from a perimeter walk, what should have been a bitterly cold mid-day in January turned into what could've been early evening.

As much as Cyn welcomed hitting the sack, the idea of going to bed without Kaden bothered her. Even if she still wanted to kick his ass for lying to her.

As they approached the camp, Rhys waited for them. Even though the lighting dimmed as time passed, Cyn could easily make out his narrowed green eyes and severe expression. Rhys, a werewolf with a tall thinner build, was often hard to read. He had a reserved nature.

"Did you see any problems?" he asked Sinister.

"Nope." He didn't look at Rhys as he headed up the path. Cyn found it amusing how Sinister walked about as if none of the werewolves concerned him.

"There's a meeting going on right now. I came out to fetch you," he said to Cynthia.

Cyn paused, but Sinister kept going.

"Keep your eyes on the path, Cynthia," Sinister grunted.

"It's pack business, Sinister. She has to be there." Rhys grabbed her arm, but Sinister advanced on them to pull her away.

"Windham wants me to keep her out of trouble. Trouble is always waiting during your," he rolled his eyes, "so-called meetings."

"I can take care of myself." After speaking her peace, Cyn tried to ignore the growing pain along her back from helping Sinister do patrol. A hint of fatigue hit her, too. She told herself that it wasn't her cancer coming back. Three days ago, she'd helped Sinister bury the body. Even though the snow cab had cleared out a hole for the snow, the body still had to be hauled into the hole and covered. Backbreaking labor, but Sinister made her help.

"Gotta keep you frosty, McGinnis," he'd said with what she thought was a grin.

Now that there was a pack meeting, Sinister was far chattier than usual.

"The game pieces have shifted position." Sinister stared at her for a moment, and within those few seconds, she caught an expression her father often used to give her: *You're strolling toward a deep pile of shit, Cyn. Watch your step.*

She wasn't going into a trap, but, without Kaden, the odds weren't in her favor. One false move, and she'd have problems.

"If you're that concerned, then come to the meeting and say hi to your *girlfriend*," she smiled and twisted out of Sinister's grip. Over the past couple of days, she teased the fellow hunter about Naomi. She turned her back on the men and headed up the path toward Rhys's cabin. "I'm ready for once."

Ready, as in she was walking into the meeting with her

good friend, Glock 37. She'd be glad to introduce it to her cohorts if they had a problem with her.

Cyn didn't bother knocking. The door was open and she strode inside. Naturally, conversation ended when she took a free seat in the back. Everyone was there, all the werewolves in the camp.

Naomi smirked when she saw Cyn. Her smirk froze when Sinister marched through the door with Rhys bringing up the rear. Instead of taking one of the folding chairs, Sinister took a spot near the door. He didn't bother to put away the rifle slung over his shoulder.

Cyn sighed. His firearm was a bit of an overkill, but this was Sinister overall.

Rhys took a seat next to his wife, Eva. "What did I miss?" he asked her.

"We were talking about emergency procedures and how to stretch out camp supplies due to the weather. We waited like you asked us." Her two boys, Phil and Peter, sat cross-legged on the hardwood floor playing cards.

"What is it that you had to wait for me to arrive?" Cyn asked. She might as well get to the point.

"As Kaden's *intended* mate, we need to discuss a plan of action since he has been missing for the past few days." Rhys stretched out the word *intended,* as if any intentions Kaden had to be her mate were for amusement. How nice.

"Isn't he out hunting for Micah?" Cyn asked.

"Yes." Eva said this with disappointment in her voice. As Micah's mother, Cyn couldn't imagine how worried she was.

"Why don't we have more wolves out there tracking him?" Cyn asked.

"I went out briefly this morning, but I couldn't find anything. Kaden is the best tracker in the pack. If we send out too many wolves, we weaken the group and leave ourselves vulnerable for attack."

Even though the camp was hidden away, the Windhams continued to be vigilant for attacks from the werewolf hunters. After doing something foolish like killing a werewolf hunter from the Cerulean clan, Cyn thought that decision was wise.

"Right now, the pack is weakened." Eva glanced at Cyn with a vicious turn of her lips. "Especially now that my brother-in-law Bastian is *gone*."

Oh, no she didn't. Cyn hid a smile. Eva seriously flashed her the evil eye. As if it were her fault that Bastian was a power-hungry jerkoff who tried to take over the pack. A few days ago, Bastian had cornered Cyn and used another pack member to attack her. If Kaden hadn't intervened, there'd be one less smart-ass hunter in British Columbia.

"Don't start, sweetheart," Rhys bit out. "We need to focus on what we need to do."

"We don't need Cynthia to figure that out," Naomi snapped. "We should do what I suggested, every twenty-four hours, we send out two pack members to search during the day. They return during the night to secure the camp."

Cyn nodded in agreement. Naomi might've rubbed her the wrong way, but her plan was sound.

"No one is leaving. We can't afford to lose anyone else. For all we know, Kaden might be dead. Micah might be…" Eva's face tightened for a moment, but she kept going. "Beyond the camp, it's not safe. Even if Kaden said he made some bullshit deal to keep the freelance hunters away, what's to stop one of them from killing anyone who hunts alone?"

"If we don't help our own, what kind of pack are we then?" Naomi shot to her feet.

"A pack that lives." Eva didn't wince or look away.

"You forget your place." Naomi growled deep in her throat, her face contorting into a snarl. "I will run the pack until Kaden returns."

"I have two boys to protect—" Eva yelled back.

"Your lack of trust is what makes you weak." Everyone glanced at Uncle Damien. Somehow, he reflected calm as he stared Eva down. She quickly looked away to the floor.

Uncle Damien continued. "Fighting doesn't help strengthen the pack."

"Why not make Damien the pack leader?" Cyn suggested. In her opinion, he was rather weird, but at least he'd yet to go batshit crazy in her presence.

No one spoke and a heavy pall fell over the room. Damien didn't even look Cyn's way.

Oh, shit what did I do now? Cyn thought.

"As much as I'd be tempted to lead, I have what you'd call *limitations* that put me in a position where I'm unfit." Damien's smile was wide and friendly, but Cyn's breath shot to her stomach when she caught the way his hands formed tight fists in his lap. His sweet resin scent flared to the point that Cyn's nose twitched in irritation.

"I see. Sorry if I misspoke." Something told her that getting on Damien's bad side wasn't a place she wanted to be.

Silence prevailed for a bit before Eva stood. "If Kaden doesn't return by dawn, I will take over the pack."

Even Eva's mate, Rhys, didn't question her, but Naomi's eyes formed slits.

During her whole little speech, Eva's gaze never turned away from Cyn. Her warning was loud and clear, though: Once she led the pack, the showdown she promised Cyn would most likely occur.

By the time Cyn left the meeting, heavy snow had started to fall. The shoveled path between the cabins had patches of white here and there. The wind blew, bringing a heavy scent of the pines and light ozone from the snow.

"I don't like this," Sinister said from her side.

"What is there not to like?" She sighed and began to head toward the cabin she shared with Kaden that lay on the edge of camp. Sinister grabbed her arm again. This time his grip was tighter. He was learning.

Cyn groaned. "Not this again. This buddy-buddy thing is getting old. I can only paint your nails so many times." She spied Naomi leaving the house. Kaden's sister looked at them with interest.

"Stop fighting me." He cocked his head to the side and then shook it. "You can act like tough shit all you want. If Eva and her cohorts want to rip you apart in the middle of the night, they'll do it."

"Let them come. I'm not vulnerable anymore." She didn't have one of Sinister's M-16s, but at least she knew where those suckers were stored.

Sinister snorted as Naomi took a step closer to them. "You're a fool. Every single day you're growing weaker. Pretty soon, I'll be dragging your ass around."

"Then why bother?" She tried to free her arm again and failed.

"I know how to keep my word to my friends."

She held in a curse. All this time, she'd believed Kaden would protect her. That he'd keep her safe, since she decided to stay, but he was gone now, and a gun-happy substitute was in his place.

"What if he doesn't return?" After she'd said those words, she wished she could have snatched them back.

"Then I'll take you to the nearest hospital. Dead or alive."

You, asshole. The need to strike Sinister was so strong she had to count to ten to keep herself from doing it. One. Two.

Three. *Screw this.* She cocked her fist back, but someone caught her arm.

"Nobody gets to hit him but me." Naomi flashed Sinister a look of exasperation before she turned to Cyn. "Look, as much as I'd like to suddenly lose you in one of those snowdrifts, I know Sinister will protect you, even against my wishes. Just go get whatever you need and come stay at my cabin tonight."

Sinister ran his hand over his baldhead to his face. He gripped his chin hard enough to make Cyn wince. "You think I'm gonna let her stay—"

"You two are camping out at my house tonight." She looked over the landscape where visibility continued to decrease. Even Cyn couldn't make out the trees past one hundred yards. "In the morning, we'll talk to Eva and get things straightened out."

Sinister finally let go of her arm. There wasn't much she could do all alone with him anyway. He probably spent his quiet evenings by the fire sharpening his knives and polishing his weapons. Old Curtis Jenkins from the Red clan was that way. He was now on permanent assignment in the Rocky Mountains. *By himself.*

"Fine. Let me get my bag," Cyn grumbled. Sinister wasn't too far behind her.

"I don't trust Naomi as far as I can throw her," Cyn said. "Do you believe she can behave herself?"

He waited at the door. "I don't trust anyone."

[4]

To Cyn's irritation, Naomi even popped some popcorn for their little slumber party. A few pieces were burnt, but the nonchalant look on Naomi's face was priceless.

This was gonna be awkward all around.

Holding her massive bowl of popcorn, the shorter woman scowled at Sinister the whole time. Her black hair was wet—apparently she'd hurried through a shower—and even though she tried to look like she didn't care, even Cyn had to admit she only showered when she cared about appearances.

Naomi rummaged through her popcorn while Cyn tried to re-read the same page in a magazine she'd had for the past few weeks. *Canadian Huntsman Quarterly* could only be read so many times without losing your sanity.

Instead of idle chatter, Sinister pulled one of the oak chairs from her kitchen table and placed the seat near the door. He took off his coat, placed it over the back of the seat and began his guard duties.

The two of them sat across from each other saying nothing. Sinister scratched the back of his head and glanced at her once. Naomi bit into a burnt piece of popcorn and looked up at him after he looked away. Anticipation hung between the two and Cyn wished they'd just make out and get their bullshit out of way.

It was like a bad date.

What she wouldn't give to be sitting across from Kaden right now.

Stop thinking about him.

Even as she faked reading an article about the importance of deer musk extraction, she couldn't stop thinking about how things had turned out. A few months ago, she was sitting in a hospital watching Zach try to breakdance and dance hip-hop style.

He had no rhythm and couldn't dance for shit, by the way.

She missed her brother, too. Nobody attempted the Worm like Zachary McGinnis. He always looked like a beached whale making a sorry-ass attempt to reach water. She laughed, and then snorted to herself.

"What's so funny?" Naomi asked.

"Oh, I'm remembering one time when my brother tried to teach me how to do the Humpty Dance. It's like this." Cyn got up to demonstrate the swaying movement, but she did it just as bad as Zach did. Even humming the song didn't help.

Naomi's face scrunched up as if Cyn had lost her mind.

At least Cyn tried to lighten the mood. "The song was way before your time. Mine too, but—"

"You can't dance," Sinister said firmly.

Cyn laughed again. "Zach can't either, but he was always trying to make me feel better. He's the kind of brother I'd die to protect."

Naomi crammed a fistful of food into her mouth. "I wish

I felt that way about my brothers. Most of the time, they piss me off." Somehow, she managed to talk between smacks.

Then her next handful of popcorn stopped on the way to her mouth.

"What is it?" Sinister asked.

"The window in the bedroom is moving." She got up to investigate, but Sinister placed his hand on her shoulder.

"No." He pulled a .9 mm from the holster strapped to his back, grabbed a flashlight, and crept toward the bedroom. "I'll check."

Cyn brought up the rear with her .45 drawn and at her side. Sinister paused at the doorway to the bedroom and leaned in to listen. He motioned to her for a five-second countdown and then placed his hand on the doorknob.

Behind them, Naomi grumbled and complained that no one wanted her popcorn as a diversion.

Cyn took a deep breath. Had the time arrived for an attack? Many days had passed. Could the Cerulean clan have got up here that fast? Maybe if they had men in British Columbia. Even Calgary was nine hours away from Prince George by car.

Sinister counted down. By the time he reached the end, she told herself she was ready for whatever was coming.

He twisted the doorknob. Cyn's calves twitched and softened as if weak. Not good.

Sinister sprang forward and burst into the room with Cyn ambling after him. The flashlight in Sinister's hand flooded the room with light. His beam cast a rapid arc from one side to the other, only to stop on two figures whose faces held mischievous grins.

"What are you two doing here?" Cyn asked.

"I was out for a walk in the lovely weather and Peter wanted to join me," Damien said. Light snow covered his shoulders. All he wore was the sweater from breakfast and jeans. Far wiser, Eva's son, Peter, was in a coat.

"Does anyone ever believe that kind of bullshit story?" Cyn asked with a laugh.

"Most pretend and tell me how delightful it is to have my unexpected company." Which meant he did this often and to other people in the camp. *Swell.*

"Hey, Cyn!" Peter strolled across the room and Sinister merely grunted. The hunter left them behind to resume his post near the door.

"You guys left the window open." Cyn tried her best to push the window closed. An inch or two remained and she needed Damien's help to push the window shut the rest of the way.

"How have you been, Miss McGinnis?" he asked slowly. His strange gaze seemed to look through her. Could he see the oncoming illness that Kaden had kept at bay since she'd arrived here?

Instead of revealing her surprise at his bold question, she slapped a grin on her face. "Great! And now we finally have some victims to eat Naomi's popcorn."

"I heard that!" Naomi snapped from the other room.

"So, umm, what are you two doing here? It's crazy outside, and your mom won't be happy to learn you're gone," Cyn said to Peter.

Peter rolled his eyes as they headed out to the living room. "I was so bored. I miss video games. Mom expected us to eat dinner and then go *read* in bed. Who does that kind of thing?"

"I do," Damien admitted quietly.

"I don't mean you, Uncle Damien. You're really smart."

Damien laughed at that.

After a fried chicken dinner, for the next hour, Cyn was wrangled into playing board games with Peter. No one else volunteered. The others remained quiet and observed. By the time her head drooped from tiredness, Uncle Damien spoke up.

"It's getting late," he said.

"No, it's only nine o'clock," Peter protested. "On Saturdays, I used to go to bed at ten."

"Then how about a story and then we leave? The tale happened a long time ago on a night similar to this one." Damien winked at Cyn. Could he tell she was tapped out?

"Which one is it this time? Is there a sad ending?" Now Damien had Peter's attention. "Your last one was *pretty* gruesome!"

"I'm going back to the beginning of the Windham pack." Damien sighed, and the line along his scar tightened. "It all began on a night like tonight. In a far more sinister manner."

[5]

"I'd been born as a man, but at the time, I believed I was a monster," Damien began. He let the words and the memories flow. The dam he had built around his hardest times collapsed.

"A long time ago, in the country that would someday be called Czechoslovakia, I was respected for my craft. No one bothered the furniture maker who lived at the far edge of my village. Until the night of a snowstorm like today." He smiled. "I guess I should explain how I became a furniture maker? No? You see, I was the village pariah. The strange man who'd been born as white as snow and somehow survived childbirth. My *matka* never wanted me, and, as soon as I was twelve, she cast me out of the house to find my own way. The late nineteenth century was a different world back then. There were many other children in the house, and, as a seamstress, she needed her customers to come to our home. With my red devil eyes, I was seen as cursed."

He paused to collect himself. "I was alone. Hungry and wet from a summer's rainstorm, I wandered the village crying until I came to the edge of town. From there, I spotted a worn hut with the smell of bread coming from the haphazard chimney. I didn't know any better and knocked on the door. The man who lived there was the area's furniture maker. His house always smelled of the pine sap he collected for his resins. When he opened the door, he looked at me like this." Damien made a sullen face in Peter's direction. The boy laughed.

"I begged for food, and he just stared at me for a moment. Then he slammed the door in my face." Damien chuckled. "That brief hesitation was enough to motivate me to stay. It took me a week to get fed. I didn't sit there waiting for a handout either. No, sir. I arranged the furniture maker's tools in his shed. I made small repairs to the outside of his dwelling. When he finally came outside to toss me a bit of bread, I caught him hobbling. He had a dirty bandage around his calf, but he never told me how he got hurt. My persistence, though, paid off. I followed him around until he died a year later from sepsis."

"What is sepsis?" Peter asked.

"It's a blood infection. You see, the furniture maker must've hurt his leg, but he never properly cleaned his wound."

Damien continued. "Time passed. My life changed for the better until that strange snowstorm I talked about earlier. A blind girl, just about a year or two younger than my eighteen years, showed up at my doorstep. Her mother left her there. The old woman never told me her name or why she was leaving her daughter there. Only that she had no place to stay and the devil furniture maker was a better place for her to be.

"The girl told me her name was Luba. At first, she avoided me all the time. But, as time passed, she began to follow me around and help. Not many people wanted the chairs I made, but once Luba came to live with me, others came by to buy or trade, and soon, we had enough money to make repairs to the house. To have a life." Damien paused a bit. His throat tightened as the memories flooded him.

"I was a happy man. And I was happier than I'd ever been on the night she told me she was pregnant with my child. The winter had come and everything was as it should be, but I was uneasy during that snowstorm. There were rumors that dark creatures were lurking in the woods from Prague to Budapest. The *vuk* hunters, as many called them, rode through our village and headed south after their trail. The snow had become deep and many didn't travel along the narrow, muddy roads. That night, I locked up all the windows and built a large fire. Armed with the only weapon I had, a bat, I was prepared for what was to come.

"Were you really prepared?" Peter asked.

"No, I wasn't," he whispered.

He continued. "The only sound I remember at first was the howling of the wind. Or maybe it was them. It was like a strange whisper. A shriek I'll never forget. The front door crumbled inward, and they came for us while we were in our bed. We never had a chance. They tried to drag Luba away and I grabbed the bat I'd made. By the time the creature had gutted her…I bashed its head in, but it wasn't hunting alone. One of the other pack members attacked me and knocked me to the wall. All I remember was the pain as it bit me in the face." He brought his hand to his face along the scar. Every ridge and line somehow brought him comfort. "The feeling of my face separating from my body. And seeing my beautiful wife on the floor of our cabin. The feeling of ineptness as my life's blood left my body. I was too weak. Too tired as the creature held me down. I thought I'd die together with my wife, but instead, the creature dragged my wife out of the house and left me there to die. It had rejected me as if my blood—my body—wasn't good enough for its next meal.

Hours passed and I waited for the end to come so I could be with my wife. In the end, with the morning sun rising and snow drifting into the house, something came for me. A man marched across the floor to where I lay next to my fireplace. I remember the warmth from the cinders through my haze and thinking that my life, like them, was almost over and turned to ashes. I remember the strange way the man leaned in to smell me, to touch the bleeding side of my face."

"*'A fast-beating heart. Perfect for revenge. You're not ready yet to die,'* he'd said to me." Damien drew in a deep breath. The others in the room stared hard at him.

"I waited for him to save me, to wrap my wounds in bandages, but, instead, he bit me on the leg. I cried out in pain, maybe this was the end that I sought. Then everything went black. Death came for me, but in a different way, the next time I woke up. The man who had saved me had watched over me as I lay in my sweat and blood. He never moved from the old worn seat Luba used to use to mend my clothes.

"As I rose, with strength in my body and resolve in my spirit, I wanted to tear the man apart. The world was different to me now. I could see better. Smell things I couldn't smell before. Everything was enhanced as if my mind were a sharpened blade. The gaping wound on my face had sealed, leaving a hideous scar.

"He revealed to me that a week had passed. Then he tossed a bit of cloth on the floor. It stank of something familiar—the same scent had been all over my body. It belonged to the creature that had tried to kill me.

"*'You can either lie there and wait for your body to starve to death, or you can seek out the Bäcker pack. They are the ones who have soiled your doorstep.'* Tobias Windham was an imposing figure back then as he was before he died."

"Father," Naomi said, her voice soft.

"I snatched the cloth from the floor. My pale fingers had claws along the tips. The need to spring on that werewolf, the same creature who had cursed an already cursed man, was strong. So strong the new feral beast within me stirred like nothing I'd ever experienced before. But the sweet smell of revenge was far stronger.

"I ran out of the house into the cold afternoon sun. No coat. No boots. Only the scent to guide me, but I didn't make it far. A few minutes in daylight and my skin began to burn. My eyesight began to blur. For some reason, unlike other werewolves, I had a sensitivity to sunlight due to my albinism. My ailment forced me to take cover for the day. The night came soon enough, though, and once I tracked them down, I killed them all. Four males and two females." His voice rose and the melody of remembering his revenge sang in his soul. He made them pay. He made them suffer for taking away the only person who accepted him for what he was.

"Tobias didn't create another werewolf, though; he created a monster of monsters. Running with another pack was impossible. Every time I saw those creatures—just smelling them made me recall the past. Made me relive the pain I'd suffered. All this time, I thought the wolf had made the man mad, but I questioned if I was mad before that point.

"Time passed. Many years. When the werewolf hunters came, I ran into the wilderness. It was there that Tobias came for me again, but he wasn't alone this time. He had others with him. His mate. He forced me out of the hole in the ground where I lived. He said something to me I'll always cherish: 'There will always be a place for you, no matter who you are and what you've done in the past. Remember that, Damek.'

"I answered to the name Damien after that point. Wherever Tobias Windham went, I followed. Across Germany. Into the British Isles. In a rat-invested boat sailing across the Atlantic. My journeys have taken me to many places, and I've seen many things. I even found a mate again. Her name was Becca, and we were happy for a brief period of time. Whenever I ventured away, Tobias always made me return. He made me return home, the place where I was always welcomed—"

The beeper on Sinister's hip chirped and everyone looked at the hunter. During Damien's stay at the man's cabin, the tiny device had never gone off. Which meant something was wrong.

Sinister stood and Cyn did the same shortly after. The human didn't say a word as he donned his coat, but to Damien, the man's heartbeat had sped up, his breath quickened.

"Did someone trip one of the perimeter alarms?" Peter asked.

"Yep." Sinister finished putting on his coat. "We got ten minutes before they reach the edge of camp."

The lights went out. Only the dim light from the fireplace cast a glow on their faces.

"Oh, shit," Cyn said.

"What's wrong?" Peter asked quietly.

"If the power is out, that means they took out the generator shed. They're already in the camp," Cyn whispered.

The glass in the back bedroom broke and a crash followed after.

Cyn exchanged glances with Sinister.

"Get the kid out of here," he said.

[6]

By the time Kaden reached the snow cab he'd parked five miles northeast of the camp, his heart jumped into his throat. Not much could be heard through the storm's howls and the snow made visibility damn near impossible, but he was certain of one thing: There shouldn't be bright lights in the direction of where the camp should be.

And those lights shouldn't look like fire.

Cyn.

At his side, Micah whined.

A gust of wind blew into Kaden's eyes and he squinted.

He looked to the snow cab and then to Micah. He'd just gotten the boy back. Would he follow him into danger?

He'd promised Zach he'd keep her safe.

There was only one way to find out if he could keep that promise. He sprinted southwest.

The snowstorm continued to rage as Cyn left the cabin with Peter. Naomi followed them in wolf form.

Cyn checked around each corner as she got off the porch, looking for anyone hiding in the shadows. The darkness seemed to swallow up everything. Visibility was no more than a hundred yards at the most. By the time they circled to the back of the cabin, to head toward camp, she noticed that they were alone. Sinister and Damien hadn't followed them.

Gunfire sounded from within the camp. Not good.

Where had the men gone? Maybe to help the others secure the power generator shed.

Hundreds of thoughts circled her mind as she tried to trudge through the knee-deep snow: *Was it the Cerulean clan who had come? If they'd reached the camp, how many pack members had been taken—or even killed?*

By the fifth step, the muscles in her legs ached. Her breaths came out as gasps. Instead of pulling Peter along, he was slightly ahead of her now.

At her side, Naomi even looked at her with slit eyes. Was Kaden's sister able to smell the return of her illness?

"C'mon, Cyn," Peter called softly.

Get your shit together, Cynthia, she reminded herself.

Through the storm and the trees, bright orange bled into the sky, lighting up the camp. Something was on fire. More shots rang out as they closed in on the back of Peter's cabin. Shadows moved ahead. Two of them.

Naomi slowed down and her head dipped.

Cyn's grip on Peter's hand tightened. The boy crouched and his body trembled with a growl.

"Quiet," she commanded. She took aim with her .45, careful to consider the wind speed, and shot the first man down before he reached the cabin. The recoil was hard, but she was ready for it. Her other target took cover.

Return gunfire came fast in Naomi's direction, forcing her to take cover among the trees. She yelped as she ran away.

Did she get hit?

Suddenly, Peter twisted to look behind them. A man tackled her hard from behind. Cyn slammed face-first into the snow.

Damn it, McGinnis you're getting sloppy. She should've stayed alert, and now, she'd left Peter vulnerable.

Arms flying about for control, Cyn wrestled with the piece of shit who hit her from behind. He threw a hard left, which she managed to dodge, but he still connected with her shoulder. The hit forced her to drop her weapon and it fell deep into the snow.

From the corner of her eye, she saw Naomi rush the cabin to attack the gunman who continued to shoot at them.

"Stop fighting me!" the man on top of her spat. He tried to hit her again with a fast right hook, but he missed and she took advantage.

She grabbed his extended arm tightly and rolled hard to the left, taking him with her. He wasn't too big; a guy any larger couldn't be twisted in such a manner. He rolled under her and she pinned his arm nicely into an armbar submission.

"Damn b—!" he grunted.

With a sharp jerk, she broke his arm and he howled.

She punched him hard across the chin, silencing him. One down. Too many to go.

Cyn searched him and grabbed his weapon, a .9 mm, and his flashlight. He wouldn't be needing them anymore.

The gunfire had ended, and Naomi plodded up to her. She'd found her target.

But then, the werewolf's head jerked to the right.

"Cyn…" Peter warned.

"Don't move, wolf!" A voice yelled from a few yards away. "Before I put a silver bullet in you." A flashlight shined into Cyn's face from a thatch of trees close by. They all didn't so much as twitch.

So they thought she was a werewolf too, huh?

She shoved Peter behind her. "Get ready to move," she whispered between clenched teeth. "Don't look back."

Naomi growled and bared her sharp teeth. Her sleek body trembled. If she pounced, they were done for.

"What a nice evening for an excursion? Huh, boys?" Cyn called out.

"Shut up." The man closed in, his rifle aimed at them. With the snowfall, it was hard to make out his features, but like the hunter she'd subdued, he wore a thick, white coat and gear for the outdoors. These hunters had money to burn.

"Let the boy go. I'm sure you just want adults," Cyn said. The light shined into her face and forced her to look elsewhere. She'd used the same tactic countless times to blind her cornered prey. If these guys were as good as she suspected, she was about to be shot. Peter would be next.

Time for a diversion. And she was prepared for what was about to happen. She was going to die, but she was taking some of these bastards with her.

"I'm not one of them; I'm a hunter."

"Like we're gonna believe you," the second man said.

"Shut up!" the first hunter said to his cohort. "We have orders to secure the camp and question the ones we capture."

"Screw our orders. She hurt Frank," the second man snapped. "I say we ice this wolf bitch. Or at least break her arms, too."

The first man chuckled and fear raced down her spine. In three seconds, she could have her switchblade from her hip and take out the first hunter, but was that enough time? Naomi still wouldn't make it. A spray of gunfire from their rifles would slice her in half. A different plan came to mind.

"Who's in command for the Ceruleans?" she asked. "Garrison? Donaldson?"

The second one twitched. Hunting clans never revealed the chain of command to werewolves to protect themselves. The men hesitated.

Gotcha. She shifted to move left and pushed Peter toward Naomi. Their guns went up.

"Run," she breathed.

The click of the hammer on their guns seemed audible to her, even with the wind. She waited for the pain. For the burst of color in her chest as they blew her away. But the hit never came as she dived in front of Peter and Naomi.

Instead, she heard the men scream. She twisted in the snow and glanced up. The hunter's flashlights danced about.

The second hunter shot in the other man's direction. "What the hell!"

A dark form came behind the first hunter. The man arched his back and screamed again, his cry turning to a wet gasp as he collapsed on the ground.

She couldn't see. She couldn't make out what happened in the darkness. Only hear begging and screaming.

"Please don't... Please..." the second man groaned. Only once in her life had she heard such sounds. They came when a hunter arrived too late to save his or her comrade.

They weren't alone. Someone else was there. Was it Kaden? Naomi still hovered over Peter.

When only the wind was left howling, Cyn dragged herself to stand. Her limbs had gone numb, maybe from the cold, maybe from what had just gone down. Her hands trembled as she reached for the flashlight she dropped.

I have to see, she told herself.

No, you don't. You've seen this before. There were no mysteries in death. It is what it is.

I have to know who did this.

If it's Kaden, do you want to see him after he's killed

someone?

Slowly, she aimed the flashlight toward the fallen men. Their bodies lay in *pieces* in the crimson snow. A single man stood near them. She brought the beam up and gasped.

It was Damien.

Covered in blood and snow. With wide eyes and a strange smile, he brought his bloody index finger up to his mouth. Bright red drops fell from the digit on the snow below.

"Shh," he seemed to whisper. He ran away from the beam of light into the darkness.

"All this time, I thought the wolf had made the man mad," he'd said, *"but I questioned if I was mad before that point…"*

She shuffled backward, the smell of blood growing stronger. "We gotta move, guys."

The boy didn't question her and followed her toward his parents' cabin. Naomi plodded after them.

I'VE COME TOO LATE. THE THOUGHT WAS HARD TO SHAKE as he raced toward camp. As much as Kaden tried to think about what had to be done and what he could do to save the others, Cyn's safety plagued his thoughts.

Micah ran hard and somehow kept up with his breakneck pace. They raced over the ridge and by the time they reached the line of snow cabs, fear was replaced with rage, an all-consuming fury that he allowed to blossom into something more.

Invaders spilled into camp along the edges, so he went after those targets. One hunter he crept up behind never saw the attack coming. The man screamed as Kaden took him out. Each target that followed got the same treatment. Sneak and kill. Swarm and attack.

But along with the victorious moments, a bitter one came as well. Two werewolves lay dead in the snow: Ash and Clyde. They were rogues who had become his friends and found a place within the pack.

Micah whimpered when he saw the lifeless bodies while Kaden's rage soared even higher. Now wasn't the time to mourn his friends. He'd take the time to memorialize them after the camp was secure.

Then he spied three werewolves running west out of the camp. One with a dark coat he recognized as Rhys. His brother was leading them toward the designated safe point west of camp.

The best thing to do now would be to sweep every corner and eliminate the vermin. Watch for the others and *destroy* anyone who dared to cross his path.

FLAMES LICKED THE THICK WALL OF WOOD IN FRONT OF Rhys and Eva's cabin. Peter released her hand, and she had to rush to catch up with him as he snuck into the dark house.

Smoke billowed from one of the windows. The inside of the house was blanketed with noxious smoke.

Naomi waited outside while Cyn raced inside.

"Peter!" she hissed, her eyes watering.

He was nimble, going from room to room looking for his family. "Mom!" he called out.

But even Cyn suspected they weren't here. The house was deathly quiet. She checked the last room when Peter went into the boys' bedroom. The master bedroom was empty—except for a dead hunter next to the bed. A woman hunter.

This could have been me.

Coughing hard from the smoke, she tried to process everything and failed. Even if this woman, who had to be no more twenty, was a hunter, she was still just a girl who was following orders.

Cyn had been born a hunter, and now she was sleeping with the enemy. The game had changed.

With just a brief glance, Cyn's heart got kicked when she saw Eva's things.

"We had to leave everything behind," Eva had said. *"All our belongings. The kids' toys."*

Two sides. No solution but to kill each other.

She spied a small photo album on a nearby dresser. For good measure, she snatched it and tucked it in her coat pocket. Something should be saved today.

"They've left, Peter," Cyn said as she returned to the living room. "We need to wait—"

She stopped short to see Eva waiting at the front door, gun in hand. The blonde woman's eyes were wild, her hair disheveled about her shoulders. Blood was splattered across her torn shirt. Peter moved behind his mother with his gaze fixed on the worn porch floor. Naomi hovered not far from them.

"I was prepared to seal you inside this house to burn with that bitch hunter who tried to attack my family," she said simply. "But you protected my child."

Eva turned to leave, pausing to check for danger, before running away. Peter and Naomi followed.

Cyn caught faint words from the boy. "What about Cyn?" he asked.

His mother didn't reply. Or maybe Cyn missed it.

She spotted a dark wolf running toward them and sighed. She recognized that wolf well. A few days ago, she'd hunted with Kaden to find the boy.

He'd made it home, but did Kaden return as well?

The Windhams headed off into the woods. She was alone now. Even after what she did to protect Eva's son, Eva had left her behind. In her weakening condition, she could never make it to the rendezvous point without help. The outsider left to die with her own kind.

~

KADEN'S HUNT CONTINUED WITH SEEMINGLY NO END, but every inch of the small camp had to be covered. Every room to every nook and cranny. No invading hunter would be missed.

He still had two more cabins to check when he heard a voice whispering near the edge of the woods, not far from the burning generator shed. Whoever hid there had been elusive so far, but with less noise from gunfire, he caught the sounds this time.

"I told you to take prisoners, Atkins," a man's voice grunted from behind a thicket of fallen pines and bristly branches. "I can't get answers unless I have someone with a heartbeat."

Kaden closed in, going wide to attack the man from the rear. Once in position, he darted from tree to tree until his target was loud and clear.

He heard the crackle of a radio. "Copy that," another voice said. "I'll see if this guy who's shooting at me will stop for a sec to chat."

"Switch targets then!"

"I almost got him. He's holed up in one of the cabins."

Who was it? Kaden wondered. *And why wasn't he at the rendezvous point?*

"I don't care!"

Fury surged within Kaden. He'd heard enough. He crept up and slammed hard into the hunter, but instead of killing the man, he loomed over his target.

This one, he decided, would *live* to be questioned.

[7]

Not long after dragging the man to his cabin and tying him up in human form, Kaden shifted back into a wolf to finish checking the camp.

The whole process had left him exhausted but still determined. He had yet to find Cyn. He finally caught her scent outside of Rhys's cabin. From there, he followed the trail to Sinister's cabin. Cyn was on the porch, trying to break her way inside. The windows had been boarded up, so she sagged against the wall.

He turned to Cyn. Her color wasn't good. Her face was as pale as the snow around them. The rise and fall of her chest was quicker. As he drew closer, her head popped up. For a moment, her eyes brightened with relief, but then they formed slits. Anger pulsed from her and nipped at him.

So she knew.

Now that a group of hunters had attacked them, she must have had an idea as to what was going on.

Slowly, he approached her. He'd waited too long to heal her, but he didn't expect a warm welcome. She didn't move when he poked her shoulder with his nose.

She winced. "Ouch."

Up closer, he noticed blood on the side of her mouth. Her scent was like black licorice again. Exhaustion and pain. But she'd survived.

She pushed him away with her good shoulder. "I don't want to look at you right now," she snapped.

He barked at her—something he rarely did—and he tried to move her again. It was too cold for her to sit out here in her condition. If she were a pup, he'd grab her by the neck and carry her inside Naomi's cabin.

"You have some nerve showing up like this." She shivered, so he nestled himself against her side. "If you were a man, you'd come in human form so we could argue."

She squirmed underneath him.

"You're heavy," she protested with a grunt.

She continued to seethe, trying her best to get away. Always the stubborn hunter he adored. "You might as well turn back into a human so I can kick your ass for what you did."

Go ahead and try, he thought.

Her gaze was toward the tree line. Now that the snow had let up, the night sky began to unfold and the stars appeared. Everything was still bitterly cold though.

Her body trembled again as she tried to push him away. No more games. He tried to let her cool her temper, but he should've expected this. He shuffled a few feet away and changed back into human form again. Without a proper meal in the last few days, changing back and forth like this would weaken him considerably. The pain should've been brief, but discomfort clawed along his joints, forcing him to breathe through clenched teeth. Maybe that was his due punishment for hurting Cyn.

He extended a hand to her, but she didn't take it. So he tucked his arms under her legs and back and lifted her up.

"Put me down, damn you!" She was trying not to cry.

He didn't answer and continued to carry her back to Naomi's cabin. They'd be safe for a little while to hash things out before they met up with the others.

The door to his sister's cabin had been kicked in. The furniture inside had been scattered about. The hunters had searched the house for its occupants. Had anyone been here when they arrived?

He placed her on Naomi's bed and wrapped blankets around her. When she tried to get up, he finally spoke. "Don't move."

"I don't want to look at you right now."

"I did what I had to do." Clothes were strewn all over the floor, but none of them were his. He searched one of the boxes in the closet and managed to find a shirt and a pair of jeans.

"You *had* to lie to me? If you had told me that man was a hunter, you know that would have bothered me, and I would have considered leaving. So you lied."

He shuffled into his pants. "To save your life."

"My life is my choice." She thrust her finger in his direction. "Whether I become a werewolf or not is *my* choice, and, after looking at all those gutted humans all over the mountainside, I'm leaning toward Team Human right now! What you did was selfish."

Selfish? "So wanting to save your life is selfish?"

"It was selfish of you to take the choice away from me. All my life, I have followed the rules of my clan. Who to follow. Who to question. Who to kill. But my life has always been my own."

"I want your life to be with me now."

"I'm sure it's because of the bargain." Her lower lip trembled. "Is that why I have to stay here?"

Now that was a *low* blow. She was hurt, so he let that

slide. "You know there's more to our relationship than that. If I wanted to heal you and cast you aside, you'd already be in Prince George on your death bed."

She snorted. "My deathbed is coming all right. Today felt like a reminder that once I make my choice, there's no going back to my old life. No more Red clan, and I might as well consider myself cut off from Zach and Ty." When she mentioned her brothers, she choked up a bit.

Suddenly, her fury climbed until she tried to get off the bed. He tugged her into a bear hug and didn't let her go. "I refuse to let you die."

"So I'm a prisoner? I can't trust anything you say at this point."

He didn't care. "If I have to make the same choice again, I will."

She fumed, even trying to head butt him.

Twenty minutes later, and still, she had fight in her.

He chuckled. That was one of the things he loved about her.

Yes, loved.

The feeling was there and tugged at his chest. As difficult as things had gotten between them, he couldn't let her go. *Wouldn't.* The wolf within him wouldn't let him consider such an idea. He'd wait until she was ready. He told himself the time would come someday. Cyn was stubborn and set in her ways, but when she exposed her softer side to him, he found himself unable to accept anything else but having her by his side.

He opened his mouth and closed it.

Straight up admitting he cared for her after getting hurt in the past was difficult.

She sagged in his arms. Her surrender.

"I'm sorry," he finally said. "My heart wants you to stay."

She drew in a deep breath, but didn't speak.

He rested his face against the back of her hair and inhaled. He took in her smell. If she was still mad, he didn't care if she tried to head butt him again.

But she didn't.

She leaned into him. "I don't want to leave yet, but I still want to kick your ass for lying to me."

Slowly, he released her and then used his right hand to unzip her coat. She sighed when his palm slid against the warm, smooth skin of her stomach.

He shuddered as an explosion of healing energy surged from his body and coursed into hers. Even though his strength was diminishing, he'd give her everything he had.

"I'd expect nothing less than a good fight from my lady," he whispered.

[8]

KADEN HAD BRIEFLY MENTIONED THERE WAS A SAFE retreat for the pack a few weeks ago, but he had never elaborated on its size or what was available. Only that she should go west in an emergency and find the others.

No one said anything as Cyn and Kaden arrived at the rendezvous point. Cyn all but expected to see a bunch of wolves gathered around a fire in the snow, or maybe a gathering inside an emergency tent. What she didn't expect was Kaden taking her to a cave. Beyond the camp, at least a mile to the west, hidden among a thick cluster of evergreens, there was an opening in the mountainside. The crack wasn't visible from the sky and the curious would have to travel by foot to reach this point.

"What is this?" she asked him.

"This used to be my home," he simply said.

"Before I discovered the camp," Kaden added, "I found this cave first while I was out exploring. Actually, it was an accident."

She glanced back the way they came. The snow added a bit of cover for their tracks, but not enough to keep this place from being found. The wolves would have to be vigilant for a while with a few guards. She followed him inside and walked past the two guards at the door.

Cyn looked around to see that the space appeared lived-in with places carved into the walls for lanterns. The whole space had to be around fifty feet from the entrance to the far side. A few parts of the ceiling were a bit low, but everyone from the camp was there.

Except one person in particular.

"Where's Sinister?" she asked Kaden. Did her fellow hunter survive? When they'd entered, Naomi had glanced toward the entrance with expectation, but her face fell to see it was only them.

"I'll need to find out," Kaden replied.

They weaved around two groups sitting around propane heaters. Those who had escaped from the camp had made themselves comfortable with sleeping blankets. A few pack members were hurt.

Kaden immediately went to each member, checked their injuries, and healed them. He stumbled a bit each time he got up, but he wouldn't let her stop him as he healed those who needed his care. He gave everything to his pack, even making sure everyone acknowledged her presence.

She'd never seen him with dark circles under his eyes, and yet they were there. He appeared…tired.

"Maybe you should rest," she suggested.

"I'll get sleep soon enough. We have to make sure our pack is well."

Our pack. The words were so simple, but they held a deeper meaning. What had Kaden's father said to Damien? She was tired, yet the words came quickly to mind: "There will always be a place for you, no matter who you are and what you've done in the past."

Kaden moved to someone else, jolting her out of her moment of reverie. She quickly followed.

"How badly is your leg damaged?" he asked another pack member.

"It's broken in a few places, but I'll be fine."

"I'll speed up your healing." Kaden rested his hand on the man's leg. "You did well protecting the pack." The man nodded and closed his eyes, most likely pleased with the kind words from his alpha. Cyn remembered feeling such when her father congratulated her. *On killing werewolves.*

Once Kaden had checked the injured, they headed to the back of the cave where they found Eva, Rhys, and their children.

"Cyn!" Peter called out and started to rise. With one look from his mother, the boy remained where he sat, but he waved nonetheless.

"Hey, Pete," Cyn said softly.

From her pocket, she plucked the photo album. All the memories were safely tucked inside. Cyn extended what she held to Eva, and the woman's eyes grew wide. Eva took the album and murmured thanks.

Instead of bitterness, Cyn felt a sliver of grief. Even though Eva had left her behind, Cyn couldn't help thinking about how important pictures could be when you needed them the most. On the day of her parents' funeral, they had to use photos because they didn't have any bodies for a casket.

Cyn sighed as Eva thumbed through the first photos. They were baby photos of her children. Memories were precious things.

Having a family *is* a precious thing. Especially when your family was taken away. It was time for her to think more about her new family.

"Thank you for finding my son," Rhys said to Kaden.

Cyn spotted Micah from the farthest side of the cave. He had a blank stare and wore clothes that were bigger than his smaller frame, but he appeared well.

"Will he be all right?" Cyn asked Kaden.

"He'll be fine," Eva quickly interjected.

"I honestly don't know," Kaden said. "His wolf is strong in him. He needs guidance. Especially before the next full moon."

"He's not leaving my side again. Ever," Eva said with her lips in a straight line.

"Eva, calm down," Rhys said, as he patted his mate's knee. A long glance was exchanged between the couple, and Cyn recognized it well. Rhys was trying to placate his jittery wife, but she wasn't having it.

"During the next full moon, he must run with an alpha and take direction," Rhys whispered.

"And who will do that?" Kaden asked slowly, his gaze fixed on Eva.

The blonde woman's jaw twitched, but instead of meeting Kaden's gaze, she stared down at her hands on her lap. "You will."

Kaden nodded.

"We need to make some difficult decisions over the next twenty-four hours. If the Cerulean clan knows our position, our pack is in grave danger."

Instead of a tart reply, Cyn noticed the others fell silent. If the Cerulean hunter had died at their hands before they had arrived, they had no one to blame but themselves. Which made this situation sadder for boys like Peter who'd have to find a new home.

During war, there weren't any winners.

"Have you seen Sinister?" Kaden asked Rhys. "He wasn't in his cabin."

"I haven't seen him since the pack had a family meeting last night," Rhys replied.

Cyn touched Kaden's shoulder. "He was with Naomi, Damien, and me until the attack began."

At the mention of her name, in a rush, Naomi left the cave entrance to join them. "He told me to take Peter to the rendezvous point. He wouldn't let me fight with him."

"I see." Kaden appeared thoughtful.

Cyn shrugged, an attempt to lighten the mood. "Don't worry, guys. Sinister's probably holed up somewhere licking his wounds." *Eating his barely cooked bacon.*

"You think he's hurt?" Naomi snapped.

"Have you seen him get hurt yet?" Cyn asked.

"There was the day I stabbed him…" Naomi remarked.

Cyn rolled her eyes. "He probably let you do that him."

"Be that as it may, we need to secure the camp and make plans over the next week," Kaden said.

"It's not safe. We can't stay there anymore," Rhys said. "What do you think, Cynthia?"

Cyn's gaze flicked to Rhys. *Did he actually call her out for advice?*

She might as well tell it like it is. "If I was the hunter in charge and I sent in a contingent of men, I'd expect someone to report back. If no one returned, I'd send in a single man to assess and determine if the threat was still present. In essence, they will be back."

"So what do we do now?" Naomi asked Cyn. "How long do we have?"

"They probably traveled here before the snow began and attacked as the storm moved in for cover. With the deep snow in place, it will take them at least a week to return."

"That's how long it will likely take us to get out." Kaden crossed his arms. "Snow along the mountainside makes the trek to Prince George treacherous. We will make plans and question the prisoner."

"Prisoner?" Naomi whispered.

"What are you saying?" Eva asked.

Even Cyn's head spun from Kaden's words.

"I'm saying that, unlike all of you, I managed to capture one of them alive," Kaden said. "I overheard him say that they wanted to capture one of us. I will be questioning him once we return to camp."

[9]

"WHY DIDN'T YOU TELL ME WE HAD A PRISONER?" CYN asked Kaden as they made their way back to camp the next morning. She wanted to add the words "what the hell," but she was supposed to be reining in the crazy at this point.

"You and I had other *pressing* matters. I planned to tell you when I told everyone else. I promise there aren't any more dire secrets." He immediately looked away after he spoke, and Cyn wished she could feel like she could trust him. Didn't he say he was willing to do anything to keep her with him? Wouldn't that meaning lying again to protect her?

"When a werewolf attaches to someone, letting go is next to impossible," he'd said the last time they made love.

She was supposed to be letting go of her past, moving on so she could be happy with him and live the kind of life she couldn't lead as a hunter. But at this point, happy wasn't happening. Crazy hot monkey sex, yes, but the happy moments were few and far between.

By the time they reached Kaden's cabin, Cyn still had her doubts, but she tried her best to bury them for now. The camp was vulnerable, and if she wanted to even consider moving forward in her relationship with Kaden, they needed to be out of danger first.

The Cerulean pack had ransacked the place, so the cabin didn't feel like home anymore. Neither of them spoke to each other as Cyn tried to pick up a bit. Kaden got a fire going in the fireplace to warm up the space.

A few minutes later, the other higher-ranking pack members joined them. Uncle Damien, Naomi, Rhys, and Eva with her children came inside.

"So the prisoner's in the bedroom?" Eva said. She ushered her children to sit in a corner.

"Are you sure you want them around when we question him?" Cyn asked. In the past, interrogations between hunters and werewolves were bloody affairs not meant for kids. "They could sit with the others in Naomi's cabin."

Eva fumed. "Didn't you hear me earlier? My children are never leaving my side again."

Naomi rolled her eyes. "We get it, Eva. She was just trying to look out for them."

"Which I will do," Eva replied.

"So what happens now?" Rhys asked in an attempt to defuse the situation.

"We question him as to why they have come here," Kaden said. "How many others are nearby? What is their operating strength?"

"And you think he'll outright tell us this?" Naomi scoffed.

"If he knows what's good for him, he will," Eva snapped as she marched to the bedroom door. "I will rip his arms off, otherwise."

None of this sounded good. Even though he was a hunter, he was still a man, and there were interrogation techniques that could be applied without brute force. She didn't know who waited inside that room, but if she knew him personally, she'd have to be given a chance to speak her mind before the pack planned to treat him like saltwater taffy.

"Wait a sec," Cyn interjected.

Eva paused.

"Let me talk to him first," Cyn said.

"I don't like this," Kaden said quietly.

"You owe me." Pulling the guilt card wasn't fair, but she did it anyway.

"You're not going to let it go, are you?" he said.

"Not on your life, pal."

"I could get him to talk," Uncle Damien volunteered with a smile and a raised hand. Almost like he was in kindergarten.

"*No*," Kaden and Cyn said at the same time.

A live prisoner was necessary for interrogation. Not a dead one for dinner. She shuddered.

"Cyn gets ten minutes," Kaden said firmly. "Eva goes with her. No one else."

Before she went inside, Cyn grabbed the first aid kit from the bathroom.

With a nod from her, Eva opened the door and she followed Eva inside. In the middle of the room, strapped to one of the kitchen table seats was a man with dark brown hair. The ropes had been laced around the man's arms and legs, as well as through the gaps in the chair.

He had bruises and dried blood all over his face. The deep scratches along his exposed torso were frighteningly familiar. The telltale sign of a werewolf attack.

Time to focus and get to work.

Cyn opened the curtains for more light. With the late morning sun bathing the room, she could make out more of the man's features. Something about him tugged at her memories. She'd seen him before. Not in person, but in pictures. He was definitely part of the chain of command within the Cerulean hunting clan structure. It wasn't as if those in command had breakfast brunches together to gossip and gab, but in order to keep a little peace between the clans, the higher-ups met once in a while to discuss matters.

Cyn gathered her thoughts so she could talk to him, but Eva made a move first. She strolled up to him, used her index finger to raise his bloody chin, and smiled. The way a predator would to her prey.

"Get your hands off me," he said.

Eva chortled and settled herself on the edge of the bed.

"I'd say good morning," Cyn began, "but this morning isn't looking too good for you."

Eva continued to stare him down as Cyn rummaged through the first aid kit. Rhys's mate tapped her fingernails against her knee. The motion was hypnotic.

"I'm going to check you for injuries first; is that okay?" Trust first, questions later.

Cyn reached for his head, but he jerked back. "I'm not going to hurt you."

"I find that rather hard to believe with scum like you," the man spat.

"Scum?" Eva scoffed as she rose. "You invaded my territory and you have the nerve to call me that?"

"Scum kills with disregard. We found the body you tried to hide."

Eva stiffened, her mouth opening and closing.

Their conversation was collapsing quickly.

The man's mouth curled into a smile. "Was it you who killed him?"

"Why are you here?" Eva lunged for him, managing to grab him by the throat, but Cyn intervened. Wasn't she supposed to do the questioning?

"Hey! We're here to question him. You don't have to hurt him like that."

"Let go of me," Eva warned. "If you find our methods unacceptable, maybe you should consider what humans do to my people." She easily twisted out of Cyn's grip. "Or maybe you should join him and see what it's like for the werewolves you interrogated."

Cyn clenched her fists to keep herself in check. The need to straight up fight Eva was coming. She could feel it deep in her bones. Like an itch that was burrowing under her skin to the point where digging it out wouldn't be possible.

"Please leave the room, Eva. I'll finish up here."

Eva stood there for a moment, maybe considering other actions, but, instead, she left. Through the open door, Cyn saw Eva glance at Kaden before she stormed out of the cabin with her children, leaving Cyn with the tied-up hunter.

Cyn immediately shut the bedroom door. Time to settle down a volatile situation.

"What's your name?" she asked as she placed the first aid kit next to his seat.

"Vince," he finally said.

"How badly are you hurt, Vince?" She checked over him and just found bruises and deep scratches. The light blue tattoo on his chest was a stark reminder of what he was.

"Are you one of their slaves?" he asked as she cleaned one of his scratches.

"Uh, no!" She drew back from him and made a face as if insulted, but the truth was the truth. In the past, a few of the packs, with more shady backgrounds, had kept humans as slaves. Some of them wanted to join the pack with the potential to run and live a long life, while other ones had particular tastes that even Cyn didn't want to think about.

"Then what are you doing here?"

"It's human decency to check on your welfare. Unlike you, I talk first and shoot later."

"My welfare?" He looked her over the way a hunter

would this time. The way she stood. The way she now assessed him. "There's no way you're a hunter."

"And what if I am?"

"Then we wouldn't be having this conversation." He glanced at the gun Cyn had placed on the bed. "I would be free, and I'd be blowing these bastards to kingdom come."

Cyn kept a straight face until the man smiled and spoke again. "A traitor among the wolves. How interesting."

"You can assume all you want, but I was brought here by force. My brother Zach left me here."

A flicker of recognition flashed in his eyes before a cloud of disdain descended. Interesting.

She kept talking. "When was the last time you ate?"

"I'm not hungry."

"After all that sledding and running in the snow?"

He didn't answer.

"I heard from Kaden that you gave your men orders to take prisoners, yet they were attacking and shooting intermittently." She crossed her arms and noted discomfort when he wouldn't look her in the eye. "What did you want to learn? How to play in the snow from the kids?"

Vince tilted his head in a half-shrug. He knew damn well what point she made. He was silent for a bit, but finally spoke.

"Why would Zach McGinnis from the Red clan be interested in taking over territory far north of Vancouver?" He paused to look her in the eye. "And now I know what happened to his sister. You've been off the radar for a while. Not unusual, but when the McGinnis boys are seen hunting without their sister, folks start talking."

"So the Cerulean hunting clan leader—is that still Garrison—sent you here to check up on things?"

Vince shrugged. "We sent a man first to check things out, but he came up missing so another one of our boys was sent to investigate and track the other one based on his embedded GPS unit."

Damn, so the hunter Bastian had killed had been sent here to investigate Zach's dealings. *Shit. Shit. Shit.* If they would've run away from that hunter, he would've probably lost their trail and all of this mess wouldn't have happened.

"So your second man discovered the camp and the cavalry was sent in based on his findings," Cyn finished.

"And what an interesting find: A pack hiding in a territory under the direction of Zach McGinnis. No bids from freelancers allowed. No reports of werewolf activity. Why was he associating with a pack?" Vince leaned forward, even though that tightened his ropes. "Especially, after the grisly murder of his parents at the hands of werewolves.

"Your parents," he added.

Cyn clenched her fists. She tried to keep herself from showing her anger, but she couldn't help herself. Especially after that shithead mentioned her mom and dad.

"Why do you care? What my clan does is no affair of yours. If my brother's interest is in the countryside instead of the cities, don't you get more opportunities to hunt elsewhere?"

Vince cocked a grin. "I'm just a hunter. Garrison's motivations are his own."

"I call bullshit."

"Call it whatever you want." He made a noise as if he had a bad taste in his mouth. "The McGinnises aren't so high and mighty now that they're working with werewolves, too. Huh?"

"What are you saying?" She closed in on him. He'd said "too." *So who else had worked with werewolves before? The Ceruleans?*

He merely smiled. A mocking grin that told her their productive conversation was done. *Fini.*

"I can leave this room and let them use their methods," she warned.

"I bet you would. You've fallen for their tricks," he hissed. "You're bedding a *few* of them, aren't you?"

Wow. What a waste of effort. She slapped a Band-Aid over his arm. Vince grunted.

"Is that the best you got?" he chided.

"That was me being nice." She opened the small bottle of alcohol and poured the contents over gauze. Then she taped the gauze on the deep scratch on his chest. "I'm good at first-aid."

He hissed between clenched teeth this time. "Damn it."

Someone knocked.

She scowled at the door. *The dude yells out once in pain, and now they care?*

"Do I need to come in there, Cyn?" Kaden asked.

"Whatever." He might as well. She wasn't going to get anything else valuable from Vince other than a string of insults on her nursing skills.

KADEN HAD LISTENED TO THE ENTIRE CONVERSATION with interest. Until the hunter had the nerve to insult his woman. He'd gripped the doorknob hard enough to break it off. The temptation to intervene and protect Cyn filled him with anger, but she was feisty enough on her own so he didn't go into the room.

He wasn't surprised to see Eva leave earlier. As a powerful female, giving up control wasn't in her nature. Eva had to feel as if she could provide for the safety of her children, but as he expected, Cyn ended up getting the answers in the end.

If a werewolf would've done the interrogation, the

conversation wouldn't have gone as well and they wouldn't have garnered as much information.

Kaden entered the room to find Cyn leaning against the far wall and Vince fuming in the seat. The male hunter flashed a dark look Kaden's way and continued to brood.

"I can see you've finished your…first-aid. Come on out. We have matters to discuss."

She followed him out of the room, but she wouldn't look at him. Even when he placed his arm over her shoulder. Almost as if a wall existed between them. What had Vince said again? *Now that the McGinnises had connections with werewolves too, they weren't so high and mighty anymore…*

"Let's walk for a bit before we meet the others," he suggested.

The others had already left so they walked alone from the porch into the snow. Kaden welcomed the moment to be alone with Cyn.

He took her hand and helped her find the best path. They walked for a few minutes before he spoke. "Do you want to talk about what happened before you give the grisly details to everyone?"

She shook her head.

"I wasn't in the room with you, so I couldn't read his body language, but he might be lying."

She was silent for a moment. "I don't think he was lying."

"How do you know?"

She shrugged. "Hunter's intuition—"

She slipped and got caught in a snowdrift, and he easily grabbed her by the hips and lifted her out. The moment was all too brief. He wished he could hold onto her longer. Maybe even pull her close for more. His body stirred to life, and their time apart tugged at him.

Ehh, the others could wait.

He lifted her into his arms and carried her away from the

cabin to the privacy of a cluster of evergreens. The trees absorbed most of the bitter wind, but he'd be more than happy to keep Cyn warm.

"Kaden, what are you—"

He swallowed her protest with his lips. With each dip of his tongue into the warmth of her mouth, the pleasure within him grew. She tasted like strawberries. At first, she resisted him and tried to add space between them. She never gave her love away easily and he relished the chase.

Each and every single time.

She cupped his cheeks with her hands and she moaned.

The outside world around him blurred away. All the distracting sounds and his burdens lifted off his shoulders. She had that kind of power over him. He missed this. He missed her. He'd do anything to take her pain away.

Breathless and smiling, Cyn backed away from him, tugging him toward the others. "That's enough. We need to return to the others."

"Are you sure? We could go to one of the empty cabins for a minute?"

Her coy smile made him want her even more. "Didn't you tell me you always needed at least an hour?"

He chuckled. "I did say that, didn't I?" He tugged her toward the camp.

Her light laugh and coy twinkle in her light gray eyes made him grin. "This isn't the time to get horny and make out."

She had a point.

He stole another long kiss.

A gunshot in the distance forced them apart.

"Was that…?" she said.

"Yes." He grabbed her hand and they ran back toward the camp.

[10]

As fast as she tried to run, Cyn couldn't keep up with Kaden. He made running in the snow seem simple. No energy wasted with each stride. By the time he was close to dragging her, she gasped, "Go! I'm coming!"

He hesitated, and at that point, she knew he was determined for her to stay by his side. They ran again—until she tripped over a fallen log and crashed in a heap in the snow. Cyn landed facedown with a mouth full of snow.

There went their glorious arrival.

She lifted her head and spit out the snow.

"Keep going, damn it," she growled out.

He tugged her up. By the time she stood, she shoved him toward the camp. "I'm fine!"

They ran together again, but he pulled ahead of her. By the time they ran into the small clearing close to camp, Cyn couldn't believe what she saw.

Naomi, Rhys, and Eva, along with two other pack members, circled around a single man dressed in a dark blue coat. He held his ground in a defensive stance with a hunting knife in one hand. Eva's children were standing off to the side next to the two pack members.

One look at the man's dark hair and her run slowed to a stuttered walk. She blinked, but she wasn't mistaken. The hunter's height and lanky build was all too familiar.

It was Zach.

What was her brother doing here?

Naomi took a swing at Zach, but he dodged her hit and kicked her away with ease.

Her brother was actually…holding his own.

Wasn't she supposed to be the one rescuing him?

Eva dived for him, but he twisted out of the way a split-second before she touched him. Cyn had only seen one man move like that before: their dad.

She tried to run faster and keep up with Kaden, but she knew she wouldn't make it in time.

Her brother would die today.

Eva came at him again, with Rhys sneaking in from the rear. The blonde woman reached out for Zach, ready to snatch his arm, but Zach anticipated her trajectory and twisted her around with her back pressed to his front.

He placed a gun to her head next.

Damn, he'd…improved.

The three others growled.

"Stop!" Kaden roared at his pack. He'd reached the clearing first. Exhaustion ripped through Cyn's legs, but she pushed herself to reach his side.

Zach turned off the safety and Eva froze.

Rhys's mouth curled into a snarl.

"Zach…," Cyn whispered.

"Not another McGinnis," Naomi groaned.

"What have you done?" Cyn murmured.

This wasn't the reunion she had planned with her

brother. There was supposed to ass-kicking—his ass getting kicked, in fact—but there would be nothing left of him but bloody scraps.

Zach cocked a grin. "Good to see you too, Cyn."

THE HUNTER'S CLAN

PART 4

[1]

My brother is going to die today, Cyn thought. It seemed inevitable, even after his cocky greeting.

From the way his hand held a gun to Eva's head, she knew he could pull the trigger, but the wink he gave her signaled that he didn't plan to do it. Now that she thought about it, why hadn't Zach shot every one of them before she'd arrived at the camp clearing with Kaden?

Because he had no plans to kill anyone.

"Everyone step back!" Kaden shouted. The edge to his voice was unmistakable, and he even made Cyn shiver.

The only people who had to step back were Rhys and Naomi. The others had kept a healthy distance. Damien, who was partially obscured by pine trees, observed the exchange at the edge of the camp with a hint of a grin.

Eva's three children stood next to one of the other pack members.

Tension filled Cyn's stomach until it soured.

"Do you know this man?" Rhys asked Kaden.

"He's Cynthia's brother," Kaden said as he approached his

brother and placed a hand on Rhys's shoulder. "He is hereby under my protection—"

Rhys growled. "He will be under your protection once he releases my wife. Until he does so…"

Kaden turned to Zach. "Enough of the showmanship. Let her go before you get yourself killed."

Zach nodded and immediately released Eva.

With a snarl, the blonde woman shifted to claw at him, but Kaden barked, "Don't even think about it, Eva!"

Eva's whole body trembled with anger. Her face was bright red against her hair. Her jaw was tight and the claws along her fingertips told Cyn the werewolf would strike the moment the opportunity came. Kaden grabbed Cyn's hand and tugged her behind him.

"You keep protecting these people, Kaden…" Eva bit out. "They have no qualms about fighting."

"Hey, I'm the one who peacefully strolled in here—" Zach began.

"Into our territory. With a gun," Rhys snapped.

"Who in their right mind would waltz into a war zone without a weapon?" Zach bit back. Her brother wasn't stupid. At least today, anyway.

"How are we supposed to know if anyone is on the 'approved list' unless you tell us everything?" Rhys asked his brother. Now that his mate was back at his side, his stance was far calmer than before.

Eva snorted and crossed her arms.

"We need to talk. We will soon enough," Kaden said.

Cyn approached her brother, the smile growing on her face with each step. Kaden wouldn't let her go for a moment. Maybe he was as surprised as she was, but once she assured Kaden with a nod, she ran to her brother and hugged him.

"If I wasn't happy to see you, I'd be choking the living

breath from your body." She rested the side of her face against her brother's chest and squeezed him tight.

The dark-haired man she held laughed. "I should drop you off on a werewolf's doorstep more often. The last time you hugged me was when you found out you were sick."

That was true. Before that time, hugs seemed unnecessary between them. Her job as big sister was to protect Zach and Ty. They needed to be men, and coddling them as hunters wasn't wise.

She stepped back from him. "Now that we've got that settled…" Her fist flew back, and she clocked him hard across the chin. Zach staggered for a moment, shook his head, and then smiled. With a chuckle, he added a healthy distance between them.

Cyn thrust a finger in his direction. "Your *little* plan worked, but if you pull that kind of shit on me ever again, I will cut off your leg and have someone reattach it to your ass."

Zach rubbed his chin. She knew the exact place to hit him. A hit any harder would've knocked him out. "You were dying. I put a lot of thought into my decision."

It was damn near impossible to be mad at someone who meant well. Worry-filled creases formed on his forehead and Zach briefly closed his hazel eyes. Their dad had done that often when he was bothered. Could the man in front of her really be twenty years old?

"Yes, I was dying. So why are you here?" Was he here to take her back to Vancouver now that the pack was in danger? Instead of exuberance at the thought of leaving with Zach, fear bristled within her.

"I had a few men on guard to the far south to keep free-lancers out. One saw smoke, so he sent a message that something was wrong," Zach said as he leaned forward. "A friend of mine owed me a favor and got me here on a private flight."

She cocked a grin. "You hate planes."

"I did what I had to do. What happened?"

With a flourish, she extended her hands toward the ransacked buildings. "As you can see, everything is fine," she added with a voice dripping with sarcasm. "The Cerulean clan found the camp, and the Windham pack is in grave danger. Anything else?"

Zach glanced at Kaden. "It appears I need to have a chat with you."

Kaden sighed. "So it appears."

THE OTHERS TRIED TO FOLLOW KADEN, CYN, AND ZACH to Naomi's cabin, but Kaden refused. This was his business. Not theirs. "There are some personal matters we need to settle. Once we're done, a decision will be made."

"If a decision is made on the pack's welfare, we should be present," Eva said. "Especially with that *hunter* walking around."

"After Zach leaves I'll reveal everything you need to know." The growl he added made it clear to Eva that a discussion wasn't welcomed, so she backed off. Her mouth opened as if to protest further, but she stormed off instead.

Once inside the dim cabin, Cyn took a seat on the couch and Kaden sat down next to her. Zach eased into the nearest chair. He crossed his arms and looked over his sister with a frown. *Here it comes,* Kaden thought.

"My sister doesn't look well," Zach began. "What about our bargain, Windham?"

Guilt tried to suck Kaden into its depth, but anger replaced the feeling instead. How dare her brother ask such a question right now? "Whether or not she becomes a werewolf is her choice. I have done my part and will continue to protect her."

"Does Ty know about this arrangement?" she asked her brother softly.

"No, he doesn't, and you know why it's best that he never finds out." The two McGinnises exchanged a hard look that spoke volumes: Ty would never approve of what Zach did.

Cyn opened her mouth to speak, but Kaden raised his hand so he could make his point. "This whole situation is complicated, but what matters is that your sister is alive, and I want her to stay with me."

"Is that wise right now when your pack is vulnerable?" Zach asked.

Kaden's stomach tightened, and he took Cyn's hand. The warmth from her palm quieted the anxious wolf within him. "I will do everything in my power to protect her. We're not safe here any longer, so we're leaving to find another safe place."

"What about our deal?" Zach sighed. "If you leave this area, it will be a while before I can protect you again."

"The deal is a moot point. This place has been compromised thanks to my brother." He slowly ran his free hand from his forehead down to the stubble on his chin. "No home is ever safe anyway."

Zach nodded. "I know that feeling well."

Cyn's brother continued. "Speaking of your brother, you need to be careful, Kaden. One of my watchmen said Bastian hasn't left the territory yet. He said he saw him leave and head south to Prince George, but he returned on foot with supplies."

"I see." The problems just kept coming. He did tell Bastian he didn't want to see him for a while, but he all but expected Bastian to head to civilization to drown himself in the whiles of beautiful women. Staying put meant his brother had other plans. And, most likely, none of them were good.

Silence settled between them so Kaden spoke first. He filled Zach in on everything that had happened so far in terms of the Cerulean clan member and the interrogation.

Her brother didn't take the news well and agreed that the best plan was for them to leave.

Zach stood. "My presence will be missed, so I can't be here for long. I brought supplies in my snow cab for Cyn. It appears you'll be needing them in the next couple of days." He looked to his sister. "Or wherever you may go in the future."

[2]

Now that matters were settled between Kaden and Zach, Cyn didn't know what to feel. They were walking through the forest toward Zach's snow cab and the conflicted feelings in her stomach were growing stronger. She finally got a chance to see and talk with her brother, yet she wasn't ready to let him go.

He was a part of her past. And his familiarity brought her a comfort that Kaden couldn't.

"You'll contact me once she's safe, won't you?" he asked Kaden.

"Yeah, first thing," Kaden replied.

As they approached the snow cab, she spotted the crate he'd mentioned. It was as if he were leaving her behind again. Her unease must have been all over her face. She followed him to the snow cab steps.

From the top step, he patted her shoulder. "You'll be fine. You're used to living on the road. Just like the good old days with Mom and Dad."

"The good old days," she murmured. Her mind went blank then hundreds of questions came to mind. Was he sleeping well? Did he find out anything about Mom and Dad's murder? Had he seen Ty lately?

"Could you stay for a bit longer?" was what she asked instead.

"You know I can't do that. The Ceruleans are watching me. The Red clan has to be kept in the dark." She waited for him to hug her, but he fake-punched her shoulder instead. "Don't waste this chance I've given you." He opened the snow cab door and then something wet hit the side of Cyn's face.

Zach wobbled above her, a crimson stain growing along his back.

She blinked, wondering if she'd heard the pop. Wondering what direction the shot had come from. Her arms went up to catch Zach, but his weight overwhelmed her, and he hit the back of his head on the way down. Kaden reached over them, shoving her to the ground as another shot broke the rearview mirror.

The need to act kept ringing in her head, but she couldn't move. *Someone shot Zach. Someone shot Zach. Someone shot Zach.*

With the side of her face pressed against the snow, all she could do was scan the forest.

Who would dare do such a thing?

She scrutinized the landscape, checking for any sign of an attacker, but saw no one. The sight was strangely tranquil. Powdery snow sprinkled from the tree branches that swayed from a brisk wind.

The forest was empty and quiet.

[3]

NOTHING MOVED IN THE WOODS BEYOND WHERE THEY stood. Even the birds had become quiet.

Kaden took a deep breath. No scent either. They'd been hit by sniper fire.

"Get him out of here, please," Cyn whispered. Panic lined her words.

First things first, he checked Zach for a pulse and a steady respiratory rate. So far, so good.

Emergency care would have to wait. They were in the middle of the forest in the cold. His pace was brisk and Cyn ran to keep up. The dead weight on his shoulder didn't bother him, but the panicked woman beside him worried him.

"Be careful with him," she whispered. She held Zach's weapon, and she covered their rear as they ran. As they got closer to camp, she grew even more bitter, but he let her words brush off him. "I hope we run into them so I can give them a first-class ticket to hell."

The camp was dead quiet by the time they walked into Naomi's place.

"Is the cabin empty?" Cyn asked.

He nodded. His sister was most likely elsewhere for now and wouldn't interfere with what needed to be done.

They still had time. He could hear Zach breathing, even if Cyn couldn't. As her brother continued to bleed, his breathing slowed.

He turned on the lanterns Naomi had left in the bedroom. The room was cold, but would heat up once he lit the fireplace.

What alarmed Kaden the most was the blood loss. They had left a trail of blood from the spot where Zach had been shot. Even after he did a cursory check, what he did see left him concerned. Two posterior entry wounds. A single posterior wound to the upper left shoulder with no exit point. The secondary shot went straight through, near his left kidney, potentially nicking his renal artery.

"Does he take any meds?" Kaden checked over his shoulder to look at Cyn. The only word he could use to describe how she looked right now was numb. Harsh lines were chiseled into her forehead. Her light gray eyes had darkened to murky smoke. A wall had fallen behind her eyes and all reason seemed to have departed.

What was left was the hunter, and that part of her was ready to lash out at anything and anyone.

Someone had to be in control right now.

"Wake up, Cyn," he said, a bit more forceful. "Is he taking any meds, or is he a diabetic like Ty? Any allergies?"

She shook her head.

"Take off his coat and shirt. Apply pressure to the wound, using a clean towel." When she didn't move, he pushed her shoulder. "Move it, *hunter*."

She quickly moved into action and unzipped Zach's coat. His whole shirt was stained bright red.

"Zach…" she whispered.

Kaden searched the bathroom and kitchen for the supplies he'd need. The emergency first-aid kit wouldn't have everything, but he could make do until he sent Cyn to fetch his physician supplies.

By the time he returned to the room, Cyn was leaning over her brother, applying pressure to his shoulder. Zach was still unconscious, which, to Kaden, wasn't a good sign. Had he hit his head on the way down?

Checking behind Zach's eyelids, he checked to see if both of Zach's pupils were the same size. Good so far. Then he felt along the back of Zach's head and confirmed a swollen spot. Likely a hematoma, and a probable concussion to boot.

"Good job, Cyn." He gently pushed her away. "Go to our cabin and grab a brown box in our closet labeled *medical*."

"Will something happen while I'm gone?" she mumbled.

"Your brother is stable for now, but I need supplies." Her brother wasn't stable, but getting her moving was much more important.

He waited for her to leave before he got to work on the wound with no exit point. Time to prepare the site to retrieve the bullet. His hands worked quickly as muscle memory took over. Over and over again, he'd sewn up the drunks, the brawlers, and average citizens who had been in the wrong place at the wrong time. Just another day in the ER. But now that Zach's life was in his hands, he trembled a bit. Would Cyn never forgive him if her brother died under his care?

Stop worrying and keep working.

Step one: remove the bullet if possible.

Most of the time, removing a bullet caused more damage than the bullet itself. Plenty of his patients walked away carrying bits of metal. Hopefully, Zach wouldn't have such a problem.

Using fresh water from the tap, he irrigated the wound to

remove any debris. At least that part was easy. Using forceps in one hand and the towel in the other, he applied pressure with the towels and opened the site a bit to determine if there was any internal damage along the entry path. Improved werewolf eyesight came in handy at times like this. With the light from the lantern, he was relieved to see no major blood vessels had been severed, but plenty of other minor ones had been obliterated.

The process was painstakingly slow. He could hear Zach's heartbeat the whole time and watched the arteries twitch every time his heart contracted. The bullet wasn't lodged in too deep.

With patience, Kaden finally plucked it out.

Damn, the bullet was tiny. They always were, and it amazed him how something like a small piece of metal could do such devastating damage.

Humans were such fragile things.

Cyn came to mind, but he brushed the thought aside. Focus time.

A box appeared next to him. She'd moved quickly.

He rifled through the box to retrieve what he needed.

Step 2: close the wound.

Using a suture, he closed the wound. By the time he dressed Zach's wound with gauze, Cyn was beside him holding a cup of cold coffee.

"I wanted to offer you the coffee when it was hot, but you seemed so focused," she began.

He took the drink. Cold coffee had been nectar during his residency. "Tastes good," he remarked as he watched Cyn place her hand on Zach's clammy forehead.

"Why is he so cold?" she asked.

"He's in shock. His temp should rise soon. We need to keep him warm." Kaden left her side to wash his hands in the dim bathroom. He briefly looked at the man in the mirror and didn't want to meet his own eyes. How had everything around him that he had built fallen apart so quickly?

His pack had been attacked on the way here. The Cerulean hunting clan had destroyed parts of the camp. And now Cyn's brother lay shot and unconscious in the other room. *Things can only get better*, he told himself.

"This is your pack now, Kaden," his father Tobias had said to him. The responsibility was the heaviest burden he'd secured in his life, but he bore it as if there was no choice in the matter. He had been born into this role.

"Stand up, boy, and quit hiding in the loo as if you can flush your troubles away," his dad would say.

He looked again in the mirror and met his gaze.

By the time he entered the bedroom, Cyn was arranging covers on her brother.

"When will he wake up?" she asked.

"Maybe an hour or two. Zach hit his head on the snow cab when he went down." He touched her shoulder and squeezed.

"What about the bullet? I want it." She still wouldn't look him in the eyes. And it wasn't fear. That scent was all too clear to him. Right how her scent flared with waves of strong black pepper: contained anger waiting to be released.

He retrieved a napkin holding the bullet and placed it in her hand. "I gave him some pain meds through his IV, but it won't last long. He'll wake up spitting fire soon enough."

Her jaw twitched. "I'm going to kill the person who did this."

Kaden didn't know what to say to that. If one of his pack members tried to harm her brother after he'd placed Zach under his protection, he'd have to punish them for their deeds. Giving them to Cyn seemed fitting.

He finally spoke. "Your brother is a stubborn son of a bitch. He'd be grateful for the fight in you."

[4]

No one dared to look at Kaden once he arrived in the cave.

Which meant they all knew what had gone down. He looked at each of their faces before he spoke. He gave particular scrutiny to Eva, Rhys, and Naomi.

Normally defiance danced in Eva's blue eyes, but, this time, she held Phil in her lap and stroked the back of his head.

"You know why I'm here, don't you?" He waited for the change in his pack. The quickening of someone's heartbeat. The stopped breath in a guilty party's chest.

But none of them reacted.

Rhys finally spoke to him. "One of the sentries saw you rushing back to camp. He said one of the hunters was bleeding."

"Zach was shot in the chest."

"Is he dead?" Eva asked. The matter-of-fact way she said it made Kaden walk past his brother to approach his sister-in-law.

"No, he isn't. Do you know what happened, Eva?" he asked.

She didn't immediately speak or react. Almost as if she were an empty husk. The only person who reacted to his inquiry was Phil. He clung to his mother as if she might bolt.

"Are you accusing my mate of something?" Rhys said evenly from behind him. "She's been with me the whole time. As soon as you left camp with your *hunter* friends, we returned to the cave."

Kaden sensed Rhys's growing anger, but he didn't turn to face him. Even Rhys knew a fight between them wouldn't go the way Rhys wanted.

"Someone shot Zach," Kaden said simply.

"I didn't do it," Eva said between clenched teeth. "Maybe one of those Cerulean bastards got away and is hiding in the woods." She snorted. "That hunter got what he deserved for threatening me."

"He got what he deserved?" Kaden glanced over her. "I don't see a scratch on you or anyone else, Eva."

She laughed. "I feel like I don't know you anymore, Kaden. The man I trusted a year ago is in bed with the hunters, and now he's accusing his own pack of shooting the very people who hunt and kill our people."

Kaden wanted to clench his fists, but he held himself in check. Things had changed, but he was still the alpha, and the protection of this pack always came first.

"*Trust,* what an interesting word," he said to Eva. "We've been running for years and hiding from the humans. I've been bitter like you, and I've wanted to kill every single one of them for what they've done to us." He looked at everyone else who listened to him. "But a single moment can change your perspective on right versus wrong, on what is more important: either accept your enemy and strive for peace or kill each other. My father Tobias didn't want us living like that. Those of you who remember him should know this." He paused. "When I met Zach McGinnis, Cyn's brother, I was prepared to kill him once I knew what he was. He came to my emergency room with a knife wound. Instead of killing him, we talked for a long time about his dying sister. I saw a side of the hunters I'd never seen before: profound grief. A drive in a man to do anything to save what was his own. Just like I feel about all of you."

"So you made a deal with that hunter," Naomi said with crossed arms.

"Yes, and I don't regret my actions. Zach did keep up his side of the bargain. His job was to keep freelancers away. Any attack from the Cerulean clan was *our* undoing. *Our* mistake."

He refused to place blame on his brother Bastian. Even if Bastian had rendered the killing blow on the Cerulean hunter. He wondered if Bastian had a role in the attack on Zach as well. No matter, they were a pack. They had to move on.

He continued. "I've learned a lot from the hunters. They are capable of generosity and selflessness. Many of them are inhuman, but not all of them. The day we become animals and strike out in fear is the day we become as bad as the ones who attack us without an afterthought."

Some pack members nodded while others remained quiet with doubts. He didn't need to read their body language to know what they felt. He had been in their place before he'd met Zach and Sinister. It really was amazing what one encounter could do to change perspective.

As the alpha, it was up to him to show his pack the possibilities and let them decide for themselves.

~

Two days passed. For Cyn, they came and went in a blur.

The pack was preparing to leave, and Zach was still in bed. Once her brother had become stabilized, Kaden moved her brother from Naomi's cabin to theirs. Their prisoner was relocated with a portable propane heater to what was left of Rhys and Eva's cabin. The building was in pretty bad shape. No one was using it.

There wasn't much for her to do except make sure her brother's wound was properly cleaned. When she got bored, she finally began to pack her meager belongings.

Stowing away her clothes in her hospital bag was soothing. Folding and arranging her belongings helped. All the while, she spoke.

"Zach, you won't believe the gun room they have here in camp," she said to him. Her brother had awakened briefly a few hours ago for broth and painkillers. He was asleep more often than awake.

"They have Bouncing Betties, Z." She tried to smile. "How come none of those suckers went off during the attack? I wonder if Sinister is slipping. He told me he sprinkled those things all over the place like they were tinsel on a Christmas tree."

Speaking of Christmas trees, there was no way she could take the McGinnis tree and all the ornaments with her. There were only so many snow cabs, and it was far more important to transport life-saving supplies like food and ammunition.

Her heart tugged. So many memories would have to be left behind.

"Why did you have to bring the whole tree?" she asked him.

Because you needed a real sign that your brother had brought you here, her heart replied.

She touched Zach's forehead for maybe the fiftieth time. He was cool to the touch as usual.

Once she was satisfied, she tried to select a few shirts for Zach from Kaden's clothes. The two had the same height, but Kaden had a more muscular build. Zach would definitely need a belt if he wore Kaden's pants. Cyn shuddered at the thought of any poor souls seeing Zach's pants fall to expose his knobby knees.

She picked up his coat to get an idea on size and noticed something hard in an inside pocket: Zach's cellphone.

Now this was familiar. Her brother tended to enjoy old school rap, but when it came to the latest and greatest in smartphone technology, Zach was the first one to buy it. Yep, even werewolf hunters lined up outside the electronic stores in the dead of winter to get shiny new devices.

"I can't believe you tried to get me to switch to Android," she remarked as she brushed his hair out of his face. "You'll have to pry my iPhone from my cold dead fingers, thank you very much."

She sat on the edge of the bed and turned on the phone. She wasn't surprised when the device, with its red military grade case with crossbones on the back, flicked to life and booted within seconds. Getting past the password screen was easy enough—he'd always used Mom and Dad's names as one word.

He had hundreds of pictures in the photo app. She browsed through them, laughing when she caught familiar faces: Clive the hairless armorer, Old Bartholomew the clan sage, and Quincy. Not much to say about Quincy other than the fact that he was the clan groupie. Couldn't shoot or hunt to save his life, but if you needed your boots shined, Quincy was there with an eager grin.

So many of these people represented family. Drinking buddies for the hard times after a long fight. In each picture,

Zach showed her how much he'd done well after she had moved here.

There had been so many things she'd missed. The Red hunting clan's winter barbecue in Old Bart's backyard. She laughed. Now that was a blast. A gang of hunters hanging out in an average, quiet neighborhood backyard, shooting the breeze. In the dead of winter. With beer, burgers, and brats sizzling on a grill. The drinking contest was legendary. Five kegs downed in less than five hours. She never won, by the way.

The next picture made her suck in her breath. Zach had taken a picture of a faded photo in a frame. One of the few pictures that had survived during their countless moves: It was the last picture they had of a thirteen-year-old Ty smiling.

[5]

FIVE YEARS AGO

SOONER OR LATER, CYN KNEW THIS DAY WOULD COME, but today seemed like the *wrong* day.

"You don't have to go in there." The hand placed on Cyn's shoulder was a large one, a steady one that could have held her up in case the weight of the world grew too heavy. "We can tell them your parents aren't coming back."

She couldn't breathe. She'd never felt so dizzy in her life. Maybe if she let go and collapsed in the corner, she'd find relief. And yet, after looking into Old Bart's rheumy light blue eyes, she straightened her back. Old Bart never comforted. He was a tall, thickset man who strengthened the weak and made them into soldiers prepared to face anything.

I'm hurting, but I have to be strong. She repeated those words to herself over and over again as she entered the North Vancouver home right off the water. If she closed her eyes, she could hear the Indian River beyond the deck that wrapped around the house.

Entering the house's living room and walking up to her

brothers passed in a blur. Most fifteen-year-old boys like Zach cried at the loss of their parents, but Zach simply nodded, hugged her, and left the house without further words. He coped in his own way.

Ty just stood there and didn't move. Finally, his lower lip trembled, and the need to take his pain away clawed at her very being.

"I'm so sorry, Ty," she choked out.

"Were their bodies found?" he finally asked. At thirteen, Ty's voice still had a high-pitched squeak that seemed child-like. Tears formed in his hazel eyes like shiny pools of amber.

Her mouth moved and she struggled to speak through her grief. "We don't know yet."

"Then they aren't dead," Ty ground out. "Dad is coming back. He always comes back. Mom will be back." He advanced on Cyn as if to strike her.

Old Bart tapped her brother's shoulder. "Channel that anger in the right place, boy. The day of your vengeance is coming."

Cyn reached out to comfort him, but the look of hatred on his face made her shrink back. *He's angry. Let him vent,* she reminded herself. But she was hurting, too. Her insides had been scraped out and all she had left was a hollow feeling that made it hard for her to stand. To breathe. To continue living.

"The day will come when we'll set fire to every place those vermin lay to rest," Old Bart whispered to him.

Ty's hands formed fists, and his body trembled.

As Cyn left the house to go check on Zach, she heard Bart say one more thing, "And the ones who scatter into the darkness will fear you and your wrath as you break down every door to seek them out."

~

NOW

When the tears stopped flowing, Cyn dared to keep going.

She went farther back into the past. The hospital pictures were next. She didn't want to see those. But instead of flicking her finger faster, she slowed down. There were pictures of her in bed. In one in particular, she presented her middle finger to Zach for sneaking a picture.

"Ugh. I look like shit, Z." She presented the phone to his sleeping form. "You're dead meat for taking this one." Her finger hovered over the delete button, but she sighed and kept going. He'd saved it for a reason. It wasn't her place to get rid of it.

Even farther back, she saw when she was well. In some photos, she saw a girl. Now this was new. None of the recent pictures included the pretty brunette.

"Nice taste," she said. "Classy and educated."

It was as if something had happened between her brother and this new girl after Cyn had fallen ill. Her grip on the phone tightened. Her brother had better not have broken up with this girl over her. Her heart would break to think of such a thing. Zach had already sacrificed so much for her.

As tempted as she was to look through his text messages and play the role of a nosy big sister, she left the text messages app.

She almost put the phone away, but a thought came to mind. With a single phone call, the Red clan could be called to take Zach away to a hospital. Maybe the pack could leave him by the side of the road and the clan could take him away. The thought came and left just as quickly. She shuddered. Keeping Zach safe was important, but there was no way the clan would simply take him away without following through.

There'd be an investigation, and, sooner or later, someone would find out about Zach's deal with the Windham pack.

She placed the phone in her pocket and told herself this was for the best. Zach's life, like her own, was in Kaden's hands.

She had to trust him.

[6]

Every time Kaden circled the perimeter of the camp, fear bounced around his head. He searched for any signs that their time to leave had run out.

They'd be leaving by dawn. The very idea tried to shake him and he always focused on something else. As he approached Sinister's cabin, he expected an unoccupied structure, but something was amiss.

The door was open a crack.

He slowly approached the door, taking care to walk along the quiet floorboards. The door opened with a yawn. He searched the room. Captain Crunch was gone.

A few days ago, when he'd swept through the camp, searching for others, the tabby cat had hid under the table in fear of the beast that looked through the window into his domain.

And yet, when Kaden lingered near the door, he didn't smell any traces of the cat along the doorway or the porch. So where had the cat gone?

A faint sound from the back room reached his ears.

Kaden stormed into one of the two backrooms. The bedroom was pitch black. This place was where Uncle Damien slept.

In the far corner, someone pointed a gun at him.

"Do you always point a gun at friends who are looking for you?" Kaden drawled.

Sinister sighed.

A few feet into the darkened room, and now Kaden smelled blood. Rich and coppery. Kaden lit a lantern and Sinister looked away. He rested his bald head against the back of the wall. One hand clutched his arm.

Stealth was Sinister's good friend.

"You're hurt." Kaden reached for the light switch, but the hunter spoke.

"Not. Yet."

This wasn't unusual, so Kaden waited where he stood. He'd played this game with Sinister before. Except two years ago, he'd been the prey and Sinister the hunter.

"Fair enough." Kaden crossed his arms. "Where's Captain Crunch?" Light conversation usually put the hunter at ease.

"After shit went down, I got him outta here."

Kaden didn't ask where. Sylvester had his secrets. As long as they didn't endanger the pack, he let his friend keep them.

"How long have you been here?" He took a step toward Sinister. The man's pain flared up and bounced against Kaden. Sinister tried to keep his breath even, but Kaden could hear the change.

"About two hours."

He was getting closer. Sinister's gun was still pointed at him. Not aimed in his direction, but the gun had been placed on Sinister's leg and could easily be used.

Something must've happened to him to set him off like this. The hunter's heart hammered in his chest like a woodpecker.

The attack on the camp.

By the time Kaden knelt before Sinister, the man's finger continued to rest near the trigger. In a flash, he could raise the weapon and fire on Kaden.

Their eyes met, and Kaden didn't hesitate to push Sinister's hand with the gun to the side.

Kaden didn't speak. Instead, he whistled a tune that made Sinister grunt.

"I hate that damn song."

Right on cue. Five bars into *Lucy in the Sky with Diamonds* always made Sinister's ears bleed. Kaden smiled as he pulled Sinister's coat open. There was a knife wound in his shoulder, but that wasn't the main problem. "They always seem to catch you there. You shouldn't be using this spot like a shield."

"No shit."

"I thought I took care of this shoulder a while ago."

"I guess you did a shitty job, Doc."

Kaden chuckled. "My handiwork is the best. Most folks who have ripped shoulder cuff tendons and broken legs are out of commission for a while. You managed to walk out of the hospital overnight." He shrugged. "You couldn't chase after me and kill me if your good gun arm wasn't working."

"I can shoot well with both hands."

Kaden rested his hand on Sinister's shoulder as the healing energy flowed into his friend. "Bullshit. You trailed me for what? Two years? And you only managed to shoot me twice. Once in the ear. Some marksman."

Sinister winced when Kaden repaired a nerve. "I don't attack my targets in public. You hid well."

"I was a resident at a city hospital. I had to be in a public place. What about an alley?"

He caught a smile on Sinister's face this time. "I've seen nuns and priests go to shadier places than you did."

Sinister relaxed against his hand and some of the tension

along his muscles faded a bit. Using his hand, Kaden checked Sinister's older injuries. Many of them he had inflicted. On one night in particular, though, Sly's hunting had gotten him into big trouble.

"I'm glad you were there that day," Sinister blurted.

"Me too. I turned down a hot chick at a bar to go home early for my next rotation. If I had gone home with her, you would've been a dead man."

Kaden remembered that night well. The bars that night had been packed, but after a long shift, longer than even werewolves could stand, he was ready to retire. On the way home, he spied a form lying in one of the alleys. It was then that he realized that his usual trailer, Sinister, hadn't followed him that night.

Another pack had been here. At least three werewolves had walked away no more than ten minutes ago. The ground was wet and the smell of garbage almost masked the smell of human suffering.

He found Sinister slumped against a wall that was covered in graffiti. His face was a mess and he gasped with each breath. At that very moment, Kaden could've walked away. Here was the very man who had tried to kill him multiple times. Now, the hunter had become the hunted and what was left of him was dying next to garbage.

Instead of letting him lie there, Kaden placed his hand on Sinister's body. Just like today.

"If you keep singing that song, I'm gonna choke the shit outta you," Sinister complained.

"I caught you humming John Lennon's *Imagine* to Captain Crunch a few weeks ago."

"Now that was a man I respected."

"Same old Sylvester." Kaden didn't have enough in him to heal his friend completely, but he'd taken the razor edge off the pain. "You'll have to immobilize that arm until your tendons are healed."

He stood and fetched the blanket off the bed. "We're preparing to leave soon. Stay here for now. I don't want the others to know you're here yet."

"Too late for that," Naomi said from behind him.

[7]

As much as Kaden wanted to stay behind to see his sister have a few words with Sinister, he left the room as soon as his sister's black gaze told him to get the hell out.

"Where you going?" Sinister asked. His face plainly said he didn't want to be left alone with Naomi. Not in his current state.

"The pack is leaving in a few hours." He glanced at his sister. He wasn't concerned for Naomi's safety. Now Sinister's safety was another matter.

As he left the cabin, he caught a snide remark from Naomi. "If your arm wasn't hurt, I'd be stabbing you in the same spot I did last time..."

There was so much to be done and not much time to do it. All the munitions needed to be packed. Those would be packed last after food and other such belongings went into the cabs.

And then there was the prisoner. Damien had offered to take Vince out into the woods for a *long* walk, but Kaden declined.

Once they were on the road, he'd handle the problem himself. At one of their stops, he planned to leave Vince tied up in the back of a random truck heading south. The man would live to see another day—unlike a few of his hunting clan members.

He sighed and watched Rhys help Eva pack up one of the snow cabs. So much money would be lost. Countless hours freelancing as a physician to the most shady characters imaginable. Hours of backbreaking labor with Sinister to construct these cabins. The man's engineering skills were put to waste, chasing werewolves across the countryside.

Time to accept what fate would bring and hope the Windham pack came through on the other side.

Traveling was nothing new for Cynthia. Time and time again, the McGinnis family had packed up their meager belongings to new safe houses or to places where their next assignment would take them.

Yet, no matter what the circumstances, leaving your home behind, as well as any of the new friendships or familiarities, was a bit hard.

The pack was now in its new safe haven, and everything should've improved. The pack had traveled to a lake about twenty miles west of Prince George. Even though they were safe, the cabins were spaced pretty far apart and the pack seemed fractured.

Kaden was still perched over Zach, who rested on the pull-out bed. Kaden's eyes, with stark dark circles under them, were closed in concentration.

After they'd arrived a week ago, Cyn always watched the healing process, but today she couldn't bear to look. Even the beautiful view of the lake didn't help.

"Will you stop staring out that window and come eat?" Kaden asked from across the room. So he'd finished his task and she'd spaced out again.

How long had she been sitting there? The loose thread she'd been pulling out of her shirt was now pooled in her lap. Like a damn fool, she kept twirling her fingers until she had a gap big enough to stick her fist inside. *Lovely!*

Kaden had made two roast beef sandwiches, and some broth was warming on the stove for Zach.

She made her way to the table as Kaden shoved a big bite into his mouth. She'd never seen that many pieces of roast beef between bread at one time. Her stomach quaked, but the discomfort wasn't from the food. It was from seeing the man she'd grown to love working his ass off to heal two people.

Make that three. Even when he thought she hadn't noticed, he kept paying visits to Sinister. And any hunter with know-how knew an injured man.

As stubborn as her fellow hunter could be, he still grimaced every now and then.

Kaden washed the sandwich down with water and then made himself a protein shake. His third one today.

She sighed. No matter how much he ate, he always seemed hungry.

That bothered her even more.

Once he finished shoveling the food into his mouth, he cocked a grin her way. "I know this arrangement isn't ideal, but..." he said this to her every day, "it's okay. I'll be gone most of the day to check on the other pack members."

With the space between the cabins, Kaden had to keep up with everyone through periodic visits. It was just as well. She refused to leave her brother's side, even though she longed to get some proper rest or take a walk to end her cabin fever.

He kissed the top of her head. “Get some sleep.”

“Of course.” She said that each and every time, but he probably knew why she didn’t rest.

There was no way in hell she was letting her brother get hurt again.

[8]

NOT MORE THAN AN HOUR INTO WATCHING OVER ZACH, Cyn's head drooped in exhaustion. She forced herself to get up and check the windows. The muscles in her thighs protested. Every day, the soreness came back, as well as an ache in her gut that told her the time Kaden had spent healing her wasn't enough. What little she got, was like siphoning with a straw.

Which meant he was growing weaker.

She was killing him.

Tears welled at the corner of her eyes, but she tried not to cry, even as the guilt in her gut forced her to slump forward and suck in a breath. The weight of the lives of others was a burden she'd carried before, but now that someone held her life as a burden, she couldn't take it anymore.

All this time, she'd thought nothing of a healing here or there. But as she looked at Zach, she truly knew, as of late, Kaden and Zach had given her everything, but what had she given in return?

Her love seemed too simple.

She closed her eyes. The right thing was never easy to do.

A knock on the door forced her to stand. She wiped off her face and realized her hand was wet. Good God, she had been crying. Her nose was a gooey mess.

At a second knock, she used a tissue to blow her nose, and she hurried to the door.

After she looked through the peephole, she gasped.

Damien glanced up and grinned. He knew very well she was standing there and his bright smile made her jump back.

"Good morning, Cynthia!" he said.

He'd said hi and the door was still shut.

Cyn immediately unlocked the door and let Damien inside. The bitterly cold wind from outside slapped her in the face, so she quickly shut the door once he entered. Damien strolled into the living room, as usual, wearing nothing more than a dark blue sweater and pants. He was all smiles, but the skin on his face was beet red and his crimson eyes bloodshot.

"Are you all right?" She peered at him.

"Just a bit of a burn. It will fade soon enough."

She nodded and turned her head to sniff and wipe her eyes. Now wasn't the time to show her weak side to this man.

"Kaden isn't here," she blurted.

"I know. He left the cabin I was staying in not too long ago."

"I see…" Her words died a bit in her mouth.

Damien stood there as if the harsh weather outside was nothing and everybody just took a jaunt in the snow every once in a while.

"I've been checking on a few friends to see how they are doing," Damien began.

Friends? Did that mean he thought of me that way?

She blinked. *Do something, Cyn.* "Can I offer you some coffee or tea?"

"That sounds lovely."

She scrambled to pick up the clothes scattered across the

only seat available. Zach was knocked out on the pull-out sofa. He lightly snored as Damien took a seat at the tiny kitchenette table.

Cyn blew her nose again, washed her hands, and went about preparing tea. She fumbled through the cabinets for moment, completely forgetting where she last put the teapot.

Every now and then, she glanced over her shoulder to see Damien no more than five feet from her brother's head.

"How is your brother doing?" Damien asked.

"Recovering well." She took a deep breath and let it out once she had the pot in her hands. The need to keep checking Zach bothered her. *Sooner or later, you have to trust, Cyn,* she told herself.

"His heart sounds nice and strong," Damien said.

Zach shifted in his sleep and burped.

Cyn sighed. "Among other things."

Soon enough, the teapot whistled and Cyn poured Damien a hot cup of tea. She added strawberry jam to a few English muffins and placed them on a plate. *There, hostess duties done.* She took a seat across from him with her own cup.

"Please enjoy," she began.

"Thank you." He took a sip. "You don't look well, Cyn."

She stopped mid-sip. Damien never minced words. She should've been prepared for this question.

"I have cancer, Damien."

"That's not what I mean." He sat with a straight back and his gaze leveled into her. Of all the people in the camp, she kind of wished it were someone else who asked her this question. Maybe for someone else, coming up with the answer would be easier.

"It's all been an adjustment, but I'm coping."

"Coping isn't living." He snagged one of the English muffins and took a hearty bite. Just seeing the red jam along his fingers pricked memories she didn't want to see. In particular, the blood that had dripped off his hands after he killed several hunters in the dead of the night.

"In a week or two, Zach will be well enough to leave, and everything will be back to normal once we find a more permanent home." Even after she said it, she didn't believe the false confidence in her voice.

She expected Damien to call her on it, but all he did was nod.

By the time they finished their tea, fatigue touched Cyn's eyelids again. By midday, it was always harder for her to stay awake.

"Cynthia," Damien said simply, "go to bed. You're practically ready to sleep at this table, girl."

She forced a smile on her face. "I'm fine. Zach might wake up and need me."

Damien rolled his eyes. "If you're worried about him, I can sit with him a few hours and read a book while you rest."

For a moment, she considered the idea, but one look at his stark white hair and strange red eyes made her blurt out, "No thanks, I can't inconvenience you like that. But I do appreciate the offer."

She'd told a boldface lie. On the inside, she cringed. Kaden had warned her that lying was easier to read on weaker humans, and, right now, she was about as strong as a dam held up with duct tape. If Damien had been disappointed though, his face never showed it.

After he finished another English muffin, he stood, and she did the same. "Then I'll leave you two to your day. Get some rest, and thank you for the tea."

The door closed behind him and shame made her head ache.

Smooth move, McGinnis. You just sent a kind man, with a skin condition, back out into the broad daylight because you can't suck it up and let someone from Team Werewolf help your family. Someone who wants to help you and doesn't care that you're a human. Why can't you accept Kaden's pack?

Our pack, Kaden had said.

Even seasoned hunters could learn a thing or two.

She took a deep breath, opened the door and ran after Damien. More like quickly walked, but the gesture was the same. By the time she caught up with him, tinges of red had touched his cheek.

"Come back inside," she squeaked. She sounded kind of crazy, but she didn't care.

Damien frowned. "Cyn, it's freezing out here, and you don't have a coat on."

She didn't have shoes on either. In horribly cold snow.

Damien picked her up and ran back into the house. Once they were inside, he took one of the many throw blankets over Zach and wrapped it around Cyn's shoulders.

"I'm so sorry," she blurted.

Good Lord, she was going to cry again in front of this man and she really didn't want to do it. "I'm really tired."

He rubbed her shoulders and no matter how much she tried to fight it, her lip trembled.

"It's all right, Cynthia." Damien pulled her into a hug and she sagged against him. Just the comfort of feeling someone run their hand down the back of her head released the anguish she'd been holding inside. No one had held her like this since her father had died.

So she gave in and cried.

And it felt damn good because she missed her dad.

"I wanted to protect my brother, and I shut you out, but that was wrong." Her voice broke.

Damien shushed. "Don't feel shame, Cynthia. I would've done the same for my Luba."

She sighed. "Why is trusting someone so hard?"

"It's human nature. Whether you're a wolf or a human, trust is earned. The moment I asked you if you needed help, you questioned whether I'd earned your trust or not."

She nodded. He spoke the truth.

Now that she had time to think, she saw every moment she'd been with Damien. Even with his dark nature, he was a protector. Just like she was. He had tried to protect his wife. Also, he protected the pack when they were in danger.

She took a deep breath. "Uncle Damien, will you please stay with my brother while I get some sleep?"

He smiled at her words. This was the first time she'd called him Uncle. "You're using your heart to see instead of your eyes. You'll do well in this pack, Cynthia."

[9]

"JUST TAKE THE DAMN PILLS, SINISTER," NAOMI snapped. "You don't get extra *man* points for enduring pain."

All she got in response was a grunt.

Some men made the worst patients ever. Naomi fisted the two pills and the glass of water. It took everything she had not to smash the glass against the side of his head.

She growled for good measure. Her patient sat on the couch and didn't so much as twitch. As frustrating as a man like Sinister could be, it was hard for her to be stern like this. Just seeing him seated in front of her was torture. Due to his shoulder wound, he didn't wear a shirt. Just pants. As much as she tried to be nice about the situation, she caught herself staring at the hard muscles on his arms to the smooth brown skin on his face. When he wasn't an asshole, he was rather handsome.

"I'm fine, Naomi."

But he wasn't fine. His scent radiated pain and practically filled her nostrils with his agony. The other signs were there. He had a line of sweat along his brow, and he hadn't so much as moved his arm when he woke up from sleeping on the couch.

The moment they arrived a week ago, she tried to make him sleep in the bed, but he refused. As big as Sinister was, making him do anything was futile, even for someone as strong-willed as she was.

So she decided to be relentless. She cooked his meals, fed Captain Crunch bacon—much to Sinister's displeasure—and took care of the litter box.

"Pups pull this shit," she said evenly.

He didn't take the bait and stayed straight-faced the whole time.

"Please take the pills?" There, she tried to be nice. Even though she wanted to cram them down his throat. She closed her eyes and sighed.

"I don't like the way they make me feel."

So he finally spoke, eh? "It's oxycodone. Kaden said it would help you."

She thrust the pills at him, but he caught her wrist. His touch made her suck in a breath and the wolf within her yearned for him to touch her more.

"They make me sleepy," he grumbled. "That's unacceptable."

"Then take a nap."

"If I sleep, I can't protect you."

Her stomach jumped for a moment, but she pushed thoughts of his chivalry aside. "You can't lift your arm up."

He stood, and yet hadn't let her go. "My other arm works just fine."

They'd stood like this before. So many times in the past. Two ships gathering at the same harbor, yet they never came to shore. Each time, her eyes devoured his lips and then she fixated on his eyes. They were always so intense, and she fell into them immediately.

She always was the first one to break the trance. This time, when he took a step toward her, she twisted out of his grip.

"Just do what you want." She dumped the water in the sink and put the pills back into the bottle. If he wanted to be stubborn, he could sit on that couch, sweat his ass off, and then take his hour-long showers.

Something curled against her leg. Every time she got mad at Sinister, the yellow tabby came purring. "Don't try to make up for him this time."

She stroked the cat's back. The cat's one eye almost winked at her.

"I'm getting more out of feeling you up than him," she whispered to Captain Crunch.

She turned to see that Sinister had left the couch to go to the bathroom.

He hadn't showered today so she left him to do what needed to be done.

But ignoring him was hard when she heard a few things tumble to the floor. What the hell was he doing in there?

She noticed the door was open a crack. Without a sound, she approached and peered through the crack.

Sinister had made an epic mess.

Watching a hulking hunter, almost as tall as the mirror in the room, fumbling with toothpaste was comical. By the time he rinsed out his mouth, he was panting and paused every once in a while.

She reached for the doorknob and paused.

Stubborn fool.

He reached for the elastic bandage on his shoulder and winced. Every other day, he changed it when Kaden didn't come by to check on him or heal him.

Fury filled her each time he left the bathroom with a fresh bandage on. In the past, the result was always the same: By the time he got the bandage off, his face would be ashen.

"Let me do it." She tried to snatch the bandage from him, but he swung out of the way.

"I can do it."

"And you're about to pass out before you can get it off."

"It's not that bad." His lips formed a tight line as if he meant to not speak on the matter anymore.

"Clamming up when you're in pain is dumb. Even I know that."

"You're hurting?" His anger faded a bit.

"No." She sighed. "Not all pain is physical." Longing caused pain.

He grunted.

"Just let me help. I won't say anything."

They stood there for at least a minute before Sinister let go of the bandage. She slowly rolled the material off his shoulder, enjoying the feel of his smooth skin. More bruised skin was exposed as she removed the bandage until something light blue appeared on the upper right side of his chest. She paused for a moment, but kept going and removed the old piece of gauze on his knife wound.

So he had a tattoo. Most men had a tattoo, but Sinister's paw print was light blue.

"Wound looks clean," she murmured, keeping her voice even. She was careful to touch, but not press against the discolored places. "There's still lots of bruising though."

The whole time, Sinister's gaze was fixed on her face. He was waiting for her to react to his clan tattoo. For her to strike out or to say something.

"Let's get a fresh bandage on you," she added.

"So you're gonna ignore it?" he finally asked.

She shrugged. "Does it matter?"

"I'm one of *them*."

"Kaden already told me you were a hunter and that I should keep that information to myself."

He twisted to help her get the gauze into position. "But did he tell you I was a Cerulean?"

"No, he didn't."

Now that made him pause for a second. "I've done horrible things to werewolves for money," he blurted.

She slowed and looked up at him. "Is that supposed to scare me away?"

"If you were smart, it would. For two years, I chased after Kaden and almost killed him once."

"Almost," she quipped.

The side of his lip turned downward. He didn't like it when she didn't take him seriously, but he was trying to push her away. Not gonna happen. "The Baker pack had wanted a piece of me for a long time, and they caught me with my focus elsewhere in Vancouver."

She cringed.

He told her about how Kaden found him, patched him up, and took him to the closest hospital. "He even paid my hospital bill, knowing damn well who I was."

She was almost done, but slowed down more. He was talking, and if she finished, he might not be as talkative. "Why do you think he did that?"

"He's not like the Bakers. I guess your old man taught him a thing or two."

"No, he isn't. He has honor and wouldn't cast someone aside when something better came along." She swallowed.

He winced as she wound the elastic wrap firmly around his chest. "What happened to you?"

She was being a bit too rough. "I lost four years chasing after a man as fickle as a pig rutting after any female." She smiled. "I wanted to be queen of the world. Not just second best, but first in all things. I thought I'd be that way the day I met Cameron in Seattle."

She sighed, waited for Sinister to interrupt her, but he didn't. Even when her free hand touched one of his bruises. "He was suave and spoke all the right words. In a few hours, he convinced me to chase after him. And like a fool, I did. I thought he was some hotshot alpha, but I learned the hard way that his paws were absolutely filthy. Robbery. Racketeering. Blackmail. The humans were nothing but a playground for him.

"One day, I even caught him talking to the Cerulean hunting clan leader. Can you believe that? But that wasn't the worst thing. It was the fact that *she* was there." Her voice skipped a bit.

"Who?"

"Hayley. The bitch who left Kaden. That woman had told Kaden she was coming to LA to look for me. Bullshit. The minute she showed up, Cameron didn't see me anymore. He even told the Cerulean clan leader that Hayley was to be his mate, and I was just some fool chasing after him."

Nothing but a fool who couldn't do anything right, she thought.

She had to be hurting him, yanking the elastic bandage far harder than she should, but he didn't move. He didn't even wince.

"Does Kaden know about this?" Sinister asked.

She chuffed. "The walk of shame coming back to Kaden was hard enough. He was hurting because Hayley had left him. I'm sure he'd really like to hear that his sister got dumped by the man who took his woman away."

A tear coursed down her cheek, but she left it there. For once, she didn't care about saving face.

A hand reach out and cupped the side of her face.

Sinister used his thumb to wipe away the streak on her cheek. The warmth from his palm set her heart aflutter.

He pulled her closer to him, forcing her to let go of the bandage. Her hands ended up pressed against his chest and her face mere inches from his.

"Your arm." She tried to push back and ended up pushing against his injury. "Oh, shit! I didn't mean to do that."

He only grunted but didn't let her go.

This was the closest she'd ever managed to get with him, and now that she was up close and personal, she reveled in his scent. The feel of his heartbeat against her palms.

"You're not a fool," he whispered. "You're just stubborn and powerful. I like that about you."

"I like that about you, too." Why couldn't she keep her eyes off his lips? Why was she so fascinated with him? He wasn't an alpha like Cameron. He didn't have wealth or power.

He was a fragile human.

But when he leaned in and his lips brushed against hers, the truth began to blossom in her stomach like a cluster of butterflies heading into flight. Sparks danced across her lips and shot down her spine.

The kiss was slow. Gentle. And the need to control the pace melted away. It was just his lips against her lips. A soft brush of his tongue along the seal of her mouth. The tension in her shoulders eased, and she settled within the safety of his arms.

The truth was, she didn't need all the things she'd sought. What she needed was such a simple thing that she'd been too blinded by ambition to find it: true love.

~

The trip along the lakeside fed Cyn's spirit in ways she hadn't expected. It took half a mile before she cut the strings in her head that tied her to the cabin.

Damien would protect her brother. He'd been quiet the whole time she'd slept, and he even had a smile waiting for her when she got up to take a walk.

"Don't forget your gloves and a scarf," he advised.

At the time, she held in a laugh. A werewolf was telling a hunter to bundle up.

So now, she was outside in the brisk Canadian cold taking a long walk. As she got farther away from the cabin, she approached another one along the lake's edge. An aroma, one of Italian spices and fresh bread, reached her nose.

She chuckled to herself. She really needed to improve her cooking skills. As much as she liked the average fare of stews and broths Kaden concocted for Zach's recovery, she'd give up a Bouncing Bettie for a fire-grilled burger overflowing with fixings.

Reluctantly—well, not exactly—she knocked on the door.

As expected, Naomi answered.

"What do you want?" The question wasn't laden with sarcasm. Her pursed lips reflected surprise.

"I needed a break from guard duty for my brother…and I thought I'd check on Sinister," Cyn began. *And I'd like more free smells, please.*

Cyn peered behind Naomi to see Sinister stirring food with his good hand. He wasn't wearing a shirt, and Cyn cringed inwardly at his injuries. He still didn't look good.

"Just let her in," Sinister grumbled. "You're letting out the heat."

She crept into the house and ignored the look of annoyance on Naomi's face.

The kitchenette table in the cabin had been set for a meal

for two. Cyn's face warmed. She was intruding on a private meal.

"I don't have to stay for long…" Her gaze flicked to the steam radiating from the fresh pasta and spaghetti sauce. Damn, everything smelled good. Sinister had golden hands in the kitchen. Even for a man with one hand.

Naomi tried to take the bowl of pasta from him, but he flashed her a look of annoyance. He was about as cooperative as Zach in terms of recovery.

As he turned toward Cyn, she couldn't miss the light blue tattoo peeking from under the side of an elastic bandage wrapped around his shoulder and upper arm. Her heart stuttered a bit. Instead of remarking on what she'd seen, she back-pedaled a bit. "I'll come back another time."

"Good try, hunter." Sinister placed another plate on the table. "What slop has Kaden been feeding you?"

"Great slop." The tasty slop was brown and nutritious. Kaden's food wasn't all that bad, but spaghetti was *spaghetti.*

"Sit." He jerked his head toward the table.

Taking a seat as quickly as possible, Cyn tried to hide the glee coursing through her. Might as well sit before he changed his mind.

The food was dished out, and Cyn didn't look up from her plate as she twirled the pasta around her fork and crammed garlic bread into her mouth. *Aww, the man knew how to crisp bread to perfection.*

"It's been a while since we talked," Sinister said.

"I wanted to give you time to recover," Cyn replied. "A lot has happened."

He looked her over, and Cyn knew what was coming. The meal was a small price to pay.

"I'm taking care of myself," she grumbled.

"Taking care? You suck at it," he said.

Ever since they'd arrived here, she'd only seen Naomi. Sinister never left the cabin.

"Kaden gave me his side of things after the attack. What happened to you?" Sinister asked.

She recounted what happened during the attack up to the point where her brother showed up. Naomi frowned at the mention of Zach's name.

"How did the interrogation go?" Sinister asked.

Cyn gave him the details between bites. She didn't hold back, and it felt good to vent, especially when it came to finding out that the Ceruleans had secret relationships with werewolf packs.

"Did you know anything about the Cerulean dealings with werewolf packs?" Cyn asked him.

He shrugged with his good shoulder. "I was just a tool who followed commands, but I might know something." He stole a glance at Naomi.

She flashed him a look.

He tilted his head and grunted.

Cyn stuffed a huge bite of spaghetti into her mouth and watched the exchange. "Uhh, do I need to leave?" The plate of food was coming with her.

Sinister took Naomi's hand and gave it a squeeze. "Baby..."

Cyn hid a smile. About time those two crazy kids got things sorted out.

After releasing a long breath, Naomi spilled on how she'd witnessed a meeting in LA between the Cerulean clan leader and the Baker pack leader. The whole time, her gaze was fixed on her plate. Had something bad happened to her while she'd lived there?

"Did you hear what they said?" Cyn asked Naomi.

"Does it matter?" Sinister said in a point-blank manner.

Knowing what they'd talked about was important, but

the way Naomi bit her lower lip and tightened her grip on Sinister's hand told Cyn she shouldn't pry any further.

"Thanks, Naomi," Cyn said softly. "I appreciate the information. It's really helpful."

Naomi let go of Sinister's hand and began to eat again. "I hope you find out what happened to your parents." She stuffed food into her mouth, but Cyn caught the next statement: "I'd hunt until the very end for the truth, too."

[10]

THE LONG WALK, AND THE VISIT AND MEAL IN SINISTER'S cabin had done Cyn well that afternoon. By the time she returned to her cabin, the daylight had leaked into the horizon, and the cold had seeped in so deep that any walk seemed futile. At least she returned to the cabin much more at peace than she had been before.

The cabin living room only had a single light from a lamp. Her brother was awake for once and sat up a bit. She had a plate of spaghetti from Sinister for him. She wasn't sure if he was ready for spaghetti, but her brother was probably tired of stew, too.

"What are you doing up?" she asked.

"Kaden just healed me," he remarked. He grinned when he smelled the food.

She checked his pillows. "He gives the good stuff, right?"

Zach groaned a bit when she checked his chest wound, but smiled again when she pushed his forehead to make him lie back down. "Okay, nursemaid."

"What happened to Damien?" she asked.

"Damien?"

"Pale guy in a sweater with red eyes."

"So that's the name of that one. I remember waking up a few hours ago, and someone gave me water."

"That was nice of him."

"He even made me eat some food," Zach remarked.

She laughed. "How horrible of him. I'll be back in a sec."

She left her brother's side to go into the bedroom. A single form slept in the bed. As much as she wanted to check on him, his deep snore told her Kaden needed his rest for now. Whenever she got into bed, he usually woke up and wanted to heal her as he did every night. So, instead of giving in to the need to be held, she joined her brother in the living room and sat down on the edge of his pull-out bed.

The quiet in the room was welcomed. The only sound in the house was the tick tock of the clock in the corner.

"You look like you have a lot on your mind," her brother said softly.

"You could say that."

Zach sighed. "I'm sorry to be such a burden."

"Whatever. You're my brother."

"I'm supposed to be taking care of you."

So he noticed she was getting ill again. "I don't need it."

"I remember vividly what you looked like before the diagnosis, Cyn. The signs were there, but we never knew what they meant. You were sick all the time and tired. It was obvious that you'd gone downhill, even if you tried to hide it from me to protect me."

She closed her eyes, even when her brother took her hand. The walk had been good for her, especially with the decision she had just made.

"I'm going to become a werewolf, Zachary."

Instead of saying anything, he squeezed her hand.

"Will you forgive me for doing this?" she asked.

"There's nothing to forgive. I dragged your ass here, remember?"

"But what about the clan? What about the pledge I made? What about…Ty?"

Zach sighed and rolled his eyes. At an important moment like this, her brother always could annoy her. "I can handle Ty."

Nobody could handle Ty but her. That was the scary part.

"If I become a werewolf, I won't be able to help you find out who killed our parents." She told him about the interrogation, and what Naomi revealed about the Cerulean clan's connections to the Baker pack.

Zach appeared thoughtful. "You know what that means don't you?"

Cyn nodded. All they had was a lead on the gang who had killed their parents. A hope to find out the truth. Just thinking about the time she'd invested to see what the lead meant made her head spin: "According to our source in Calgary, the gang's location was out of LA." That area was Baker pack's stronghold, but they didn't have any evidence that the Bakers could have been involved.

Until now.

"Our parents' last mission was to take out the Baker clan leader," Cyn added.

"And they got the lead on his location from the Ceruleans," Zach finished.

When jobs were too big for one clan, they hired freelancers or hunters from other clans. Getting a lead from another clan wasn't unusual. Betrayal was.

"I'm so tired," Cyn said. "Do you remember anything else about the details on the assignment?"

Zach rubbed his eyes. This was the worst time for them

to be digging into the past. They were both worn thin. "Ask me tomorrow when I feel less like shit."

Cyn chewed on her lip. Anytime she thought about her parents leaving and not returning home, a familiar pain kicked her in the stomach and made her breath hitch. It was as if her mind and body didn't want to go there. She didn't want to churn up the bad memories from the past.

Zach tapped her knee to draw her away from her reverie. "Even if the Ceruleans and the Bakers killed our parents, what happened in the past won't change the fact that you're dying."

"I know..."

He cleared his throat. "As the district manager of area 19438, I hereby resolve you of your duties and allegiance to the Red hunting clan."

She snorted. "I'm being serious."

"So am I."

"You're not doing it right."

"I'm recovering in bed after getting shot. I think, so far, this ceremony has gone great, and you should give me one of those cookies Damien baked to celebrate your new life in the pack."

"He baked, too?" And somehow managed to hide the evidence.

"What matters is that I love my sister, and, from the beginning, I wanted you to make this choice. I wanted you to become a werewolf to save your life. If that means I have to meet you secretly or lose ties with you forever, I was prepared a long time ago to pay that price."

Just hearing those words filled her with relief.

"Thanks, Z."

"Not a problem. Although, I am kinda pissed I had to get shot in order for you to make this decision."

She groaned. "You getting shot isn't the main reason I am doing this."

"It better be. This shit hurts like a motherf—"

"I'm doing it because I love him," she blurted. Her heart fluttered as she made her confession.

Zac chuckled. "About time. I've seen the way you look at him."

She'd never made a confession like this before. "Yeah, I just needed to see with my heart instead of my eyes."

AFTER THE LONGEST SHOWER OF HER LIFE, CYN FINALLY left the bathroom and plodded into the bedroom. Each footstep was hard to take and she almost wished Kaden were asleep so she'd have more time to chew on her thoughts.

By the time she slipped under the covers, his arms snaked out and pulled her toward him. She sighed, enjoying the warmth of his body against hers. The room was cold, but she could always depend on Kaden to keep her warm and comfortable.

"I was wondering if I'd have to go Baywatch and send a lifeguard into the bathroom to rescue you," he murmured against her neck.

"A David Hasselhoff rescue doesn't sound bad." She blinked, searching for something to say. This was the part where she'd find some clever, off-beat way to say that she loved him and wanted to stay forever with him as his mate.

Her mouth opened and then she closed it again.

I got nothing.

Most of the time, whether she was interrogating a werewolf, or training wet-behind-the-ears hunting recruits, she knew the exact words to say. The orders to bark or the lessons to be given, but this time she just lay there.

Say something, you fool.

But how do you say the very thing that exposes your soul? Was this how men felt when they proposed? Or when they first said they loved someone? Her heart was beating so fast and her hands grew clammy.

He chuckled. "You okay?"

He rubbed the sides of her arms. "Your heart rate just shot up like a racehorse…"

"It's been a long day." She wanted to smack herself. He had given her the perfect opportunity to say something suave. She could've turned to him, kissed his lips and said that he was the one who made her heart beat like that. That he was the one who made her feel this way each and every night.

Run with it, girl! Before you forget.

So she twisted into his arms and found his lips. She nibbled at the corners of his mouth and relished in his immediate response. It was so easy to forget about the world. By the time their lips parted, that was pretty much what happened. Every single cool phrase she had waiting in the wings vanished with the Arctic wind.

So she cupped his face. In the darkness, she could barely make out his features, only the dark circles under his eyes, but she knew he could see everything about her from the faint scars along her cheek to the knick on her ear from an attack a few years ago. Every imperfection she had was laid out for him to see. And yet, he wanted to be with her. He still cared for her, even as her human body grew frailer.

His hand ran down her hip and then rested against her stomach. She knew what was coming and stopped him.

"Not this time," she whispered.

"I told you that you'd have no choice in this matter, Cyn."

"I do have a choice," she began. A lump in her throat

made it hard for her to continue, but she somehow found her voice. "And I choose you. I don't want you healing me anymore."

His jaw twitched, and his body stiffened.

"I'm not done yet." She reached in and kissed his cold nose. *My protective little wolf.*

"I love you, Kaden Windham." She closed her eyes as her face warmed. Other than her immediate family, she'd never told a man she'd loved him before, even the man she thought she would've married over a year ago for a perfect picket-fence life. "I don't want you to heal me anymore because I want to stay with you as your mate. I want you to make me what you are."

He paused as if to consider what she was saying. "Are you sure about this?"

"I've had long enough to think about it."

He sighed against her. "I would've waited years. I can *still* wait."

She pushed his shoulder. "Okay, I've just confessed that I love you, and you're telling me to wait?"

He cocked a devilish grin, and her heart skittered. He was so beautiful.

"I'm just saying I'm willing to wait. I've always been willing." He pulled her closer until their lips met and he kissed her so fervently that she moaned from the heat he generated from her toes up to the top of her head. Her head tilted naturally into the kiss and everything that plagued her all day seemed trivial. This moment was true happiness.

Finally, she pulled them apart. "I want you to change me tonight."

His eyebrows rose as if he hadn't expected her to say that.

"Unless there's some kind of prep I don't know about?" Did he have to do some kind of mumbo jumbo or magical spell? Based on the story she remembered from Damien,

Tobias bit Damien and then he transformed from a human to a werewolf.

"There's no preparation per se. Just an alpha's will." His tone grew serious. "There's no going back, though, Cyn. I can't undo this once the process has started. There will be *pain.*" He ran his fingers down the side of her face. "There will always be pain."

She shrugged. After countless hospital visits and chemotherapy, transforming into a werewolf every month seemed trivial compared to the constant pain and fear of dying.

"I can live with that. But I was kind of hoping for a free boob job with the process, too."

"I'm not joking, Cyn."

"I know; I am..." She paused. "It's easier to make light of this situation so I can move toward what I will gain instead of what I will lose."

He nodded, knowing all too well what she was letting go of if she did this. The things she tried so hard to hold onto: her humanity, her hunting clan, her brother Ty. Finding out who killed her parents and exacting her revenge.

She presented her neck to him. "Just do it now while I'm ready."

He frowned. "I'm not a sparkling vampire."

Her mouth formed an "oh."

He gently took her palm. She waited for the bite, even anticipated the pain, but he kissed the spot between her thumb and index finger. A sweet brush of his lips against her skin. She sighed from the pleasure. He nibbled along the back of her hand, his heated gaze fixed on hers. All the while, his body hardened against her leg.

He was as turned on as she was.

He pressed his lips against her fingertips, kissing each one as she relaxed. She couldn't help smiling at him. It was hard not to enjoy the warm, wet edge of his tongue as he swept it over the middle of her palm to her pulse point. Her thighs clenched when he nicked the skin near the place where her heartbeat thumped.

Then he bit her. The whole time, he'd hidden his incisors, but she briefly saw them when he withdrew from her.

The bite on her hand immediately began to throb, even after he kissed the spot.

So that's it? she thought.

"Did it hurt?" he whispered.

Barely any pain. "Not at all."

"Now we wait." Instead of drawing her to him to sleep, he kissed her again. Tugged off her shirt and shorts. Nipped at the skin from her earlobe to her breasts. Each caress was done slowly, carefully placed to maximize her anticipation.

He drew his tongue from one nipple to another. A lazy lick that made her toes curl. There was no reason for him to hurry. No one would bother them tonight.

There was no place he didn't venture. He trailed kisses along her legs, ran his tongue down the length of her back, and even tickled her feet.

When he caught her watching, he winked.

Bite? What bite?

He kept going until she was practically ready to manhandle him and ride him into the sunset.

Finally, he settled between her legs, and, with one thrust, he was inside. The burning sensation in her hand worsened with each stroke as her pleasure rose higher.

"Cyn," he murmured from above her. His pace was agonizingly slow, but she moaned and trembled with each hard thrust. By the time she climaxed, he followed not long after.

As her breathing slowed, the honeyed feeling in her stomach churned into a painful stab from her stomach to her sternum.

~

SEEING THE GLOW OF CONTENTMENT DIE FROM CYN'S face filled Kaden with fear. The whole time he made love to her, the rising tension in her body was not only from the pleasure he gave her.

Her nostrils flared and she clenched her teeth. The waves of pain along her gut slammed into him, and all he could do was kiss her forehead and hope the process would finish quickly.

"Rapid healing is a gift," his father used to say when Bastian did something careless and almost died. *"You have no idea what gift you squander. Countless men have fallen before my feet, seeking the bite that will render them virtually immortal. None of them deserved such a gift, and, right now, you don't either."*

Bastian hated whenever his father chastised him in such a manner, but now that Kaden held Cyn, he truly understood. Every once in a while, a patient's life had been in his hands. With one bite, they could've become a werewolf and changed the outcome. ALS patients. Terminal cancer patients.

"Shit..." Cyn held her breath for a moment as if punched in the stomach.

But not every man used such a gift wisely, and, as such, like his father, he didn't bite a single soul with the intent of transformation. That is, until he met Cyn.

The scent of her sweat flared. He wiped the sweat away as she blinked and her body sagged.

She'd sleep soon, but, again and again, she'd stir as if experiencing a bad dream.

Each person was different, based on the extent of their strengths and weaknesses. According to his father, the process took Damien several days. For Cyn, maybe less.

[11]

Forty-eight hours later, Cyn still hadn't awakened.

As much as Kaden wanted to rest, the thunderous knock on his door couldn't be ignored. It was nearly sunset, and the house was quiet and still. He untangled himself from Cyn and hurried to the door.

Zach had tried to stand, but Kaden pushed him back down. "Stay down."

Before he reached the door, he knew very well who stood behind it. The scent was unmistakable. He steeled himself as he opened the door.

"Bastian," Kaden said.

"Kaden." His brother didn't blink once.

"What do you want?" They were way past an invitation to kick it for casual conversation or even dinner.

He looked over Bastian. Living in the outdoors had changed his brother. Gone were the flashy expensive coats and the boots more suited to going from club to club in the city. Bastian was dressed in a brown coat, dirty jeans, and hiking boots. At least he didn't look hungry.

"You and I have *business* to settle. Meet me a half mile to the west. I'll be waiting on the frozen part of the lake." The coldness in Bastian's demeanor turned Kaden's blood to ice. "If you don't come out, I'll come in after you."

Bastian spun on his heel and turned his back on Kaden. The wolf within him bristled. Under his grip, he crushed the doorknob and the crumbled ceramic fell to the floor. How dare his brother do this to him? Out of all the days to have a pissing contest.

"Kaden…" Zach whispered, entering the din of Kaden's churning anger.

The need to lash out at someone—anyone—almost overwhelmed him for a moment, but he swallowed hard and turned to Cyn's brother. "You heard that, huh?"

"It's kind of hard to miss that big dude. So you got a duel coming up? Should I prepare your pistol?"

"I'll need some white powder, too. Gotta look my best." He appreciated the bit of humor for the somber moment.

He rubbed his face. Leaving Cyn behind when she needed him the most was unacceptable. Last time when the Ceruleans attacked, she could defend herself, but today was different. "I can't leave Cyn…"

Until she woke up, anyone could bust down the door and attack. But, if he stayed, Bastian would bring the fight here. Damned if he did leave, damned if he stayed.

"Go handle your business," Zach said from behind him.

Kaden grunted. "Like you're in any condition to hold down the fort."

Zach trembled, but he managed to sit up with an effort. "I'm weak, but I can hold a gun, and it don't take much to pull a trigger."

The two exchanged a long look.

This is a bad idea, he tried to convey through a frown.

I got this. Zach jerked up his chin with a casual nod. Didn't most gunshot victims make great guards?

"What's the worst that can happen?" Zach added. "I raid your fridge and leave protein bar wrappers everywhere."

After some thought, Kaden reluctantly nodded. He had no choice in the matter, and he didn't expect to be gone long. A pack fight was coming, and when two men vied to be an alpha, only one of them walked away alive.

COLD WIND FROM THE LAKE STUNG KADEN'S EYES, BUT he didn't blink as he walked with purpose to the meeting point. A bit over a mile from the house. The need to look over his shoulder nagged him already.

By the time he was halfway to where Bastian stood, a crowd was gathering not far from his brother.

Shit. Only twice in his life had he fought for the Windham pack. In those instances, he'd fought the opposer all alone. Having the curious eyes of his pack members wouldn't be good. Who'd want to witness a man laying his hands on his brother?

No one looked at him as he passed through the crowd. Tinges of excitement surged through many. A fight was coming and the wolf within them all was eager to see blood spilled.

Naomi and a somber Sinister flanked the back. Sinister used his good arm to tap his side. So he came prepared to offer backup. Kaden subtly shook his head. *Not today, man,* he thought. Sinister jerked a nod.

Kaden weaved through more members until he reached Bastian. Rhys and Eva stood along the edge of the crowd. He ignored the triumphant grin on Eva's face. No need for him to speculate where her allegiance lay. He glanced at her children. This would be their first formal pack fight. Looks of uncertainty crossed their faces and Kaden wished he could make this process easier for them. Pups needed to see real pack life, but seeing one uncle harm another was going too far.

"Was calling the other pack members necessary?" Kaden asked between clenched teeth to Bastian. A growing fury pulsed in his chest, but he held himself in check. He'd waste precious energy letting Bastian get to him. "Do they have to see this?"

No reply.

When his heartbeat settled, he found his voice. "Answer me, Bastian."

His youngest brother smirked the whole time. "They should see their new pack leader's victory." Bastian shifted from one foot to the other. "You let me worry about the pack. Soon enough, you won't have to worry about anything."

"Don't do this."

Bastian laughed. "Do what? Take over the pack? That I can do. I will admit, though, the first time I tried to attack you was foolish. I should have waited for a better moment to make my move." His smile widened. "An opportunity fell right in my lap when that hunter showed up. Using Eva's help, I got into position and made the perfect shot. Not a fatal one, but I wounded him just enough for him to need your care."

A murmur fluttered through the crowd, and Kaden sighed. He knew what was coming, but he couldn't fathom that his little brother would go this far to take over the pack.

Bastian continued. "You healed her. You healed him. All the while, you grew weaker."

That piece of shit had no interest in a fair fight.

"You're a coward." Kaden's lip curled into a snarl. "I'm

not surprised you couldn't face me like a man. I guess you couldn't do the same for me like I did for you."

Bastian closed in on him, but didn't touch him. "A coward? If I wasn't merciful, you'd be full of bullet holes right now. Just like that hunter."

"Which hunter? The one you killed that brought the Ceruleans down on us? Some alpha you'd make."

"I'm tired of talking to you." Bastian thrust his index finger in Kaden's direction. "Every time I look at you I see Dad. I see that look of disappointment. Well, I won't have to look at you anymore, since, from now on, things will be done the way I want them done."

Kaden grabbed his brother's finger and jerked hard to the right. The finger snapped like a tiny twig. No more bullshit. No more talking.

Bastian howled in pain and rushed Kaden with his shoulder to Kaden's chest. They slammed hard to the ice, but the surface didn't give. His brother's claws dug into his neck to choke him, the broken finger hanging limp on Bastian's hand. Kaden tucked in his legs and kicked upward. With a snarl, Bastian flew backwards, all the while ripping the skin along Kaden's neck. Glorious air filled his lungs.

No time to celebrate, Kaden.

His brother came at him again, fists swinging. Words weren't necessary at this point. Several clocked Kaden in the head. Dizziness swept over him, but he kept his arms up.

Others around them shouted and barked.

"Kick that punk's ass," Sinister belted out.

"Kill him, Bastian!" Eva screeched.

"Tear him apart!" another yelled.

Bastian kept coming at him, snarling and snapping, almost as if he had no qualms to kill him. Blood ran down the side of his face and now he had two broken fingers. Things had gone far enough.

"Bastian, stop it!" Kaden yelled.

His brother's claws dug into the meat of his neck as Bastian slammed him into the ice again. The faint sounds of ice cracking reached his ears. The hit sucked the breath from his lungs. His vision blurred. *Damn it.*

Kaden threw a hard right hook and sent his brother sprawling to the right. He didn't give Bastian time to recover and swung at him again and again, until his knuckles hit hard against bony flesh that gave in. How much did he have to hurt Bastian to make him back down?

He threw back his fist to knock out another set of Bastian's teeth when his brother's eyes grew wide and the promise he made to their father kept ringing through his head: *"Bastian is your responsibility. No matter what he does, it is your place to take care of him."*

So he stopped.

Then Bastian rammed his forehead against Kaden's and split the skin along Kaden's scalp open. Black dots popped up along his peripheral vision and a strong metallic taste slid down the back of his throat. He'd bitten his own tongue…

All round him, the pack members had steadily grown quiet. Did they see an ending to this fight that he refused to see?

Was he playing the fool?

"You keep backing down," Bastian murmured. His grip on Kaden's coat tightened as he drew Kaden to stand. "You keep saving someone who doesn't want to be saved by you anymore." Bastian's breath was hot against his face. "You choose to not understand the truth. The moment you allowed yourself to become weak was the moment I knew you and I *couldn't* live in the same world."

So not the fool. He was just a man who needed to realize the promise to his father was no longer binding.

Bastian had made his choice.

Now Kaden had to make his.

Bastian swung his elbow towards Kaden's chin, but Kaden blocked the blow. In a flash, Kaden used the block swing to force his brother to turn around.

He didn't hesitate to render the next punch on Bastian's upper back. It wasn't the power behind the punch that mattered, it was the placement. A hard blow at just the right spot in the spinal column above the fifth thoracic vertebrae.

Bastian landed hard as if he'd dropped dead on the ice. His face was turned to the side. His breaths were shallow and wet.

Now that Kaden had a moment to catch his breath, he closed his eyes. As a physician, he'd never harmed another in this manner.

Being the cruel bastard he was, Bastian laughed. "Do you think incapacitating me like this will work? I'll heal in a week or two." His eyes formed slits. "Every time you turn your back on me, I will be there waiting for the opportunity to kill you."

A dead silence fell over the pack. He sensed their shock from Bastian's words.

Kaden said a prayer.

Then he hunched over his brother and snapped his neck.

His brother moved no more. Shock among the pack turned to horror. When Naomi cried out, he stumbled as if someone had struck him again.

"I'm so sorry," he whispered again and again. He collapsed to sit beside Bastian and placed his hand on Bastian's back.

You did what you had to do.

This was how Bastian wanted things to end.

If he had killed you, what would have become of the pack? What would have happened to Cyn and Zach?

But no matter how many times he told himself these

facts, it did nothing to lessen the pain. It did nothing to stop him from squeezing his eyes shut as anguish crushed his lungs until he could hardly breathe.

Every fight ended like this, but the loss of his brother still seemed unreal.

~

CYN SLOWLY BLINKED.

That was about all she could do. All that existed was the fog she drifted within and whatever was on the other side in the real world.

Glass broke, interrupting the quiet. Next came the hard crunch of wood breaking into many pieces. The muffled sound of a silencer going off.

And then silence.

Silence, along with pain during her moments of wakefulness, were an all too familiar companion during the long hours she lay in bed.

But fear grew in her gut as well. Something had gone wrong. Horribly wrong.

A familiar yawn reached her ears. Was the door opening?

The footsteps across the worn hardwood floor got closer until they were right by the bed.

No matter how hard she tried, she couldn't so much as move a muscle. She tried to beg, even curse, but her mouth refused to function. She tried to do anything to lift the fog enveloping her. Her intuition, which had never failed her, rang off horrific alarms in her head, but there was nothing she could do.

Someone was leaning close. Their fingertip ran along her jaw to her pulse point. They leaned closer. They were so close, they could cut her throat if they wanted.

Eva? Bastian?

"Cynthia…" the voice said her name through clenched teeth. Bitterness rolled through each syllable.

"How could you?" She knew the voice. She could've been in a coffin ten feet under the earth and she'd know that voice above all others.

"You stink like they do," the man said. "If Zach would've turned up dead, you'd be joining him right now." He chuckled. "Thanks to Zach's technology addict ways, tracking him down was all too easy. Now I can rescue you."

She wanted to gasp out his name. Do anything to stop what was about to happen. But her muscles had no substance, and the single blink she managed revealed a murky sight: a familiar face with lips curled into a dark smile.

The McGinnis reunion had come to pass.

Ty McGinnis had found them.

[12]

NIGHT HAD FALLEN BY THE TIME THE PACK BURIED Bastian in the woods not far from the lake. As Kaden added the final layer of dirt, it seemed as if Bastian wasn't truly dead and his body wasn't laid to rest.

"I've been gone long enough," Kaden said quietly to Rhys. He'd only left Cyn's side for less than two hours, but he was uneasy the whole time.

He was only a mile away before he saw that the door to the cabin was missing.

The inside was dark. Not a single light illuminated the inside. His whole body tightened with fear as he broke into a hard run.

With each step, he told himself, *she's there. She's fine.*

He bounded through the door into the living room. The couch, along with the sofa mattress, had been turned. Kaden gaped as he checked the room.

There was blood on the floor, but it wasn't Cyn's.

He stooped and inhaled. The blood belonged to Zach.

Kaden searched under the overturned table and found

Zach lying on his stomach. His breath was uneven, but his heartbeat was strong.

The rest of the house was silent.

His body ached all over from his wounds, but the pain faded away as his panic rose.

The bedroom is empty. The bedroom is empty.

But he still ran into the room. He had to see with his eyes.

The room was empty as he'd suspected.

Not a single drop of her blood was on the floor or the bed. She hadn't been harmed. Yet.

A new scent was here. A human who *smelled* like Zach, yet wasn't Zach. A blood relation. Anger settled into his stomach and blossomed into a growing rage that filled his vision with red. The wolf within him bristled until he couldn't suppress his fury anymore. He smashed his fist through the thick door. The blow knocked the door off two hinges, but he didn't care.

A hunter had taken Cyn.

That person knew who she was.

But that hunter had no idea that he had just snatched a newly born werewolf.

THE HUNTER'S MATE

PART 5

[1]

Not all of the boxes of shells Kaden crammed into a duffle bag made it. Several scattered across the ground. His grip crushed a few of them. As much as he tried to hold his temper in check, he couldn't shake the feeling that something was very wrong and, if he dawdled, he wouldn't reach Cyn in time to help her. So far, he'd packed his bag, patched up Zach, and was now outside in the cold stuffing ammunition into a bag.

If he had to face the entire Red clan to get Cyn back, he'd do it.

And what about the pack? The thought circled his head over and over again but pushing the concern away was easy. Countless times, he'd chosen the pack over her. Time after time, he'd done what was necessary and returned to find that Cyn was safe. But not this time.

His luck had run out.

He had to choose her this time, and he wouldn't fail her like he did Bastian. Just thinking about his brother added further to the ache in his gut.

He hadn't eaten since this morning. After fighting Bastian and getting beat up, he could barely stand.

If he had to crawl to Cyn, he'd do it. He still had money, and he'd use every resource he had to reach her.

Someone approached him from behind.

"I saw from across the lake that you were fixing your front door," Rhys said. "What's going on?"

"It's not good. Cyn's brother Ty tracked Zach somehow and that man barreled in here while I was tied up with..." He couldn't say his brother's name because if he said it, the agony inside of him would worsen.

"Is the other human still alive?"

"Zach's pretty hurt, but he's fine." When Kaden had left him in the cabin, Zach had been as mad as a pit of vipers left to bite their own tails.

Rhys glanced at the duffle bag Kaden held. "How long until you leave?"

His brother didn't question his decision, and for that, he was grateful. "As soon as I finish loading my supplies, I'm driving down there."

"I'll get my things, too."

"No, you're staying here," Kaden said. "You need to tell the others what happened and keep things under control." He sighed. "This is my fight. I made the decision to accept Cyn into the pack."

Rhys appeared uncertain. He was always the thinker who'd do anything for his own. "Of course, Kaden."

From behind them, Kaden caught the sounds of shuffled steps. He cringed. He'd hoped to be gone before Zach tried to get up.

He'd failed.

Kaden moved faster and headed to the car to dump the gear.

"Where do you think you're going?" Zach barked. He clutched his stomach, but each of his steps was sure.

"I'm leaving you here to recover," Kaden replied.

Rhys nodded to him. "Do you want me to carry him back into the cabin?"

"He has a gun," Kaden said with a chuckle. "I doubt you'd want to try."

By the time Kaden shut the trunk, Zach had slid into the passenger seat with a curse.

"I guess you're not going alone then," Rhys remarked.

"I guess not," Kaden said.

Rhys placed a hand on his shoulder. "Be careful. You're not in the best shape right now either."

In more ways than one. But if Ty planned to take her back to where the Red clan was settled in Vancouver, he had a few hours on the road, so he could recover.

By the time Kaden got into the driver's seat, Zach had popped a few pills from a bottle he'd pulled from his pocket. Aspirin. Based on his injuries, he would need more than that.

The road leaving the lake was bumpy with gravel, but Zach endured it with silence. Until they reached the highway.

"Head to the airport in Prince George," Zach whispered.

"Why? If they made any stops at the gas stations along the way, I might be able to track them."

"He's taking her back to Vancouver. There aren't any Red clan safe houses this far north. He will have to take her straight to our territory."

"And from there?"

Zach sighed. "That will be the next problem for us to face when we get there. For now, we need to buy time. Once we get to the airport, I can secure private transport to Vancouver."

"How much pain are you in?" Kaden had asked the question earlier, but Zach ignored him. Asking again seemed wise.

Zach smirked. "Not as much pain as Ty will be in once I wrap my fingers around his throat."

AFTER SEARCHING CYN'S APARTMENT IN DOWNTOWN Vancouver, Kaden's frustration grew. "How many more places do we need to check?" Kaden asked Zach.

Not a single thing had been touched in the one-bedroom condo in the False Creek neighborhood. Compared to the cabin, she'd lived a comfortable life in a high rise. Seeing her personal effects bothered him the most. He tried to tear away thoughts that she might be hurt, but he couldn't.

"All of them," Zach bit out.

Before checking her apartment, Zach had stalked into the Red clan headquarters in East Vancouver, then they checked the marina, and now Zach seemed as frustrated as Kaden was.

"There are a few hunters Ty trusts with his life," Zach grunted. "We'll check those places first before we try the last place he'd go."

"Where's that?" Kaden asked.

Zach snorted. "There's no way he'll take her back to our parents' house. The place is a closed-off location, but it's a rookie move. Ty's too smart for that."

[2]

THE FIRST THING CYN WANTED TO HEAR WHEN SHE woke up for the first time as a werewolf was Kaden's voice. Like all the other mornings, she wanted him to wrap his arms around her and pull her closer to his warm chest. He'd rain kisses along the nape of her neck.

But, for some strange reason, while she lay in bed trying to shake off the last bit of sleep, a fly kept her company. The pesky insect buzzed at her ears. The sound was deafening as it dive-bombed down to her ear, only to buzz as it flew away. The fourth time that little bastard landed on her hairline and danced along her roots. Every twitch and jerk of its wings registered in high definition sound: *thwap thwap thwap*.

So she waved her hand to make it go away. Her hand moved so fast, she clocked herself in the head with her open palm.

Oh, the pain. I just smacked the shit out of myself, she thought with a grimace.

Her right eye socket throbbed, and the skin along her cheek sang. *What kind of fool slaps their own face in the morning?* She opened her eyes a bit.

Then blinked.

She wasn't in the cabin on the lake.

Instantly awake, she shot up in the bed and glanced around.

She was home.

Not her old apartment in Vancouver, or the old cabin she had shared with Kaden before the attack from the Cerulean hunting clan, but her parents' home before they'd died.

Her old bedroom in this house hadn't changed much since she'd last been here a few years ago. The old dresser, which had survived three moves over the years, still tilted slightly to the right. Knicks and pokes, which she hadn't seen before, covered the old piece of furniture. A jewelry box, her mom's old one, sat on top. She still remembered the tinny tune the box played: *Moon River*.

There was so much to see now. Light from the mid-morning sun peeked through the lavender curtains and lit the corners of the room. The old wallpaper, which should've been white with purple violets, was now a bit yellowed. A fine layer of dust covered everything.

As acute as her senses had become, what bothered her most were the sounds coming from outside the room. *Breathing sounds.* If she focused and closed her eyes, she could almost hear the steady inhale and exhale. Beyond that, she heard the hum of the fridge.

Then a new sound: a chair scraping against the floor.

The sounds of footsteps grew louder. The unsettling feeling in her stomach worsened. Someone was coming.

The door opened and Ty came in. His face was unreadable.

Her heart sank and a sour feeling crept up the back of her throat. She forced herself to speak.

"What am I doing here?" she managed.

Ty was shorter than Zach, but he made up for the lack of

height with his thicker build. Where Zach had speed, Ty had strength. He didn't have gray eyes or black hair like their mom. Flickers of their dad shined in his hazel eyes and dark brown hair.

He was dressed in jeans and a black *My Chemical Romance* T-shirt, but the casual clothes didn't fool her. Ty always carried a weapon.

"Ty takes this wolf hunter thing a little too seriously," Zach said once while they were drinking during happy hour. *"I once stumbled in on him while he was on the crapper. Dude had a machete while he was reading* War and Peace*."*

Cyn had laughed at the time, picturing her brother anticipating an attack while reading in the loo.

Right now, the joke wasn't so funny.

Ty was a talented hunter.

His gaze swept over her face. "You look better."

He also had an uncanny intuition.

Think, Cyn. There were tells. And werewolves gave them away eighty percent of the time: smooth movements, the slight flare of the nostrils when a scent passed through their nose.

Cyn averted her gaze from his eyes and slumped her head forward.

"My head hurts pretty bad...You never answered my question, Ty."

She pushed her hands through her hair, wrestling to grasp onto memories of her symptoms that no longer existed. Weakness in the limbs, pain in the joints.

"Perhaps I should ask you first why I found you and Zach in a werewolf camp in the middle of nowhere."

She groaned and settled on the edge of the bed. Taking things slowly, she added a twitch to her right hand. Stretched her wrists. After a few doses of chemo, her wrists hurt when she tried to use them.

"It's a long story. I'm not sure you want to hear the details," she said.

He crossed his arms. "Oh, this I gotta hear."

Cyn frowned. The house was deathly quiet. What she wouldn't give to hear another person in the house. Maybe the sounds of Zach snoring. Had Ty kidnapped him, too?

"Just get Z, and we'll explain everything."

Ty's face remained impassive. "He spoke when I *broke* into the cabin. There's nothing else I needed to hear from him."

Oh, shitty shit. Cyn's heart sped up and hammered against her ribs hard enough to hurt. To hide her anxiety, she took a deep breath. "Is he back at the lake?"

"Oh, I left his ass back there. Especially after he had the nerve to pull a gun on me." Ty took another step toward her. She caught his scent. The acidic smell of his sweat mingling with the aftershave he wore. Was he afraid? She'd never smelled fear before, but something told her Ty didn't trust her.

"You two have kept secrets for a while now, and the moment he disappeared off the map for a long time, I got curious."

Cyn made a rude noise. Time to turn the tide so she could get some space. "So now you care?" Slowly she stood and added a cringe. Nothing snapped in her knees, but she made a show of it. "I distinctly remember the day I came here after spending a long weekend of chemo, and you left right after I arrived."

His eyes formed slits. "Don't you dare throw that in my face. I came a few times."

Cyn chuffed. "I guess I missed out on your company while I was delirious from my chemical cocktails."

Keep moving, get to the living room where there's a phone. Slow, jerky steps. She ambled to the dresser to find socks.

Her feet used to always be cold in the morning. Her pink fuzzy socks were still in the top drawer.

"Stop stalling, Cyn. Why were you in Prince George?"

She shuffled backwards to the bed and put on the socks. She stiffly feigned arrogance. "Unlike you, Zach gave a shit and wanted me to live. He found an alpha and made a deal for my life. The alpha agreed to heal me to prolong my life a bit." She left out details like mating with that alpha and becoming a werewolf, and prayed Zach hadn't spilled such.

"So you've been there this whole time?" His eyes were incredulous. "You didn't try to escape?"

Now that she had finished with the socks, she stood again and approached him. "Do I look like I'm in any condition to face a pack of werewolves? Let alone an alpha male?"

"You've gained weight and your color is back."

"How kind of you to notice." She angled past him and left the room. Just a few more feet to the nearest phone. "Other than the fact I had to live with those freaks, I managed to tolerate the alpha's presence so I could recover. I can't run away if I'm a half-starved hunter who can barely hold up a toothpick."

"You've been gone for a while, Cyn. Long enough to raise suspicion."

"Bullshit. The moment I pulled back from the clan because of my cancer, nobody came for me. I was knocking on death's door, and everyone knew it." She twisted to confront him and had to remember to slow her movements. It was far too easy to get angry over this topic. "Clive and Quincy came to see me a few times at my apartment, but when I really started going downhill and didn't attend any functions, you disappeared and so did everyone else."

His jaw twitched.

"This is the world we live in, Ty. Hunters do their job and some die in the field. Unlike our parents, I was going to die slowly and painfully. Nobody but Zach took the time to witness that. He made a choice—a stupid one—and I have to live with it."

The phone, which should have been next to the television in the living room, was gone. The living room was sparsely decorated. Unlike the home Eva had, the McGinnises didn't have as many memories after moving so many times. What they did have were weapons. A set of spears on the wall. A crossbow in a locked cabinet in the corner. Another cabinet with shotguns.

Would she be fast enough to escape if necessary? Or would she have to fight? Anticipation crept up her spine as she scanned the room for the phone's new location.

Ty stalked behind her. There was a new scent she hadn't smelled before. It emanated from him and hit her back in waves. Almost as strong as black pepper. Enough to make her nose twitch, but she kept herself in check.

Until Ty tapped her shoulder. "Stop treating me this way! I know I messed up—"

The unexpected touch came faster than she expected. She caught the whistle of his movement, but her reaction couldn't be controlled. One moment, he touched her shoulder, and in the next, she turned to growl at him.

Of all the foolish things for her to do, a growl was what did her in. The very act had to be instinctual. She controlled everything else, from her stance to the way she walked. But never in a million years did she think she'd open her mouth and a growl would come out.

Ty froze and she did, too.

His heartbeat, which belted her ears from where he stood, stuttered for a moment and then beat faster like a cornered rabbit. A feeling of incredulity washed over him, and the sour stench from the sweat along his brow flared in her direction.

He inhaled sharply and his shoulder jerked forward half an inch.

Holy moly, he was about to strike, and she could see it coming. The subtle muscle twitch of an arm about to extend.

He reached out to snatch her shirt along her shoulder, but she slid out of the way with ease.

"I know what you're thinking," she whispered.

The loud scrapes of his footsteps on the hardwood were like someone raking their fingernails on a chalkboard. The long muscle that stretched from his collarbone to his ear twitched. Even with blinks, she didn't miss a damn thing.

He took another step toward her. His fingers flexed open and shut, a miniscule initial movement to reach for the knife at his hip.

"What did you do, Cyn?" his voice was stiff.

She crept backwards toward the front door. "I chose life and love."

His hand was closer to the knife hilt. A blade lined with silver.

She'd never reach the front door in time. The windows all had bars over them. The McGinnises weren't stupid when it came to home defense. Instead of family game night, they sharpened knives and munched on popcorn.

She placed her hand on her hip and settled her weight on one leg. *Gotta keep things cool.* "Was your plan to shoot first and talk second when you stormed into the cabin?"

His right eyebrow rose. "I knocked. Zach answered with a gun."

She would've done the same in such circumstances, but that was the past. "Dad told us to always analyze the situation. Ask questions before we react in a manner that could potentially kill us."

Neither of them spoke for a moment. Long enough for the sinking feeling gathering in her stomach to fall to the floor. How often in the past had they fought to where she thought they'd never speak to each other again? Countless times. But they always forgave and forgot.

So why was she deathly afraid this time? *He is my brother. I'm his sister.*

With practiced ease, Ty pulled a gun from behind his back and pointed it at her. For the first time in her life, she could see inside the barrel.

Might as well skip the knife and get the gun.

Would Ty even consider shooting his own sister? "Stop being an asshole and put the gun away."

"Dad would want me to end your suffering."

Under normal circumstances, she wouldn't have caught it, but a muscle in Ty's arm twitched. He released the safety.

Oh shit, he's actually trying to save me by shooting me. In a way, that's kind of twisted...yeah, he didn't take our parents' death well at all...

By the time he placed his finger on the trigger, she sprang forward with a front snap kick, jettisoning the end table in the gun's direction. Forced to duck or get hit, Ty shot into the ceiling. With a roar, Cyn surged forward and pushed his back to the front door. The gun fell to the floor. Ty grunted from the blow, but he didn't stop struggling. The fire in his eyes grew brighter.

"So everything I did for you meant nothing? All those gigs I had to work to put food in your mouth after Mom and Dad died?" The strength in her limbs seemed never ending. She held him by the arms against the door with ease until she caught the sound of an audible click and jumped back. Right before he tried to kick her with his knife-tipped boots.

She added space between them. Would he pick up the gun? "Before you became a hunter, I was cleaning up the bed you wet every night."

Instead of grabbing the gun, he feinted to the left, but spun right over to the spear case. He used his elbow to break through the glass and yanked the escrima sticks from the top.

"Oh, c'mon," she groaned. Damn, he knew she preferred long spears to those little toothpicks.

With a snarl, he came at her swinging with the short bamboo sticks and she vaulted to the couch to avoid a wild swing. He kept coming, forcing her to roll over the coffee table when he followed up with a high jab. The sticks whistled with each swing, each strike barely missing her head. Twice he hit her forearms as she blocked.

Raw pain shot up her arms, but she ignored it. No broken bones yet. Pain wasn't anything new, but when he managed to thrust the tip into her stomach, she grabbed the end and twisted the stick from his grip.

Now the big bad wolf had a toy, too.

He came at her again, forcing her to retreat. She took backward shuffling steps, avoiding furniture while she kept her eyes on him. She mirrored his actions down to the last twitch, but now she had nowhere to go but the kitchen.

The need to hold back overwhelmed her to the point where she had to stop herself from swinging her weapon to the side of his face. Again and again, she pushed him out of the way. "Stop it, Ty!"

Ty edged her past the breakfast nook and she kept backpedaling until her side hit the granite countertop.

He tried to reach for the knife on his hip, but she kicked his forearm. Then he changed tactics, diving for the knife holder on the counter and tossed the holder at her. She dodged the holder before swinging out with her right leg, catching his arm, and knocking his remaining stick from his grasp.

The look on his face was feral. This wasn't the brother she remembered.

He isn't playing. This is for real. No more games. She turned to find a way out.

He leaned down and pulled up his pants leg.

Oh, hell no…

That tricky little shit had another gun.

She dove to get out of the way, but not fast enough. The pop bounced against the walls and pain blossomed in her upper thigh.

Run. That was the only thought she had left. Get the hell out of there. She'd never unlock the front door in time, so she raced for the door to the basement and thundered down the steps.

The darkness swallowed her whole, but she knew her destination without an afterthought. Her hands encountered the cold metal door to the safe room, which she quickly opened and locked herself inside.

All the while, she couldn't shake the uneasy thought running through her head: *He shot me. Oh, God. He shot me.*

[3]

Wet warmth continued to course down her leg. The gunshot wound burned and nothing she could do eased the discomfort.

Muffled footsteps moved outside of the door.

"I never expected you to come here," Ty shouted.

She caught the sound of a blade scratching the metal door from one side to the other. Almost as if he were cutting someone's neck.

"So honor trumps family?" she bit out. "The clan trumps family?"

"After you left me behind, it was the clan who supported me. When you took our parents' place, it was the other mothers who comforted me. Don't you dare try to play the martyr!" His rage battered her. "Our parents died for our way of life. If I let you out of this house alive, I'm not honoring them!"

Their dad would never do this. Neither would their mother. But no matter what she said, she'd never get through to him. He'd been a fervent supporter of the hunting clans.

She encouraged the behavior, never thinking that every word, every action, would drive him to this point: a man bent on killing any werewolf who crossed his path, even if that werewolf were his sister.

She bumped the back of her head against the door. "I'm sorry I made you like this."

That got her silence back.

"After Mom and Dad died, I should've taken you and Zach away from all this." She closed her eyes as her leg throbbed. The silver in the bullet slowly melted away her muscles as it sank toward the bone, but she kept speaking. "We could've gone anywhere. A farm in Utah. A ranch in Texas." A tear fell down her cheek. "But I made you stay. I let you become the man you are today. A killer."

The faint sound of someone prying open the lock box jolted her insides, but she kept talking. There was no place for her to go. Ty knew that.

She got up and stumbled to the first aid kit on one of the shelves. She kept talking while she took out tweezers from the kit. Time to repeat what she saw Kaden do to Zach.

It wouldn't hurt that bad, right?

"I should have taught you how to find—" She opened the wound wider.

Hot damn that hurt.

She dug into the bleeding wound with the tweezers, cringing from each jab until she hit the pain source. That stubborn bullet refused to come out until the fourth try. Even after she got rid of the bullet, the burning didn't stop. It was as if she'd placed her leg over an open flame.

She finished speaking. "I should have taught you how to find the beauty in the beasts we chased." There had been countless bodies in Ty's wake. He'd learned well from the Red hunting clan. He'd learned well from her.

Once that door opened, she'd have to face him and she'd

have to subdue him. What sucked was that she'd have to use a body that seemed foreign to her right now.

The bullet tumbled to the floor and rolled away. With a hint of light from the overhead bulb, the silver glinted. A few months ago, such a sight was salvation. Any werewolf she tracked could be found using the blood trail.

Now she was the shot werewolf. Using her teeth, she ripped open a few packages of gauze. Then she unscrewed the cap to a bottle of peroxide. Dousing the wound to clean it out didn't make the burning end.

She shook her head with disgust. The bullet must have fragmented a bit. Now she had silver filaments in her leg. Until her body forced them out, they'd burn like hell.

The click of the first lock drew her out of the moment. The door had four locks. All of them could be triggered with manual levers. In case someone got stuck inside, someone else could fish them out. She had less than a minute until he released all the lock mechanisms.

She glanced around the room, searching for ideas. The room had nothing more than two beds, a bookcase with supplies, and a weapon rack.

The rack was empty. *Lovely.* How was this room a *safe* room?

Using tape, she quickly secured the gauze on the wound. That would have to make do for now. *Keep moving*, she told herself. She hummed softly to herself as the second lock disengaged. She flipped the mattresses over and placed them in a protective pile as far away from the door as possible. She turned over the rack, praying he wouldn't notice that the rack was empty. Maybe he'd think she had an Uzi or something.

The first aid kit didn't have anything resembling a weapon. Unless she planned to burn his eyes out with rubbing alcohol or stab him with the tweezers.

The third lock disengaged.

Next, lights out. She smashed the light bulb.

Her leg hurt like hell, but she bit down on her bottom lip and scaled the wall next to the door. As a human, she wouldn't have been able to place her weakened fingertips into the crevices in the wall and pull herself up, but now she stretched upward with ease.

The fourth lock clicked.

Time's up.

With her legs locked, she formed at T right above the doorway. Her stomach muscles tightened to keep herself in position. She held her breath as the door yawned a bit. *Wait for it. Wait for it.*

Would he creep inside?

Ty stormed into the room with a flashlight and the dark corners filled with light. He spotted the pile of mattresses and that cocky shit opened fire with a shotgun. After two rounds, he waited.

Slowly, he approached the mattresses.

"I want to make this easy for you," he whispered. "I couldn't turn you over to the Red clan, but I want you to have the mercy you deserve. The sister I knew from a year ago would want me to end your life."

Fury clutched her throat. How dare he make such a choice for her? Just like Zach did when he left her behind at the werewolf camp.

Sweat gathered on her forehead as her anger skyrocketed. The need to spring on him grew stronger. Almost like something inside of her churned and gathered. A spring waiting to be released. A rumble gathered in her throat, but she quieted herself.

The stench of gunpowder from the fired weapon forced her back under control. That was what the foolish werewolves did. They struck first and thought about the consequences later.

When Ty cleared the door, she held her breath. It was now or never. She could hear his rapid heartbeat. Smell the fear coursing down his back. He truly thought she would hurt him.

Hurting him was too kind. She planned to beat his ass first.

She tucked in her legs and propelled herself from the ceiling to the floor. She landed hard on his back and they tumbled to the concrete floor. Her leg screamed in pain from the movement, but she ignored it. Medicine later. Ass-beating first.

Once she had him down, she plucked the shotgun from his grasp. There wasn't much space to move around the small room. He tried to throw a punch, but she dodged the swing with ease and kicked him in the gut. He still made the same mistakes when he fought.

"I told you not to expose your life side when you swing," she whispered.

"Like this," he roared. He tried to swing again, but instead of exposing his side, he jerked into a front kick. She jumped out of the way of that one, too.

"I'm faster now, Ty. I'm bleeding and cornered, too." She caught his fist in mid-swing. "The thing that separates us from them is this." She used her other hand to tap her heart. "I could be on top of you right now and it would be all over."

He wrenched his hand free and twisted sharply to the left with his elbow. He caught her on the chin, but she glanced off the blow to slap him across the face.

"I'm not going to hurt you, Ty!"

"Then I guess you're weak now. Maybe you forgot about Ketter."

The name made her start for a moment, but she gathered her composure as Ty stepped back, clutching the side of his reddened face. She hadn't meant to hit him so hard. Hopefully, she hadn't broken his cheekbone.

"He made the choice to not harm a child."

"And he ended up dead for it," he spat. There was a reason why Ty was willing to kill younger pack members, and Ketter was the reason. He'd been one of Ty's mentors.

"It was a freak incident," Cyn said. "You just can't let it go, can you?"

"That little boy ripped Ketter's throat out and left him to bleed on the street."

"Not all pups are that way."

"Pups?" His eyes widened, Ty backed out of the room toward the basement. "Those things aren't pups."

Cyn eyed the shelves outside of the room. There was a .45 sitting on the washing machine, tucked under soiled clothes. He had about eight feet to reach the weapon.

"They are still innocents in the middle of an adults' game. They are people who have learned hate from their parents. From the very people who have hunted them."

Ty took another few steps backward.

"What will killing me solve?" she asked. "It's over now."

"No."

"Let me go, Ty."

She approached him.

With a frown, he chuckled. "And if I do, what's to stop your alpha from taking revenge on me? What's to stop Zach from killing me?"

She pursed her lips. "I can't stop stupidity everywhere, but I can control the people who are close to me. Werewolves are capable of love. They know about promises and forgiveness."

He looked upwards in a manner that she knew meant he was thinking. "And what if I don't know how to forgive anymore? What if my hate is the only thing keeping me going?" He was closer to the gun now. "What if killing every werewolf takes away the pain for a split second?"

Hearing those words cut deep. She'd told herself over and over again that it was her responsibility to care for Zach and Ty, not the other way around. She knew he was bitter, but they'd never spoken to each other like this before. They'd never talked about the depth of Ty's pain.

"That's not living," she whispered. "That's surviving."

"Well, that's all I got left."

"Is that all that you and I have left?" Her gaze swept over the room and she spotted the marina supplies. She'd have to hurt her brother to do what needed to be done.

If he dived, he could reach the gun. She searched his light brown eyes, waiting for his decision. A flicker of indecision touched them, but when his eyes jerked to the right in the direction of where he needed to go, she knew the decision had been made.

Ty's tell.

For those who knew him best, he had the worst poker face.

Cyn hurled herself at him, rammed into his side to drive him toward the marina supplies. His back hit the shelving pretty hard, but he recovered fast enough to throw a few jabs at her. She let him hit the shelf behind her as she grabbed the rope. Ten feet of rope exactly. By the time her brother tried a new attack, she swept his leg and drove him to the ground. She was on him again with her knee pressed into an old shoulder injury.

"Damn it," he grunted. "You always play dirty."

After shooting her, her brother had the *nerve* to complain about the fact that she took advantage of his weaknesses?

For good measure, she didn't hold back when she punched him out cold and tied him up.

Cyn was certain of one thing at this very moment: No McGinnises would die today.

[4]

TIME PASSED AND NONE OF THE PLACES THEY CHECKED turned up Cyn. They didn't even find any Red clan members. Which left them with one final place. Zach reluctantly relented about going to his parents' last home. Irony could be a mean bitch.

Cyn's brother grew quiet as they drove north on the Trans-Canada Highway into North Vancouver.

After a bit of time, Kaden broke the silence. "Anything I need to worry about in terms of your brother?"

"He's an asshole."

Kaden held back a laugh. "Cyn said the same thing."

"It's true. Ty didn't take our parents' death very well. Matter of fact, he changed for the worst."

Zach continued after he rubbed his face. Kaden had no idea how the man kept his eyes open. The hunter had an open Cheetos bag in his right hand, orange crumbs on the stubble on his chin, and one big piece in his left hand that still hadn't made it to his mouth for the past fifteen minutes.

"He was really close to our mother," Zach said. "Every

time dad left for a job, she'd rocked Ty to sleep. He always had nightmares about dad not coming home."

The city turned into woods. At first, Kaden thought Zach had fallen asleep, but he started speaking again.

"When we moved here from Calgary, my parents picked a place they thought would help us feel like kids." He sighed. "It was too late for that, but the house in Brighton Beach was beautiful. It's this little town you can only reach by boat that's northeast of here. The river views are incredible." He smiled for a moment as if a pleasant memory flashed before his eyes. "The woods are endless. Cyn and I even got a chance to visit Raccoon Island at low tide. When we weren't worried about moving some place new, we liked to pretend we were conquerors."

Zach gave him directions to a marina where they could rent a boat that would take them to Brighton Beach. The boat ride up the Indian Arm toward the northeast lasted about a half hour. By the time they reached their destination, Kaden was surprised to see unexpected company along the small town's shore.

"Is that what I think it is?" Kaden asked Zach.

From their boat going slowly upstream, they peered at a cluster of men lounging in a pontoon boat. The guys were slamming down beers and eating snacks like any group of vacationers, but they smelled like hunters all the same. The signs were all there: no fishing equipment and one of them was on guard for trouble.

"Shit," Zach whispered. "The gang's all here."

"You recognize them?"

"Yeah. They're all Red clan members. Old Bart is probably about to grill some burgers."

Kaden nodded. "We could go up farther along the shore and double back?"

"We'll have to do that. I don't know if they placed

sentries in Brighton Beach, so we'll have to be careful." Zach's brow furrowed. "If Old Bart is here, that means Ty asked him to be here for Cyn."

~

WHILE TY SLOWLY CAME TO, CYN LIMPED UPSTAIRS AND changed into sweatpants and a clean T-shirt. Her clothes had been covered in blood. The whole living room was in shambles with glass everywhere, so she donned an old pair of boots. The soles were worn and the laces ragged, but they fit perfectly and brought memories of a life she didn't live anymore.

Suddenly, pain raced down her leg and she cringed. What the hell was she supposed to do now?

After grabbing a bottle of meds on the kitchen counter, she carefully lumbered down the stairs to face Ty's death glare. He hadn't loosened the bindings a bit, but he had inched closer to the shelves where additional tools lay. As to be expected.

"Your ankle switchblade is on the third shelf. Once I leave, you can get it," she said.

He didn't answer. Nor did he stop glaring.

"When's the last time you took your insulin?" Once she left, she didn't want him stuck here for a prolonged period without his diabetic medicine. Knowing Ty, he wouldn't be stuck for long, but she couldn't take that chance.

He still didn't speak.

She placed the bottle on the shelf next to the switchblade. The need to leave grew until that nagging feeling was stronger than the pain in her leg. But, the need for closure pecked at her.

"Ty, don't make me leave like this," she begged.

He finally looked away.

She swallowed the lump in her throat. Time passed. Maybe less than a minute, but she wasn't counting.

If he wouldn't settle things, at least they could part from each other with some news he needed to know. "I know who killed our parents."

Finally, his mouth moved. "I don't want to hear your voice anymore."

"I tied up your body, not your ears." She fought clenching her jaw in annoyance. "It was the Baker pack. They made a deal with the Ceruleans."

His gaze flicked her way. Now that got his attention.

"If I hadn't met Kaden or the Windham pack, I never would've found the missing pieces to bring everything together." She shook her head as her mind whirled from what went down. "Once I learned that the two heads had met previously, the Ceruleans' lead on the gang from LA and our parents' last mission finally made sense."

"The Baker pack alpha mission," he mumbled.

"Yes. Their last mission was a referred case from the Ceruleans: corner the Baker pack alpha and kill him."

"So it was a setup."

"Yes. The Ceruleans were in on it the entire time. If they eliminated our parents, there would be less competition among the elite ranks."

Ty let out a long slew of curses.

She waited for him to say anything else, but he didn't.

You can't stay here, Cyn, she thought.

Let him go.

All this time, she'd worried about him. Whether he ate properly and took his medicine. She'd still worry after she walked through that door. Her throat grew dry, but somehow she managed to say the words she needed to say. "Goodbye, Ty."

By the time she walked across the living room, she swore

she heard a sad whimper downstairs.

~

THE TRIP FURTHER UP THE RIVER TOOK A MINUTE OR two before they reached a clearing in the trees and the shore. Zach grimaced as he got out of the boat, but he didn't ask for help.

Kaden was tempted to ask him if he wanted to wait, but Zach took point toward Brighton Beach.

The air here was warmer compared to farther north. The breeze from the lake warmed his cheeks and almost put him at ease.

As hopeful as Kaden was to be reunited with Cyn, he couldn't deny that he was restless inside, thinking about his pack he left alone back at the lake.

The time would come when he'd find a way to right all the wrongs he'd done and return to the time when his father led the pack. So far, there had been more mistakes than successes.

By the time they reached one of the side streets of Brighton Beach, everything was quiet. The small village didn't have much. Almost like a cozy hideaway that was only reachable by boat. The place seemed ideal as a hunter's haven.

Zach checked along the road before they walked down the street. The place seemed empty. Kaden couldn't hear any sounds coming from the two houses they passed.

"Is this a vacation community?" Kaden asked.

"A few of them used to be empty when we lived here. The place is a lot busier during the summer time. Of course, there are folks who live in town year round. It's been a long time since I've visited the house, so I'm not close to the locals."

No one stopped them as they darted from street to street

until they came to the front of a dark green house. The lawn wasn't mowed and the windows were curtained, almost as if the house had seen little maintenance over the years. A home that had been cast aside by time.

"Do you hear anything?" Zach whispered.

"It's quiet," Kaden replied. He strained to listen, but then he caught the faint sounds of footsteps heading toward the back of the house. Ever so faint that he had to focus and tune out the other sounds around him. He pressed against the side of the house as if such an action would help him find her.

"Why can't we just storm the castle?" Kaden grunted.

"This house might not look like much, but Mom and Dad put in enough safety measures to drive back a T-Rex on a rampage."

Kaden glanced around, but he couldn't see much other than the bars on the windows and the thick front door.

"There's a reason why I didn't use the front door," Zach said. "When I was a kid my old man added explosives. If you kick the door down, you're not gonna have a leg anymore."

A sound from the nearby river floated his way. Was it Cyn? The sounds in the house had ended.

Someone was moving in the backyard. Not taking any chances, Kaden found a safe spot to hide in the tree in the front yard.

Sounds from the front door locks disengaging caught his attention. From so high up, he couldn't see a damn thing. He'd have to wait for Ty to come out to act.

Kaden crouched, prepared to spring. He'd do anything to protect Cyn.

Footsteps plodded along until he caught a glimpse of black hair. The woman reached the bottom steps and spoke to her brother who continued to hide next to the house.

She placed her hands on her hips. "Took you two long enough to get here."

[5]

CYN STROLLED TO THE TREE WITH A WIDE GRIN.

Don't cats hide up in trees and not dogs?

She opened her arms to the sky. She only had to inhale and Kaden was there to wrap his arms around her. The warmth of his body surrounded her. In seconds, he scooped her up and hurried northward. Zach had to run to keep up.

"You never answered my question. What took you so long, hero?" she mumbled against his chest.

"Timing. We had no idea where Ty had taken you."

By the time they reached a cluster of trees that provided cover, Kaden stopped.

"What are you doing?" she asked.

He pulled back the sweatpants along her leg. "How bad is it?"

"A gunshot wound with a silver bullet," she replied. "The pain is manageable. I just want to get out of here."

He didn't look happy at all. "You smell like you're in pain."

"So that's what that smell is." She chuckled and ran her nose along his chin. There were so many delicious smells here from his aftershave to the underlying smell that was him. Kaden. She could even smell the last thing he had eaten. A greasy burger, fries, and maybe some onion rings. She kissed his chin. Definitely onion rings.

While Zach tried to gather his breath beside them, Kaden kept questioning her. "Ty shot you? Is the bullet still inside?"

"I dug what I could out, but I think the bullet fragmented," she replied.

Kaden nodded. "I'll carry you back."

Cyn snorted. "You should probably carry Zach back."

Zach made a rude gesture with his middle finger. *Same old Zach.*

She asked her brother how he was feeling and he shrugged it off.

"I'm on enough painkillers to be borderline high," he remarked.

Kaden picked up Cyn and they made their way to the boat. The trip back to Vancouver was a quiet one. For Cyn though, it didn't matter. Kaden didn't let go of her and she didn't let go of him. Not once did he break off contact with her skin.

By the time they pulled up to a nondescript apartment building in a South Vancouver neighborhood, everyone was morose and seemed exhausted.

"What's this place?" Zach asked.

"An old condo of mine," Kaden replied. "I still own the property."

The apartment was sparsely decorated, but still furnished. Kaden had to open the windows to circulate the air.

Cyn hobbled to the couch and brought up a cloud of dust. "When's the last time you've been here?"

Kaden laughed and she smiled just hearing the sound. "A few years. Post residency."

Kaden's smell was here, too. Faint but in all the corners.

"There's no food," Kaden added, "but the place is warm and I know enough delivery places around here until we move on."

While Zach took some time alone in the bathroom, Kaden gathered Cyn in his lap. Everything felt…right again.

"I don't know what I would have done if something had happened to you," he murmured against her hair.

Cyn tried not to think about that. She'd seen what Kaden was capable of doing. What he was willing to do to protect the pack.

"I'm sorry I didn't return in time. I…," he began. He paused a moment and Cyn caught his shudder and long exhale. Something had gone very wrong. "I got caught up in pack matters and things went poorly," he whispered.

"Kaden, what happened?" She touched the side of his face and ran her fingers along the stubble there. He still refused to shave since the attack on the camp.

He didn't speak for a bit. Only his stomach quaked as if he fought to gather his senses. "Bastian challenged me. This whole time, he waited for me to be weakened so he could win…"

"And…"

"He told me he shot Zach. We fought and I won."

The word "won" seemed so final and she knew very well what winning meant in an alpha fight: Bastian was dead.

Kaden had to kill his youngest brother. The very idea that Bastian was the one who shot Zach filled her with anger, and then guilt. Guilt that she'd thought for a moment of harming Kaden's kin.

"I had to kill him, Cynthia." His eyes were barely open and he spoke through clenched teeth as if the weight of what he had done crushed him.

"Kaden..."

"I promised my father that I'd protect him, but I couldn't do it anymore. A line was crossed and the only thing that was left for me was to do the one thing I thought I could never do."

"I know exactly what you mean." A tear fell down Cyn's face as thoughts of Ty came to mind. Would she ever have to face the same thing someday? Would she have the strength to subdue Ty each time he tried to kill her? Would she always be on the run with Zach for the foreseeable future?

The truth made the lump in her throat hard to swallow. This whole situation, the events from the first time she woke up in Kaden's cabin up to now, seemed like a strange dream. One with beautiful moments and horrific ones.

She pressed her lips against his cheek and peace settled within her. Every nerve ending in her skin sang and contentment seemed possible.

"So what now?" The ultimate question. There was no going back to her old life.

"First, we eat. Then we sleep." He captured her lips and they shared a delicious kiss. Hell, even kissing as a werewolf was better. "Then we do other *stuff.* I haven't claimed you yet as my mate. No more sneaking off in the night for you."

She tried to stop herself from giggling but couldn't. "And what's this *stuff?*"

Kaden's right eyebrow rose. "Stuff I don't want your brother hearing us do."

~

CYN WOKE UP IN PURE BLISS. THE PAIN IN HER LEG wasn't so bad anymore. After everything she'd been through, this had been the soundest sleep she'd ever had.

She wanted to lie there and bask in the thick silence in the condo, but the man lying beside her had other plans.

Ever so slowly, Kaden's large hand on her hip rode the curve from beginning to the end. *Sneaky little wolf wanted to play.*

She turned around and pressed her lips against the hard chest muscle.

His heart skipped a beat. *For her.* The sound was so loud and clear.

He had yet to claim her like he said he would. But she didn't move. She enjoyed this moment. Hearing him. Feeling him in ways she never had before.

Slowly, their lips gravitated toward each other. Almost as if the action were inevitable. Undeniable. Just the very sensation of his lips against hers sent a shock from her lips to her toes. The kiss was tentative. Quiet and soft. The beginning of a symphony she couldn't wait to hear. As her head tilted to deepen the kiss, she reached up to cup his face. Her fingers traced every ridge, memorizing every contour.

His mouth opened and his tongue brushed against hers. She moaned into his mouth. The pleasure was intense.

This kiss. *Remember this*, she thought.

She shuddered as he pulled her leg over his hip.

This touch. *Remember this.*

"You're mine," he murmured.

She smiled against his mouth.

With a final kiss, his head lowered to rain nibbles from her collarbone down to the V between her breasts. Awash in pleasure, all she could do was hold onto the top of his head while he nipped and licked and sucked everywhere. Marking what was his.

Staying quiet became harder when his fingers explored the warmth of her thighs. The place that couldn't wait for him to touch her.

"Kaden," she whispered. She called out his name again and again. The name never grew old.

Every place he touched filled her with a growing need. A growing urgency she'd never experienced before. Tension gathered along her inner thighs. She squirmed against him. Their limbs intertwined as he stretched over her, silent yet always moving. The bed yawned with perhaps a happy groan when he entered her body. The pleasure flowed all over her and she surrendered as he slowly pumped his hips.

Skin against skin. Heartbeats matching as his lips claimed hers. Every time they'd made love, she never realized that there could be more, that she could feel more. It was as if a wall had been between them and now that wall was gone. She could feel every secret he had. Not only could she see the passion in his eyes while he thrust deeply inside her, but she could feel it. She could smell how his body responded to hers. She could truly understand the pleasure flowing through him every time he growled in her ear. He trembled above her as his climax approached. The pleasure grew overwhelming as he claimed her with each stroke. Marked her with each bite along her shoulder. The pain was brief. Her stomach muscles clenched tighter and tighter. The need to speak overwhelmed her as she climaxed. "I'm yours," she finally whispered.

Above her, he kissed her again, his eyes intense enough to make her want to avoid the heat from his gaze. She was being swallowed whole, and she was scared she'd never escape.

His back stiffened first and a growl grew in his chest as the pressure built. He trembled under her fingertips. Another climax was approaching and she welcomed it as he turned to steel.

You're mine, his eyes said. *You belong to me*, his kisses along her neck claimed.

Best reunion sex ever.

By the time she settled with a contented sigh in his arms,

she was shocked to hear Zach moving about the living room. Her face reddened.

"We weren't loud, were we?" she whispered.

"Of course not." Kaden kissed her cheek, but he didn't *sound* so confident.

She just caught her first werewolf lie.

"We've probably traumatized him for life, haven't we?"

His devilish grin seemed downright wolfish. "Possibly so..."

[6]

The next day was a hard one for Kaden. After reuniting with Cyn, the joy he'd experienced seemed to fade with the onset of reality.

He put his cell phone into his pocket and sighed as the trio drove into Seattle. The conversation with Rhys had gone as expected. Their sister still hadn't taken the fight between her brothers well. The Windhams had been born into pack life, but none of them expected to have to bury Bastian like this.

A pain spread across his chest, but he ignored it. Facing Naomi once the pack reunited would be difficult. There was no way around it.

"She keeps telling me you should've walked away," Rhys had said. "I told her walking away wasn't possible."

For the pack's safety, he couldn't let Bastian go again.

At least Sinister could comfort her until he faced his sister again.

He'd made plans with Rhys for the pack to converge in Seattle. Staying in Vancouver wasn't possible. The Red hunting clan territory was a deadly place and staying there wasn't wise.

Even Zach, with his ever-present injuries, seemed restless. "The sooner we get on the road," he'd said, "the sooner I can sleep in peace."

As Kaden drove down Highway 169 into the small town of Mirrormont, he wished circumstances would have been different. This whole new situation for the pack had been unforeseen. Inner-city Seattle had plenty of werewolf hunters, but outside the metro area, towns like this were more or less freelancer territory. Everyone here was fair game in terms of the packs.

The house he'd found nestled in the woods was idyllic. Practically a hideaway in one of the most expensive places to live in the country. The scenery might have been nice, but the house would be full soon and more space would be needed for fifteen pack members.

He let out a long sigh. His dad would have knocked him on his ass for letting things get this bad.

Cyn turned to him. Her fingers flew across her phone. "Rhys didn't sound happy."

"A few members will be angry and bitter for a while."

"Like Eva…" she added.

Now, that was a woman he didn't want to think about.

"You were typing for a while there," he remarked to change the subject.

She bit her lower lip and rubbed her fingers along her hairline. Her black hair had practically thickened overnight. "Ty," was all she said.

"Is it wise for you to message him?"

During the long travel time to Vancouver, Zach had told him how Ty was quite savvy with phones and tracking others.

"This is a throwaway phone; I plan to crush it before we

reach our destination." She looked out the window to the woods. Did she find solace in them already? Like he did?

"Want to talk about it?" he asked.

"I said goodbye pretty much. I apologized for tying him up. For wrecking the house…" He took her hand when she trailed off. "I don't expect a reply back. Maybe it's for the best that I throw away this phone and move on."

"You don't have to move on. I can tell you still love him."

"Even after what he did, the need to protect him is innate."

Kaden nodded.

She continued. "For the last couple of years, it's been us three. Zach, Ty, and me. The idea that there will be Christmases without the crew getting together for a barbeque seems surreal. Like a bad dream."

Her grip on his hand tightened and her sharp inhale conveyed her pain. She fought the need to cry, so he didn't speak. Life changed too easily. He'd seen that far too often as a physician. In one moment, the world that seemed to go on and on forever changed, leaving people who were not prepared to cope.

Soon enough, they arrived to the house.

The place in Mirrormont was comfortable, but, for Kaden, the weather change took an adjustment. The Seattle area in early February was brisk compared to the Arctic cold. The woods were nothing more than wet mud and trees.

A few days passed and the pack arrived without problems. The reunion was a somber one.

Instead of saying her peace, Naomi avoided him altogether.

She walked in through the front door and kept going to the kitchen where Cyn was brewing coffee. As alpha, he should have said something, but he let it go for now.

"Hey, Cyn," he heard Naomi say.

"Naomi."

"So I guess you finally did it."

Cyn left the kitchen to go into the living room. Naomi followed. His mate took a place beside him on the sofa while other pack members found whatever space they could around the four-bedroom house. They'd have close quarters for a little while until he made formal plans for the pack's permanent home.

Cyn spoke. "The time seemed right…although plans didn't go as I'd expected."

Naomi's gaze was fixed on Cyn. "Many things didn't go as planned."

Cyn sucked in a long breath and glared at his sister. He placed his hand on her knee. "Naomi, Kaden did what he had to do—"

"Cyn!" a boy's voice squeaked.

She didn't have time to finish before Peter bounded into her arms. The boy was pretty big and stumbled onto Kaden, too.

"Whoa, there. Werewolf attack," she said with a laugh.

Naomi looked away while Cyn and Kaden tickled Peter. Eva entered the living room with Phil, carrying a suitcase of clothes. Briefly, Eva exchanged a glance with Cyn, one Kaden couldn't read. Now that her co-conspirator was gone, he hoped Eva had moved on. Too much blood had been shed already.

One thing was certain though: he'd never trust her again.

While everyone found a place for the night, Kaden got a fire going and Cyn pulled out the fixings for s'mores for the kids. Sinister had sequestered the kitchen already, kicking out anyone who dared to make the pack meal.

Kaden wasn't surprised.

The pack mood was morose, even with Cyn's attempts to make the children laugh. He smiled at her as often as possible, even if a part of him felt broken. He wasn't sure when those feeling would go away either.

As the pack ate, he recounted everything. He didn't hold anything back. Repeating everything even for those who had heard the story before. His deal with Zach. Bastian's treachery. The murder of Cyn's parents. Cyn's kidnapping. Her rescue up to the point where they were now.

His confession didn't lift the mood, but others nodded. They agreed it had been best to leave the camp due to Ty McGinnis tracking Zach.

"We should run tonight," Rhys suggested after they ate Sinister's excellent prime rib dinner.

Kaden nodded.

"Can we run with you, Mom?" Phil asked. He sat on the floor playing with a new-looking toy. Just seeing the boy make do with what he had, made Kaden feel guilty. How much had his nephews left behind this time?

"I don't think it's a good idea. I don't know the area," Eva said softly.

"Aww, Mom!" Peter said.

Damien offered to stay behind with the kids.

So it was settled. The Windham pack would run, and Cyn would join them for the first time.

THE MOMENT CYN DREADED WAS COMING, AND THERE was no escaping the inevitable. Kaden's grip on her hand never loosened as he led her away from the house into the woods. There was no running away. She would become a werewolf tonight.

My body is about to change in ways I can't imagine.

Other pack members ran past them, whistling and shouting with a growing excitement that sparked her senses.

The only other time she'd ever felt this way was right before she tracked her targets.

They reached a small clearing. Fear pulsed through her. Would this hurt as badly as Kaden told her it would? Who in their right mind looked forward to pain?

She glanced at her free hand. The moon's glow made the limb seem inhuman. Yet she still had five fingers. Three pinkish lines arcing across her palm. She flexed her fingers and glanced at the tips. No claws. No fur along the back of her hand.

Kaden took her chin with his free hand. "You'll be fine," he whispered.

Even with the other conversations around them, her mate was loud and clear. His green eyes shone with amusement.

He placed his hand on her chest. Did he feel her thundering heart? "Remember Micah's first time?"

She nodded and couldn't help but turn to see Rhys discarding his clothes into a neat pile. Dark hair already sprouted on his back by the time he bared his ass to the world.

Cyn looked away. More pack members were naked now. She didn't feel any different as she watched Eva hunch over. The blonde's face contorted into a painful grimace. Her slim legs jerked and snapped backwards into hind legs.

All the while, Kaden remained as a human by her side. "Why haven't you changed yet?" she asked him.

"I'm the alpha," he said simply. "You and I must protect our pack while they complete their transformations."

He drew her close to him and kissed her forehead. She shuddered from the intense heat his skin radiated as he rubbed his nose down the side of her face. "Your scent is different. You smell so beautiful."

He tugged at her T-shirt and helped her pull it over her

head. Her bra came next. She reached up to cover her chest, but stopped when Kaden chuckled. "Would you like to go behind a tree for your first time?"

She shook her head and took off her pants and panties. Like any seasoned hunter, she'd adapt. If everyone else was naked, she'd do it, too. Even if she didn't like everyone seeing her curves.

A quick glance around her revealed no one else looking her way. *See?* she told herself. *Everyone else is too busy sniffing other folks' butts.*

So what about her? Was something supposed to happen? Then an itch crawled up her spine. At first, it was a mere tingle, but the sensation grew until her entire back seemed covered with tiny little black ants, biting and scattering all over the place until the unnerving feeling turned to pain, utterly raw and powerful enough to send her to the ground.

Kaden was naked now.

"Ride through it," he said with his hand on her back. "What comes next is the most beautiful thing in the world."

Through her fog, she recalled he'd said those words before: during Micah's ceremony.

Her fingers trembled. Searing pain bit into the fingertips. She watched with horror that turned into amazement as claws sliced through her fingertips and midnight black hair spread across her limbs.

The change consumed her, almost like a firestorm sweeping across the forest. As the flames of transformation ate away at the human, what was left underneath was the wolf.

When Cyn's head finally rose, the forest floor up to the canopy of trees overflowed with life she hadn't seen before. So many new scents. From the massive western red cedars, maple trees, and to even decaying vegetation. Each one had a signature and now she knew them all with stark clarity. The overwhelming moment made her wobble on her feet, but she managed to amble over to Kaden.

He ran his flank along hers in greeting.

Others followed suit and, soon enough, she was surrounded by wet noses and familiar forms. She didn't need their faces anymore. Every werewolf had a distinct scent, and, with it, she could discern their identity and emotional state. Rhys had a pungent musk while Kaden had citrus undertones.

Twice she ran along the edge of the clearing with her nose on the ground. She couldn't get enough. There was so much to learn—but she didn't get a chance to dawdle. Kaden circled her twice before he nipped at her backside.

His message was clear: *move it, woman.*

The pack set a hard pace into the forest. Micah took the lead, darting between trees to take them deeper into the wilderness. The destination or time of night didn't seem to matter. She reveled in the feeling of the fresh air against her face and the other werewolves yipping and barking around her.

Light rain began to fall, but that didn't stop their hunt. Eventually, they caught the scent of a cluster of wild rabbits. The small animals scattered from their hiding place in a rotting tree trunk. The pack split as everyone chased a target.

Cyn yipped with delight and raced after a dark brown male. Chasing after prey as a werewolf was just as thrilling as tracking prey as a hunter. Her heartbeat hammered as she wove around corners and dove under lower branches. The faster she went, the faster the rabbit ran. But her drive to end the chase was stronger. Her eyes were sharper. With a hard swipe of her paw, she knocked the rabbit off its feet and she swooped in to grab it. The rabbit squirmed within her clutches, emitting a high-pitched squeal.

Dinner time.

Her mouth opened wide, poised for a killing bite, but she stopped mid-strike. Never before had she eaten a living thing. Yet the hunger was still there. It clawed at her belly, but hearing the rabbit's frightened cry made her let it go. The animal scampered away into the night. Rarely did she let any prey go, but tonight was a night of new beginnings. She might be a werewolf now, but she was also still a human.

That very fact set her at ease.

[7]

A FEW HOURS LATER, THEY RETURNED TO THE HOUSE. The run had been good for everyone, including Cyn. She relaxed with Kaden on the porch with her brother. Cyn sat next to Zach on a porch swing, while Kaden watched them from a bench on the other side of the porch.

"I can see you survived while I was gone," she remarked to her brother.

"Sinister and Damien play a mean hand of blackjack," Zach replied.

"How many times did you lose?" she asked with a groan.

"What makes you think I lost?"

Just watching those two made Kaden feel better. With a tug at his heart, he wished he had that kind of relationship with Naomi. They'd never been close. She'd been closer to Bastian...

Cyn and Zach were quiet for a while. Cyn rested her head on Zach's shoulder.

"Are you thinking about what I'm thinking about?" Cyn whispered to Zach.

Zach closed his eyes for a moment. "Yes."

"I just can't stop. I thought I had closure after I left Ty."

What were they talking about? Instead of asking, Kaden continued to sit quietly.

Zach continued. "You're alive. I'm alive. Going after the Bakers and Ceruleans won't make the pain go away."

"It'll make something go away..." She sat up. "I just can't let it go." She formed fists with her hands. "I feel like I can punch a hole through a wall right now."

Uhh, don't try that, Kaden thought.

"I have all this power, but I can't use it to make them pay for what they did," she said.

"What can we do?"

Cyn hummed a bit as if in thought. "In every dream I've had since they died, the guilty party got what they deserved. Karma bit them on the ass, and what they did to our parents turned around on them."

Zach nodded and his face broke out into a toothy grin. "That just might work."

"Excuse me?" She turned to him.

Kaden was dying to ask what he meant too, but he kept his mouth shut.

"I need to think for a bit." Zach got up from the porch swing and strolled out into the woods beyond the steps. "I'll be back."

Cyn took a place next to Kaden after Zach disappeared.

"What was that all about?" he asked her.

"I don't know, but he's only done that twice before. Up and left like that."

"When were those times?"

"After I told him I had cancer and after I told him our parents died."

A half hour later, when the night sky was cloudless with a half moon, Zach emerged from the woods with Uncle Damien at his side. As to when the two found each other in the woods would be a question he'd have to ask his uncle later.

Neither Kaden nor Cyn spoke when Zach and Damien approached them. "I heard back from Ty," Zach said.

Kaden's eyebrow rose. "You contacted him? What for?"

"The McGinnises have unfinished business," Zach said simply.

Kaden had never seen Zach look so serious since the day Zach brought Cyn to his doorstep.

Zach continued. "I had a long talk with Damien and then I told Ty our thoughts on getting back at the Ceruleans and the Bakers. Ty said he wants in on the action."

THE NIGHT STRETCHED OUT UNTIL CYN AND KADEN went to bed.

Cyn had trouble sleeping that night, though, so she slipped out of the room and headed to the kitchen to grab some leftover food. She hadn't felt this hungry since high school.

On the way back to her room, though, she was surprised to see Eva waiting at the bottom of the stairs.

"I heard you plan to have us sacrifice ourselves for your vendetta against the Baker pack," Eva said with a sneer.

Why couldn't that woman move on? she thought.

She was rather proud of herself for avoiding Eva after what Eva did with Bastian against Zach. "You don't know when to stop, do you?"

"What?"

"Let's get something straight here." Cyn inhaled sharply. Keeping quiet was gonna be hard. She was balancing an overloaded sandwich in one hand and a cold beer in the other. "You don't have to do anything except take your precious children to the pack's new home and continue to be a *back-stabbing* bitch."

"What did you say to me?" Eva trembled with growing anger.

Cyn had been waiting a long time to say how she really felt. "If you hadn't betrayed the pack, my brother wouldn't have been shot. I should knock you on your power-hungry ass right now, but I happen to have something you lack: self-control."

Eva tried to close in on her, but Cyn had several inches on Eva in height and didn't back down. *If that woman made her drop her sandwich…*

"Are you ready to take things outside?" Cyn asked. "'Cause I've been itching to see if you'll deliver on all those crazy threats you've made over the last couple of months."

Eva's blue eyes locked on hers and Cyn didn't even flinch. She wanted Eva to challenge her, was practically thirsty to drink from the fountain of an all-out bar brawl, but Eva was the first one to look away. When Cyn took a step toward her, it was Eva who backed up.

"I'm not sick anymore. I'll even give you permission to take a swing at me." Cyn edged forward until Eva was forced to go up one step.

"No comments from the crazy club?" she asked. "Good. Go to bed, Eva."

Watching Eva march up the steps felt damn good, but the moment Eva disappeared into one of the rooms, Cyn let out a long deep breath.

Never thought you'd have it in you, McGinnis, she thought.

She wasn't surprised to see Kaden was awake and waiting right outside of the door to the room they shared.

Her mouth flapped open a few times. "I didn't need backup."

"No, you didn't."

"What are you doing up?"

"You got up, so I did, too."

She rolled her eyes. "I can't stop thinking about the plan. And Zach. And Ty's role in all this…" The very idea that Ty could be trusted had made Cyn burst out with laughter at first, but once Zach told her what he had planned after talking to Damien, the idea was crazy cool.

Okay, crazy cool was a stretch. Mission impossible was a better term. So many players and pieces had to line up perfectly for everything to work.

"Are you sure Ty and your Red clan will do their part?" Kaden asked her.

"Without a doubt," she replied. "The McGinnises have a long history with the Red clan. The loss of our parents was a loss to them."

"I'm not worried so much about the Red clan, I'm talking about Ty." Kaden eyed her as if to remind her of what had gone down between brother and sister.

Her brother had *shot* her. Remembering wasn't a problem.

"Do you believe you can trust him?" he carefully asked her.

Good question.

She thought a bit before she answered. "I'm not sure about his anger, but what I am sure about is his thirst for vengeance. That I trust unequivocally."

[8]

A WEEK HAD PASSED BEFORE KADEN FOUND A LOCATION that was much more ideal for his pack. A property in Montana came up with over five thousand acres. Plenty of space to start over again. He had no desire to fight for breathing room with rival packs.

Now all they had to do was relocate. Which was easier said than done with the plans a few of his pack members made.

Damien paid him a visit in the house's small office while he was researching moving companies.

"Good morning, nephew." As usual, Uncle Damien was bright-eyed and in good spirits.

"It's nice to see you. You disappear quite often," Kaden replied.

Damien settled into the seat next to the mahogany desk. "Wanderlust can never be sated."

He looked at the man who had always been in his family since his birth. Usually, Damien had a quiet, refined nature, but right now, the older werewolf stirred like a pacing cougar.

The muscles along Damien's shoulders were stiff and a persistent twitch flexed in his jaw.

"You know why I'm here, don't you?" Uncle Damien began.

"I have an idea. The McGinnis plan."

"I've been waiting decades to finish what I started so long ago against the *Bakers*." His European accent slipped in a few times.

Kaden took a deep, cleansing breath. A day like today should've been anticipated, but he had been distracted. "I have reservations about the role my pack has to play." He'd been feeling guilty as of late, and a rash action such as going against the Baker pack wasn't wise. Even if he had no plans for a major war.

"You have had your moment of revenge, Uncle," he added. "Haven't you shed enough blood?"

The side of Damien's mouth curled upwards. "Cameron Baker's sire escaped my wrath all those years ago when his pack stormed into my cabin and *killed* my pregnant wife. The day I woke up as a werewolf, I swore that I'd sever that line and never doubt my decision."

Kaden held in a sigh. He respected his uncle, but revenge wasn't his way. Killing the Bakers wouldn't solve anything or satisfy Damien's hunger for vengeance. What if any of the Bakers escaped? They'd come for the weakened Windhams.

"The pack is vulnerable right now," he said simply.

"I wish I had doubts, but the people who had plotted and killed my parents are still alive and well." He turned to see Cyn in the doorway. Her chin-length black hair was messy, but the fierceness in her gray eyes was quite clear. "They live day-to-day without fear that the past will come back to haunt them."

With Zach not far behind her, Cyn crossed the room and stood before them. Now he had a crowd.

"I'll be honest and say I'm pissed that the Cerulean hunting clan conspired with the Bakers to take out Mom and Dad," Zach said. "I'm not as angry as I used to be a few years ago, but the idea of delivering some poetic justice is so tempting, I can taste it."

This was a turning point, and even Kaden felt it. Would he help deliver justice or keep the pack on the path to Montana? If he refused Cyn, who would stop her from moving forward with her plans with the others?

After everything that had occurred, leaving her side was unacceptable. The only way to keep his mate safe would be to stay by her side and see this journey through to the end. He closed his eyes.

He nodded to the others around him. "The only way I'll agree to this is if the other pack members are in transit to our new home. That's in two weeks."

"Absolutely," Uncle Damien agreed.

Kaden continued. "After that, we'll rendezvous in Vancouver to settle our personal business." Apprehension flicked at him with each word. Maybe he didn't want to confront Cameron because of what he took away from him: The woman who willingly walked away from him.

[9]

THE TWO WEEKS FLEW BY FOR KADEN. WITH SINISTER, he'd visited their new home in Montana. Then he packed up the Windham werewolves and sent them on their way to the east. Next, he went over the attack plan countless times with Cyn, Zach, and Damien. The two weeks were over and now he had to do his part: meet with the Baker pack leader about possible territory rights in southern California. A complete sham, but he got Cameron to come to town.

As he walked to the Cottonwood Club Hotel concierge desk to learn the meeting location, he couldn't shake a sinking feeling. They were past the point of turning back now. Ty had done his part with the Red clan and sent a message to Zach who relayed the text to Kaden: *"The Ceruleans know the Windhams are in town to meet with the Baker pack. You won't be vulnerable to attack until dusk."*

Tonight he'd meet with the Baker pack leader. The arrangements had been made and now he had to learn where and when they'd meet. Cameron trusted no one.

"I've been a target before with those damn hunters so you

will go to the hotel lobby for details. No flunkies. Ask the hotel concierge for the meeting place and time," Cameron had said over the phone.

Seemed like an easy enough request.

What he didn't expect after he'd spoken to the concierge desk was for someone to walk up to him and pat him on the shoulder. He turned around to see Hayley standing there.

She was pregnant.

"Hello, Kaden," she said softly. Hayley wasn't the kind of woman one could forget. She had a heart-shaped face, beautiful brown hair to her shoulders, and a body most women envied. Her heart wasn't as pretty.

"Is there a reason why you're here right now?" He hadn't meant for his words to come out so stiffly, but they did.

"I came to check out the meeting space."

"So he sent you out here alone," he gestured toward her stomach, "like this?"

Hayley smiled smugly. "He is very protective of me. Believe me; I'm not alone right now."

He glanced at the corners of the lobby and spotted five werewolves looking them over as they spoke.

"What do you want?" Kaden asked.

"Why did you contact him?"

"You already know why I contacted him."

She licked her lips and the look of discomfort passed over her face. "After what happened between us, I expected you to never contact me or Cameron ever again."

He gave a dry laugh. It took everything he had not to say, *"I didn't want to ever see your face again."*

Instead, he settled for, "Circumstances change. For the betterment of my pack, I had to speak to him." He leaned forward.

"You still shouldn't have, Kad."

He used to love that nickname. Now, hearing her call him that rubbed his fur the wrong way.

She ran her hand over her belly. Based on her stomach size, she had to be around seven months. He looked away. That could have been his child, but things had gone for the best. He'd dodged a bullet.

Hayley's right eyebrow rose. "All this time, I thought you were plotting your revenge for what I did to you. I had Cameron increase security tenfold." The side of her lip curled into a smile. "I almost wanted the man I remembered to come for me and try to take back what was his."

He found none of what she said humorous at all and just stared at her with a face resembling stone.

"Stop looking at me that way. I didn't mean for things to happen between Cameron and me."

"Don't—" Wow, he couldn't believe she went there.

"Just listen. I want to speak my peace. I want to say I'm sorry for what I did to you and Naomi."

"Naomi?"

"I tried to call her, but the last phone number I have for her is bad."

His face soured. "What did you do to my sister?"

Her face dropped. "She never told you."

He took a step closer to her. "What did you do to my sister?"

Hayley stared at the large Oriental rug not far from them on the floor. In the past, she'd rarely avoided his gaze. "There was a misunderstanding. She thought Cameron had feelings for her, but he didn't. He fell for me the moment we got together and I couldn't help but reciprocate, even if that meant hurting you."

"You did more than *hurt* me." Kaden shook his head with disbelief. He couldn't look at her anymore with that feigned sorry look on her face. She had hurt both him and, now, Naomi.

"There's nothing I can say to make things better, but I hope this meeting you have with Cameron goes well and you find what you seek for the Windham pack."

He didn't say goodbye. He left the lobby and didn't look back.

[10]

CYN'S OLD APARTMENT WAS THEIR BASE CAMP FOR THE day. The minute Kaden walked through the door, he marched right up to his sister.

"I need to speak with you on the balcony. Alone."

He didn't bother waiting for an answer, went to the condo's balcony, and closed the sliding door. He didn't have to wait long for her to follow him.

"What do you want?" she asked when he didn't say anything at first.

"Why didn't you tell me?" Kaden whispered. The wind blew into their faces, but his sister caught what he said. "Why did you really leave LA?"

A frown filled her face. "So you met Cameron already?"

"No, Hayley wanted to meet with me."

"Why did you meet with that bitch?"

"Don't call her that. As much as I hate her, you're too good of a person to sink that low, Naomi." He tentatively placed his hand on his sister's shoulder and she didn't shrug it off.

"I was ashamed. All right?" She wouldn't look at him.

"Don't you think I felt that way too after Hayley left me for another man?" He swallowed deeply as he said it.

"That's why I couldn't say anything. You were in as much pain as I was. Why make you suffer more?"

He strolled to the edge of the balcony and placed his hands on the iron bars. The city hummed under their feet. Carrying the burden of someone else's faults wasn't a burden he wanted anymore. "I've moved on with my life, and I'd like you to do the same."

She slowly nodded. "I want to move on, but the pain seems to give me focus. The pain makes me feel normal."

"It's not normal. It's just a shield that protects you from what you could have in the future."

"My shield isn't doing that good of a job of bringing Bastian back."

Kaden's grip on the fence tightened. "It never will." He turned to briefly look at her. "But, if you want, you can give that pain to me and live your life. I'm the one who was *responsible* for him. Not you."

"I can try…" she whispered.

They stood side by side for a few minutes before she finally spoke. "So what now? Are you going to get revenge for your sister?"

Same ol' Naomi.

Kaden sighed. "Until today, I was prepared to do anything, but now a change of plans is in order." He motioned for Naomi to follow him into the living room where Cyn and Zach gathered.

Kaden knew one thing was for certain, though: They couldn't go through with the attack tonight.

"We have to call off the attack," he said to everyone.

"Are you sure about this?" Cyn asked.

He was quite sure. "I only see this going badly. If the Baker pack has increased security ten-fold, then we won't make it to the hotel penthouse. I don't even know if Ty will be able to take out the contingent of Ceruleans in the parking garage."

Zach was nodding in agreement. "And there's no guarantee Garrison will be there—" Zach began.

"But there is a chance!" Cyn said.

Kaden wished he could say what she wanted to hear.

"All this time, you told me you wanted to protect Ty," Kaden said. "That he was your responsibility."

She twisted away from him, but she nodded reluctantly.

Kaden wanted to reach out and pull her to him, but her turned back spoke volumes. "You've been hungry for the truth for so long. I've been there, but, this time, we have to back down."

Cyn turned to face him and his heart tugged painfully. With slumped shoulders, she shut her eyes. A tear ran down her cheek and she wiped it away.

Zach stood. "I'm going to call Ty and see if I can call off the mission." He left the apartment and his disappointment was evident in his slow exit.

Kaden took a place next to Cyn and held her hand. By the time Zach returned, his face was hard to read.

"It's too late," Zach said. "Ty left me a message that he's already left for the hotel."

Cyn's face fell as suspicion crawled up Kaden's backside. Where was Uncle Damien? He hurried into the spare bedroom where he'd last seen his uncle. That old wolf had most likely heard everything.

His suspicions were confirmed when he entered the empty bedroom with the window wide open: Uncle Damien had also made an early escape.

~

"WHO IN THEIR RIGHT MIND SCALES TO THE TOP OF A skyscraper to reach the penthouse in another building?" Cyn asked Kaden.

He should've been prepared for such questions, but didn't want to think about what they meant.

"Someone who isn't afraid of heights," he murmured.

Namely, Uncle Damien.

Downtown Vancouver buzzed around them. Rush hour had ended a while ago, but light traffic remained.

From across the street to the Cottonwood Club Hotel, Kaden scoped out the building. Kaden, Zach, Sinister, and Cyn arrived not too long ago to bring an end to the madness. Somehow, someway, they had to get Damien and Ty out of there.

"You sure you want to go after Ty in the parking garage?" he asked her.

Cyn was a strong hunter who could hold her own, but if he had his way, she would be back in the apartment waiting for him. Unfortunately, the situation required all hands on deck.

"Oh yeah, the roof is all yours, pal." She glanced upward and shook her head.

He had to agree. No one in their right mind would take the same route Damien had. Half of the time, he questioned whether Uncle Damien was in his right mind.

Cyn wrapped her arms around him and planted a quick kiss on his cheek. "I don't like goodbyes so I'll just say, 'See you.'" She tried to leave his side and he wouldn't let her go. "You could wait for me to return and I'd take care of Ty?"

"Not happening. I got this."

He expected as much, since Ty was her little brother. She tugged free. "Besides, you need to watch your ass, since you're about to become Spiderman going from one building to another." She left his side and headed down the street to join Sinister and Zach, who had given them a moment of privacy.

Just watching her leave filled him with apprehension. Was this the right thing to do? Leaving her behind to take care of Ty? She had fully recovered and had settled into her werewolf skin well, but he didn't know what waited in the parking garage with the Cerulean clan going head to head with the Red clan.

She is stronger than you can even imagine, he reminded himself as he headed to the high-rise condo building next door. *She is the most stubborn person you've ever met,* he reminded himself as he rode up the elevator toward the roof.

By the time he reached the roof, the sun had set and the sky was dark purple with hints of pink. The wind whistled in his ears and the smell of the sea reached his nostrils. He stood on the edge and glanced below.

Kaden had never been afraid of heights. There were other things to fear that were far more frightening than falling. One could control falling, but the actions of others were another matter. He walked along the edge. So how did Uncle Damien get down to the Cottonwood Club roof? He grinned when he spotted the scaffolding for the window washers. *Clever Uncle Damien got a ride.*

Usually, the scaffolding was rolled up to the top, but someone had ridden it down to the thirtieth floor below, which meant Uncle Damien jumped from the thirtieth floor down to the Cottonwood Club roof. At least ten stories.

Kaden whistled. Now that was a tall order. Damien had some years on him and that meant experience as well.

He nimbly climbed onto the scaffolding and rode down the rope to the window-washing ledge.

Jumping ten stories was nice and all, but he noticed the window washer platform could go down about five more floors.

Uncle Damien always was the show off...

At the twenty-fifth floor, Kaden took a deep breath and made the leap. The building came at him far faster than he'd anticipated, but he was ready. He landed with ease and rolled to stand. He glanced around him and saw the hotel roof was empty, but Uncle Damien's scent was here. Kaden followed it.

At the far end of the roof, he spotted the caved-in doorway. From there, he entered the hotel.

[11]

Cyn and Zach, with Sinister not far behind them, walked into the well-lit basement garage at the Cottonwood Club Hotel. Down at the far end of the garage, a large window of glass led to a set of elevators to the hotel. Cyn's gaze swept over the place. There weren't many hiding places among the rows of cars. Cameras were perched in the corners. How the hell did Ty expect to ambush the Ceruleans?

At her side, Sinister assessed the space as well.

"Two emergency stairwells. A few pylons to hide behind," he grunted.

If the Ceruleans expected Kaden to park on the second level and enter the hotel through those doors, that would be the ideal place to take Kaden out.

The trio darted to the closest wall and moved from car to car. Not many vehicles flowed in and out around them. To Cyn, the ones she passed smelled like money. The expensive cologne and polished leather seats practically stabbed at her nose. The guests shelled out quite a few bucks to stay here.

Along the way, Cyn observed a white van going by.

Vince was in the passenger seat. *Lovely.*

Now that wasn't a face she expected to see. Kaden had told her he'd left Vince in the back of a semi hauling sex toys to Southern California. That greasy bastard should be at the beach by now, but instead, he'd be a nuisance bent on revenge.

When the van parked at the far end of the garage, two men dressed in casual clothes ambled out while Vince, and a few others, continued to wait in the van. The guys who got out chatted with each other about how much they couldn't wait to finish such a shitty job.

If they were smart, they'd forget about this *shitty job* and just go home. The garage was too wide open. Only a fool would come down here with all this light.

A thunderous sound rumbled from inside the building, shaking everything around them. After that, a sharp pop broke the glass windows to the hotel elevators. Debris from the ceiling fell to the floor in front of the elevators.

Then all the lights went out.

KADEN SAW THE FIRST DEAD BODY BEFORE THE LIGHTS went out. One of the Baker guards, posted to watch the hallway to the roof, had been slaughtered like a small animal. A single emergency light flickered to life as he approached the mangled form. The werewolf's legs were bent at awkward angles and the man's mouth was open wide as if he'd been in the middle of a scream when Damien had found him.

He swallowed and kept going. Only once in his life had his father warned him about Damien's true nature. The conversation had been a casual one while Naomi was playing with her toys not too far away, but Kaden had caught the warning hidden within the words.

"I don't regret making Damien what he is," his father had said at the time. *"But now that decades have passed, I never anticipated what time and the past would do to a man. Most men should die after such a traumatic experience, but I let him live."* His dad sighed. *"I released a wild dog from his cage and let him run free in the hopes that love and time would heal him."*

Many times, Kaden thought Damien had found peace, but as he found another two bodies in pieces on the stairwell to the next floor, he questioned that thought. The tiny dim light in the stairwell didn't hide the carnage from his eyes or keep him from smelling the wet, coppery scent that had doused the walls.

"I want my revenge," Damien had said to him.

Was this revenge or slaughter? All these guys were most likely hired men and not true members of the Baker pack. They were casualties.

The hallway led to the service stairwell. Kaden plodded down the stairs, expecting to run into someone, but the path was clear the whole way. As much as he tried to find a path that led to a floor, all the doors were locked.

Finally, he came to a door that was open a crack. Open a crack was the wrong term. Someone had *ripped* the door open with claws. The scent of desperation was all over the place. Someone had fought to keep the door shut and Uncle Damien had forced the door open.

Through the doorway, he reached the landing to the penthouse suites. Two double doorways at the end of a large foyer with a single elevator. The sconces on the walls were out, but a single emergency light over a mirror was on. Shadows danced. Then a scream filled the air: a woman's screech that turned into a choked growl.

No, it couldn't be.

Even though it had been a long time since he'd heard Hayley scream, the sound was unmistakable.

He rushed to the sound from the left. The door wasn't locked, but it wasn't exactly unblocked either.

Dead bodies were in the way.

Once through the door, he staggered from the sight.

At the far end of the room, he spotted Hayley and Uncle Damien.

Bodies littered the floor. Splattered blood wet the floor like a slaughterhouse kill floor. The stench of death smacked him in the face, and the wolf within him wanted to cower, to force him to turn away from what was unnatural.

The gun Hayley held quivered in her outstretched hand. Had she emptied the clip yet?

The couches had been overturned and bullet holes filled the sides. But the men who had pulled the guns had had their limbs ripped off from the werewolf who lumbered toward Hayley. The only thing Kaden recognized was the crimson-stained white hair all over his body. Damien could barely be considered human with bloodshot red eyes and fingertips extended to sharp claws. Only his mouth remained in a form close to being human.

Damien's mouth extended into a wide grin, revealing bloodstained teeth.

INSTEAD OF DARKNESS SWALLOWING HER WHOLE, THE garage blossomed into view. The emergency lights left little to be desired, but in this new body, she could hear the hammering of Zach's heartbeat next to her, his muffled curse as he pulled his gun from behind his back.

Sinister was a bit too calm.

"Fish in a barrel," Cyn whispered.

"*Bang. Bang. Bang,*" Zach replied.

Sinister chuckled.

The first pop came from the general direction of the elevators. From there, Cyn spotted Ty, who was using night vision googles, heading toward the nearest emergency light. Once he took out all the lights, the death games would begin.

This wasn't a new tactic for the Red hunting clan. Flush the enemy to the optimal position and then take them out.

"We need to get him the hell out of here before the Baker pack's security gets involved." She tapped and pointed toward the direction of the elevators. With the power out, any reinforcements would come from the stairwell to the main building.

Unless the explosion took out the stairs, too. *Worry about that later.*

"Take point near the garage entrance and cover me when I bring Ty back," she whispered to Zach.

"You sure about this?" he asked.

Sinister rolled his eyes and disappeared first to find an ideal cover point.

Cyn left his side next, racing from car to car. As she veered around a corner, she had to dodge a Cerulean who was stumbling to find his way back to the white van. Another nearby light went out and the man bumped into her shoulder.

"What the hell?" his muffled curse was subdued as she grabbed his arm and twisted it behind his back. With a hard shove, she rammed his head into the closest vehicle.

"Don't move," she whispered to the knocked out man on the ground.

Cyn hurried to follow the path of knocked out lights. Ty was getting closer to the elevators as he took out more Ceruleans on the way. Once they heard gunfire, they scattered like frightened cockroaches. Many of them fired into the dark, searching for their attacker.

At the far end of the floor, near where the Ceruleans were trapped behind cars, shadows gathered behind the broken glass.

The Baker pack reinforcements had arrived.

Oh, shit, no.

"Damn it, Ty," she grunted. She leapt over a vehicle. *Stealth be damned.*

Two Ceruleans fired at the shifting shadows she created, but they missed as she reached Ty.

Just a few more steps. He was taking out Cerulean clan members with no mercy.

"Somebody's shooting at us. Cover our asses!" someone yelled to the Baker pack.

From the corner of her eye, she spotted one of the Baker pack members storming through the broken glass door with something large in his hands. He placed an RPG-7 onto his shoulder and Cyn's insides turned to liquid.

Oh, no freakin' way.

The fish in the barrel had missiles.

There was no way they'd avoid getting hit. She just reacted. No thought. No second-guessing. She grabbed Ty by the arm and pushed him toward the closest car. Bright lights blossomed to their left as an SUV was blown to bits. Blinding lights forced her eyes shut. Her ears painfully popped. The explosion battered her backside as scorching heat fanned her back. She covered Ty with her body and took the brunt.

When everything quieted, her ears rang, but she forced herself to move. *Gotta keep moving, Cyn.*

Holy hell, everything hurt. Each inhale burned. Blood coursed down one ear. Her trembling fingers reached for the back of her neck and found scorched bits of hair.

Some of my hair is gone, she thought.

But Ty was alive.

He shook his head as if to jolt himself out of shock and she grabbed his arm to lead him past the thick smoke into safety. With each step, she found the energy to go faster, until the point where she was dragging him. Zach and Sinister weren't far behind them and covered their rear.

By the time they reached the garage entrance, a crowd had gathered. Cyn shouldered her way to the sidewalk and pulled Ty down the street. Two blocks later, she veered into an alley. Collapsing seemed the best plan of action, but she kept going.

"Keep moving," she grunted.

"Where's Zach?" Ty asked. He sounded funny. He must have a popped eardrum, too.

"He's behind us." Cyn's backside still hurt and the burns on the back of her neck had turned into a stinging coldness, but when she touched the back of her head, the skin was already better and the burnt hair had fallen off.

Gotta love this werewolf healing.

"We need to get you to a hospital," she said.

"Don't touch me." Ty yanked himself free and staggered toward the brick wall. He sank to the ground and ended up banging his head against a dumpster.

She snorted. *Serves him right for being stubborn.* "You probably took some shrapnel back there, and I don't think you want Old Bart pulling that shit out of your ass for the next couple of hours."

Ty groaned and Cyn could smell his pain. It was bitter and filled her nostrils like black licorice.

Zach joined them. "How is he?"

Cyn's right eyebrow rose. "He's ready to bring them all down."

"I almost had them," Ty grunted.

"Them? You mean the small army of Baker pack members who had rocket-propelled grenades?" Cyn couldn't contain her dry laugh, but then she blew out a long sigh. She'd learned a valuable lesson today. "I thought revenge would be so easy, but we're in over our heads here. You two are more important to me than getting back at people who don't give a damn what happens to us."

Ty twisted toward her. He pulled a gun out from the holster under his arm and pointed it at her. Zach snarled and stepped in front of Cyn.

"Don't," she snapped at Zach.

"So you're gonna shoot me after I saved you?" Cyn said to Ty next. "I saved you so that we could *live*. Dying while we seek revenge won't bring Mom and Dad back…"

Ty's finger on the trigger trembled, but Cyn resolved herself to not move this time. He'd already shot her once. She'd survived that time and she could endure it again.

Ty's lower lip trembled and Cyn could still see the boy from the day she told him their parents were dead.

All of her brothers were alive. That was enough for her for now.

She'd almost lost Ty.

The staring contest continued until Ty slowly lowered the gun. "I won't accept what you are, but I'm willing to let you go."

"*Thank you?*" She crossed her arms and winced from the pain in her back.

She turned to Zach. "Take him to the hospital before he does decide to shoot me."

Zach placed Ty's arm over his shoulder and helped him stand.

"But if the time comes—" Ty threw over his shoulder.

"I'll be sure to watch my back." Cyn smiled.

Ty nodded.

A cease-fire was good enough for her. Especially if his hate kept him alive. Seeing the McGinnis boys together felt good.

"I guess I'd be disappointed if you went soft on me," she whispered.

[12]

KADEN SLOWLY APPROACHED DAMIEN. THE EARLY evening's moonlight spilled into the room through the expansive windows that went from one wall to the other.

Streaks of tears wet Hayley's cheeks. "Kaden," she whispered. "He killed Cameron..."

"Quiet," he replied to her.

The floor was slick with Cameron's blood. He kept his footing, all the while his gaze was locked on Damien's. Blood from a head wound coursed down Damien's face and dripped off his chin. Parts of his white hair were crimson stained.

"You're hurt badly. We should leave," Kaden began.

"You should leave, nephew. Before I stormed in here, Cameron had called for reinforcements."

Hayley edged backwards toward the nearest door, but Damien growled. "Not so fast..."

"Don't touch her, Damien." He still had more of the room to cross. If his uncle lunged for her, it would be all over.

Instead of closing in on Hayley, Damien stopped. "I can take away the pain she has given you."

Now where did that come from? Was his pain that visible? "If you hurt her, you'll give me more pain."

"You've been blinded, boy," Damien said softly. "She wears a mask to the world, but I see behind it."

"I'm not blind anymore. She's cruel, selfish, and doesn't give a damn how much she hurt me." Kaden caught the faint sounds of footsteps thundering up the stairwell. So many men. *Time's running out.* "But I'm not like her. Neither are you."

Damien took a step back from Hayley. "Are you willing to give your life for hers? Even after what she did to you?"

"Yes, I would protect her from you to save what humanity you have left."

The yawn of the stairwell door was the final warning. Death was coming.

Damien rushed past him and ran through the double doors to the elevator hallway. "Guess I'll have to find other toys to play with. *Goodbye*, nephew."

Shots fired the moment Damien closed the door behind him.

Kaden rushed away from the door as a spray of bullets spewed through the door. He swooped up Hayley into his arms and ran for the penthouse's nearest room.

"Is there a safe room in the penthouse?" he asked her.

She shook her head, her eyes wide. "He came out of nowhere…"

"I know…" He shushed her.

"Please don't leave me. I'm so sorry…" she begged. "Don't let him kill me."

"You don't have to say you're sorry." Kaden cringed on the inside. He was bitter, but he wasn't a cold bastard. "Don't worry; I'll wait in hiding until the Bakers show up."

Her white-knuckled grip on his arm loosened. "Thank you." She shuddered. "Your uncle kept screaming about a woman named Luba. Cameron never told me about what his father did…" Her voice broke, but she kept going. "What *he* did. Cameron had been there the night that man's wife was killed. Did you know that? I guess we reap what we sow, right?"

He stared at her for a moment and the meaning of those words hit him in the gut. What would he reap from what happened tonight?

Time stretched out to the point where Kaden couldn't wait any longer. Cyn and her brothers were still downstairs. Had she found Ty and escaped unharmed?

"Goodbye, Hayley." He didn't look at her, but the least he could do was be civil.

By the time he reached the elevator hallway, there was no one there. The hallway was empty again. More bodies. More dead. None of them was his uncle. Uncle Damien's scent went down the stairs. As tempted as he was to follow, he promised Hayley he'd watch over her until the Bakers showed up.

He sighed.

This wasn't how today was supposed to go.

His phone buzzed in his pocket from a text message: *Are you all right? I'm safe. I love you.*

Relief filled him for a moment. He wasn't all right, and he wondered if he would ever be. But Cyn was safe. The pack was safe in Montana. For that, Kaden would always be grateful.

EPILOGUE

THREE MONTHS LATER

Kaden jerked awake and clutched the side of the bed tightly. For the past three months, he had been waking up in a cold sweat as the memories from the Cottonwood Club Hotel slammed into him. He closed his eyes in the dim room and fell back into his recurring nightmare, seeing Uncle Damien closing the doors, hearing the shouts and screams that filled the air as he took Hayley's hand and hid her away in the penthouse bathroom. He tasted the death lingering in the air as he returned to the door and burst into the hallway.

Only to find an empty room. More blood. More bullets. More bodies that led to the staircase from whence he'd arrived. His uncle had led the men away to save him, but now there was more blood on the floor: blood that belonged to Damien.

His heart raced in an offbeat manner as he was hit by the very real possibility that his uncle was dead. That his uncle was lying in a heap somewhere in the hotel. That he was dead just like Bastian.

Before his breath turned into a wheeze, the woman lying next to him touched his cheek. *I'm here*, the caress seemed to say. *You're not alone*, the comforting kiss to his forehead implored. Cyn cradled him close and whispered words that chased away his nightmare.

He wasn't alone. Whatever guilt plagued him could be driven away. Whatever sadness lingering in his body could be purged. As long as Cyn was next to him.

Morning arrived in Montana and the cool May breeze through the closed curtains brought scents from what would be a wonderful day.

He strolled over to the window and opened the curtains. Cyn groaned and placed a pillow over her head.

"Just two more hours, Mom," she mumbled.

Beyond their house lay three more houses. Real ranch homes. The beginnings of a new town hidden near the Tobacco Root Mountains. There wasn't as much forest out here where the pack had settled, but beyond his field of vision, there was nothing but rolling hills and a stream carving a path through the landscape.

This place was theirs and it was home.

The sound of a knock on the front door drew him from his reverie.

Cyn's head darted up. Her black hair was pointed sideways. "Did I hear a knock?"

"Yes, you did."

He wasn't expecting anyone this morning, so he quickly walked to the door. After what happened with the Ceruleans and the Baker pack, everyone was on guard. There weren't any sounds or scents, so it could be any number of people. Maybe one of the pack members.

Kaden opened the door and stopped cold. "Now this I didn't expect."

Right in front of him was a tiny oak chair, about big

enough for a toddler to sit in. A breeze from outside weaved through the chair's ornate carvings of hounds and brought the scent of pine resin to Kaden.

Pine resin. Handcrafted furniture.

The pleasant thought made Kaden smile.

From behind him, Cyn rushed over to the tiny chair. A note had been tied with a red ribbon. The penmanship was easy to decipher:

Kaden and Cyn,

For when the time comes in the future, I'd like for you to put this chair to good use. My sweet Luba wanted me to make this, but I never got a chance.

There wasn't a signature, but he knew very well Damien had crafted the chair. He tried to follow his uncle's scent, but Damien's trail led off the porch and disappeared out into the wilderness.

"Will he return?" Cyn asked wistfully.

He wrapped his arms around her waist and she leaned against him. The wolf within him was at peace. "He always does. Love has a way of bringing people to the place where they belong."

"That it does," she whispered.

THE END

ALSO BY SHAWNTELLE MADISON

COVETED SERIES

Collected (Prequel Novella) #0.5

Coveted #1

Kept #2

Pocketed (Novella) #2.5

Compelled #3

Cursed (Collection of Short Stories)

FLEA MARKET MAGIC SERIES

Thrift Store Trolls

Deceptive Dime Store Demons (Coming soon)

HEROES RUN IN PACKS SERIES

Hadley Werewolves

Windham Werewolves

McGinnis Werewolves (Coming soon)

URBAN FANTASY/PARANORMAL ROMANCE

Bitter Disenchantment

Repossessed

Taming the Viking's Dragon

AT YOUR SERVICE SERIES

Bound to You

Surrender to You

ABOUT THE AUTHOR

Shawntelle Madison is a Web developer who loves to weave words as well as code. She'd be reluctant to admit it, but if pressed, she'd say that she covets and collects source code. After losing her first summer job detasseling corn, Madison performed various jobs, from fast-food clerk to grunt programmer to university webmaster. Writing eccentric characters is her favorite job of all. On any given day when she's not surgically attached to her computer, she can be found watching cheesy horror movies or the latest action-packed anime. Shawntelle Madison lives in Missouri with her husband and children.